JONATHAN KELLERMAN
and JESSE KELLERMAN

THE
LOST COAST

A NOVEL

BALLANTINE BOOKS
NEW YORK

Published in the United States by Ballantine Books, an imprint of Random House, a division of Penguin Random House LLC, New York.

BALLANTINE BOOKS & colophon are registered trademarks of Penguin Random House LLC.

Hardback ISBN 978-0-525-62014-3
Ebook ISBN 978-0-525-62015-0

Printed in the United States of America on acid-free paper

randomhousebooks.com

2 4 6 8 9 7 5 3 1

First Edition

Frontispiece photo: Adobe Stock/Tobi

Book design by Susan Turner

To Faye
—*Jonathan Kellerman*

To Gabriella
—*Jesse Kellerman*

THE
LOST COAST

ONE

CHAPTER 1

I'd been off the force and out on my own for a year when I got a call from Peter Franchette.

We met in downtown Oakland, at the same sushi restaurant where I'd last left him on a rainy afternoon, sitting across from a sister he'd never met. I'd tracked her down for him—a bit of extra-curricular activity that was part of why I was off the force and out on my own.

The summer sun was harsh as he stepped in from the street. "Sorry I'm late."

"Not at all. You shaved your beard."

"And you grew one."

I'd grown my hair out, too. The extra length masked a scar running from temple to nape.

"My wife likes me better this way," I said.

We took a booth, put in our order, made conversation. Peter told me he'd kept in touch with his sister, closely at first. Then less so.

"She has her life, I have mine."

I nodded.

"And you?" he asked. "Charlotte must be—what. Four and a half?"

"Good memory. We have a son now, too. Myles." I showed him my phone.

"What a bruiser. Am I wrong, or does he look like you?"

"Yeah, he's a clone."

"Cute. So how's life as a private citizen treating you?"

"Can't complain."

"Thanks for meeting on short notice."

"No problem," I said. "What can I do for you?"

"This kid I mentor, Chris Villareal—super-bright guy. His company does interesting stuff with AI and traffic grids . . . Anyhow. He showed up to a recent meeting looking pretty distraught. His grandmother passed and named him executor of her estate. Without warning him."

"Always a fun surprise."

"From what I gather, there's not much in terms of dollars. It's just disorganized, and he's run across some things that don't feel right."

"How so?"

"You'd be better off hearing it from him."

"Has he spoken to an estate attorney?"

"I set him up with my person. She thinks it's not worth the trouble, Chris should drop it."

"Sounds like good advice."

"I think it's a matter of principle. He and his grandma were very close. The lawyer was the one who suggested a private investigator. She had a name but I thought of you."

"Appreciate it."

The server approached with our food.

I split a pair of chopsticks and sanded them together. "Have him call me."

"Great."

Toward the end of the meal, he said, "You know, you never cashed my check."

The check in question was made out to my daughter for $250,000—a reward for my efforts. At the time I was still a county employee, sticking to the rules. Most of them.

Crazy money for the job. Peter's venture capital success had earned him more than I could imagine, but mega-rich isn't necessarily mega-generous.

"I tried to," I said. "The bank wouldn't accept it. They said it was too old."

"When?"

"Last year."

"What'd you wait so long for?"

"I didn't want to get fired."

He shook his head. "What I get for using paper . . . Well, look," he said, digging out his phone, "at some point I decided you weren't going to deposit it. So I made an end run."

He began tapping at the screen. For a moment I thought he might zap me the money electronically, a quarter of a million dollars in a quadrillionth of a second.

Instead he turned the screen around as if to show off pictures of his own kids.

I saw a banking app, with one account, labeled CHARLOTTE EDISON—529 PLAN.

"Technically it's in my name. I didn't know her Social. Happy to transfer it whenever you'd like. You can see for yourself, it's done pretty well."

The balance was $321,238.77.

"What do you think?" he said.

"I think I should remind you," I said, "I have a son now, too."

CHAPTER 2

I met Chris Villareal at his grandmother's house in Daly City, a suburb of San Francisco also known as Little Manila. Her neighborhood, scaled with postwar tract housing, was walking distance to the Asian bakeshops and markets along Mission Street.

He'd arrived early. Boyishly handsome, he leaned against the door of a silver BMW coupe with a laptop pinned under his arm, tapping a sneaker and straining to smile beneath a crest of black hair.

Branded start-up T-shirt: the Bay Area's tribal signifier.

He removed his sunglasses and hung them on his neckline to shake hands.

"My condolences," I said.

"Thank you. She lived a good life. But it's still hard."

I nodded.

"All right," he said. "Let's get it over with."

The house was a stucco box, pastel pink, jammed between pastel neighbors. Concrete steps rose to a decorative security gate. Chris slipped off his shoes and left them on the doormat. I did the same.

He shut off the alarm system and led me past an entryway altar crowded with Catholic figurines. Everything was old but cared-for, living room furniture polished to a dull glow, sofa and chairs upholstered in a vivid floral pattern. The extended family was large and well represented on the walls, as were members of the Holy Family and various saints. A crucifix loomed.

"She'd be mad if I didn't offer you something to eat or drink," he said.

"I'm good, thanks."

He'd commandeered the dining room for his workspace. Accordion file folders labeled in black marker covered the table: B OF A, CHASE, CITI, VA, LIFE INSUR (LOLO JOHN), MEDICARE, SOC SEC, 81-2 TAXES, 83 CAMRY, 09 CAMRY, UTIL, RECEIPTS.

Wrinkled cardboard boxes brimming with loose paper lined the baseboards, awaiting their turn. More boxes and folders piled on the chairs. It looked like an all-you-can-eat buffet for goats.

"She kept everything." He tapped his temple. "Immigrant mentality."

We sat beneath a giclée print of *The Last Supper*, and he ran me through the basics.

Marisol Santos Salvador, born 1938 in Manila, arrived 1957 in the United States along with husband John (deceased 1995). Five children, of whom Chris's mother, Asuncion, was the youngest. For most of her life Marisol had worked as a health aide.

"When did she pass?"

"April 6. She had a stroke so it was fast."

"You didn't know she'd named you executor."

"No. Maybe she meant to tell me. She had another stroke, about fifteen years ago, and it affected her. I don't get why her lawyer didn't say something sooner, though."

"Who's he?"

"Mr. Pineda. He's a family friend. At the wake he came up to me. 'We need to talk.' I go to his office and he hands me *lola*'s will. Like: Tag, you're it."

"Is he helping you?"

"Not really. He's almost as old as she was. I don't think he's completely with it, either. Basically I'm having to figure it out on my own."

"Do you know why she chose you?"

Chris shrugged. "I'm the only one who's not married with kids. She used to ride me about it. 'You're thirty, I had four kids by thirty.' I told her I'm building a business, that's my baby."

"I'm sure she found that very persuasive."

He laughed. "She also thought I was the smart one. She called me Henyo. It means 'genius.' 'Look at Henyo, he can talk to computers but not to girls.' Or, I don't know. Maybe she wanted to punish me. Whatever. Lucky me."

"What does the will say?"

"Sixty percent to her kids, thirty percent to the grandkids, ten percent to the church."

"Pretty straightforward."

"Yeah, till you look a little closer. The house is the main asset. But she's got money squirreled away all over the place. Not just multiple bank accounts. I found three thousand dollars in cash under the bathroom sink. I'm trying to be fair, and everyone's calling me up all mad. 'What's taking so long? Why haven't you finished?' Why? Because look at this mess."

Bright young guy applying artificial intelligence to traffic grids but struggling to wring meaning from piles of paper.

"Peter said you noticed some irregularities," I said.

He nodded. He opened the laptop. "I started itemizing her bank statements."

"Is that necessary?"

"Peter's lawyer said the same thing."

"I admire your diligence. It just seems like you have enough on your plate as is."

"I wanted to make sure there's no huge discrepancies. It's how I roll. For all I know she has a million bucks buried in the backyard. I'm seeing all these payments I can't figure out. Look."

He showed me a QuickBooks entry from March 17, a check for $135 to SFRA.

He scrolled back to February 17. Another $135 check to SFRA.
January. December of the previous year. November.

One hundred thirty-five dollars, SFRA.

Identical entries appeared monthly for the previous two years.

"That's as far back as the online accounts go," he said.

He drew over the B OF A folder and began taking out sheaves of paper, secured by alligator clips and bristling with tape flags. "So then I started going through by hand. Same deal."

Each flag indicated a $135 check to SFRA.

"Do you know what it stands for?" I asked. "San Francisco something?"

"I tried googling it. I get so many hits it's useless."

"How many payments are we talking about?"

"The earliest I could find is from 1996. All in all it works out to around forty-seven thousand dollars. It might not seem like much, in the grand scheme of things, but she wasn't a rich woman. She wasn't poor, either. I gotta say that or she's going to descend from heaven and scream at me."

I smiled. "Understood."

"She was a kid during the war. She and her sisters were living on the streets, eating from the gutters. She knew what it meant to have nothing. She bought day-old bread until my mom made her stop. She kept the same car for twenty-five years. It died and she got another just like it. This," he said, placing a hand on the bank statements, "isn't like her."

I said nothing.

"You don't agree," he said.

"I didn't know your grandmother. I get that it seems inconsistent with her behavior."

"But."

"Inconsistency is human. And the payments could be innocuous."

"Then what the hell is SFRA?"

"Maybe a membership fee? Or a subscription."

"She didn't belong to clubs. She bought the *National Enquirer* once a week."

"Something to do with her church."

"I asked the priest. He said no."

"A mortgage or a loan."

"The house was paid off in 2007. I'm not aware of other loans. It's possible. I haven't finished with everything yet. All I know is I'm seeing a pattern. It reminds me of when I get recurring charges on my credit card, stuff I signed up for without realizing."

"Okay," I said, "but this is analog. Your grandmother's physically writing checks. She must've believed she was paying for something. What does the rest of your family think?"

"They're clueless. My mom gets so emotional it's hard to have a conversation. My uncles, too. They're like, 'It's your job, you deal with it.' "

"Can you access her bank account? I'd like to see an image of the most recent check."

He logged in and clicked open the March 17 payment, filled out in Marisol's tidy handwriting. *SFRA. One hundred thirty-five dollars and 00/100.* The back bore an illegible scrawl but no account information, suggesting a mobile deposit. Likewise for the remaining online images.

"What about canceled checks? Do you have any of those lying around?"

From the B OF A folder he removed a manila envelope stuffed to bursting.

"Immigrant mentality," he said.

He hadn't gotten the chance to sort them. We started in, one by one. Chris was sweating. I was, too. The house had no AC. He told me, laughing, how *lola* would sit on the living room couch, watching *Days of Our Lives* at maximum volume and fanning herself with a *pamaypay*, which she also used to whack anyone she felt deserved it.

"She sounds tough."

"Oh yeah."

"I guess you'd have to be, to survive what she survived."

"Yeah. But whatever she did was out of love."

"You miss her."

He nodded.

We found a check, dated December 17, 1998, $135 to SFRA.

I turned it over. In addition to the same indecipherable signature was an account number, a routing number, and the time and date of deposit.

Chris leaned in. "Can you use that to tell who it is?"

"I can try. You mind if I hang on to this?"

"Take it all." He sat back, rubbing absently at his chest. "The lawyer thinks I'm wasting my time. But I can't get it out of my head. You know?"

"I do, yeah. In your position I might feel the same way. As to whether it's a waste of time, that depends on what you expect to get out of the process. Can I be straight with you?"

"Please."

"I'm happy to look into this for you. I think it's important to acknowledge that you may have already found everything there is to find."

"You're preparing me for disappointment."

"I'll run with it as far as you want. But sometimes when people come to me with a request like this, what they're really after is closure."

He stared at the pile of canceled checks; fuzzy edges and yellowing paper.

"I don't have any expectations," he said. "I just feel like I owe it to her. What if she was stressed out over this, and it contributed to her stroke? It's fifty grand. It's not nothing."

He turned to me. "It eats at me. What else am I missing?"

CHAPTER 3

My office sits behind a Laundromat. What it lacks in ambience, it makes up for in convenience: half a mile from my house, half a mile from my parents, and catercorner to a killer ramen shop. I grew up in San Leandro, and since Amy and I moved back, I'd been getting reacquainted with the city. It fascinated me to see how it had changed and not changed. Prices climbing. More and better restaurants. But the meters still took quarters only.

I ran the canceled check through a specialist data broker. The most they could tell me was that it had been deposited at a Wells Fargo. But they couldn't specify the branch, and the account was closed, no way to retrieve the owner's name.

Per Google, SFRA was the Science Fiction Research Association.

Or it was the South Florida Radio Amateurs.

Store Front Reference Architecture. Student Financial Responsibility Agreement. Software Frequency Response Analyzer. School Funding Reform Act. Scottish Flood Risk Assessment.

It was a protein found in *E. coli.*

It stood for innumerable groups in San Francisco, city and county: Redevelopment Agency; Rugby Academy; Resonant Acoustics.

The California Secretary of State business entity registry returned eleven entries, all of which I ruled out based on filing date:

They'd come into existence after Marisol Santos Salvador started making payments.

I checked UCC filings. DBAs. Civil courts. Bankruptcy courts. Liens. Credit records. Regulatory bodies. Telephone directories. Newspaper archives.

Nothing.

Marisol faced no outstanding judgments and was not party to any legal actions in San Mateo County or any of the surrounding counties. Her credit was good, her driving record was clean, and she had no criminal record. She possessed neither watercraft nor a pilot's license. Her sons and daughters had chosen to settle within a few miles of her. A robust, close-knit clan.

As Chris had said, she owned outright the house in Daly City, having purchased it in 1963 for $14,200. Currently its estimated value stood at $799,000 to $1,000,000. The increase said everything you needed to know about Bay Area real estate.

In 1996 she'd spent $57,500 on another property, 8 Abalone Court, Swann's Flat, CA. Currently its estimated value stood at six to ten thousand dollars.

Swann's Flat.

The SF of SFRA?

The date of purchase aligned with the start of her monthly payments.

The decrease in value told a story of its own.

I'd never heard of Swann's Flat. With good reason: It was scarcely there, a census-designated place, population thirteen, perched at the western edge of unincorporated Humboldt County. The Wikipedia article was brief and read like chamber of commerce copy. Amenities included hiking and horse trails, an inn, a boat launch. The nearest post office was in Millburg, twenty miles to the east, as was the nearest elementary school. The nearest high school was three hours away in Eureka. Notable local events included the annual Queen of the Salmon pageant.

Google Images showed dramatic cliffs, savage waves, black sand, gloomy forest, fog. Isolated houses dotted a tongue of land that poked out into the Pacific as if to taste its salt.

From Marisol's house in Daly City, the drive was six hours, twelve minutes, the last leg along private and unpaved roads. Street View chickened out well shy of her address on Abalone Court.

I called Chris. "Did your grandmother own a second home? Like a vacation house?"

"What? No. Why?"

"I'm seeing another property in her name."

"Where?"

"Swann's Flat."

"I don't know where that is."

"Up the coast. Humboldt."

"What the hell," he said.

"She never mentioned it to you."

"No way."

"Can you ask your mom or your uncles?"

"Let me call you back."

I put my new search term to use.

The second hit after Wikipedia was the official Swann's Flat website. I clicked the ABOUT tab.

We are a private residential community located on the Lost Coast of California, established in 1965 pursuant to the State Public Resources Code Section 13000-13233 . . .

The rest of the text matched the Wikipedia page, word for word. Impossible to say which had been lifted from which.

The HISTORY, BOARD, and FAQ tabs all read *Under Construction!*

Returning to the search results, I clicked the third hit, Swanns FlatRealEstate.com.

The name and the feel suggested a real estate agency. But there were no agents, only a list of properties for sale. I scrolled down.

Golden opportunity to own an unspoiled piece of California coastline with fabulous vistas and fresh ocean breezes. Outstanding quarter acre lot a short distance from beach. Seller financing available for qualified buyers. Come join our friendly seaside community!

Photos showed a sunny verdant patch. Pine trees framed a peekaboo view of sparkling ocean. Asking price was $45,995. Contact Diamond Vacation Properties.

I scrolled on.

Hidden gem! Unique south-facing .19 acre lot on a quiet cul-de-sac. Greenbelt in the rear creates privacy and protects your view of the stunning King Range. Qualified buyers ask about seller financing. Find your heart on the Lost Coast!

The photo gallery was so similar to that of the first listing that I had to check to make sure they weren't the same. Asking price was $21,700. Contact Omnivest Services.

There were about thirty listings in all, every one of them for undeveloped land.

I went back to Google.

Hit number four was SwannsFlatHomes.com.

The color scheme and font differed from SwannsFlatReal Estate.com. In every other respect the two sites were identical.

Same for SwannsFlatProperties, SwannsFlatLand, and Swanns FlatLostCoast.

Same for the next ten pages of search results.

Chris called. "They have no idea what I'm talking about. Could it be a mistake?"

"The databases aren't perfect, but not likely. Have you run across any property tax stubs?"

"They're probably mixed up with the other tax stuff."

"Search for a check. Humboldt County Tax Collector. Something like that."

I heard him typing and clicking.

". . . Humboldt County Treasurer–Tax Collector," he said. "Two hundred fifty-nine dollars."

"Do you see a parcel on the memo line?"

The number he read matched the one on my screen.

I said, "Not a mistake."

Chris said, "Shit. Why didn't I see this?"

"You weren't looking. You were focused on SFRA."

"Do you know what it's about?"

"I'm not sure yet. Let me poke around a little more. I'll be in touch when I have something concrete. But Chris? Do me a favor. Resist the urge to stay up all night googling."

He laughed. "Yeah, sure."

I'd been squinting at the computer since noon. My eyes were sand, my neck felt permanently crooked forward, and I had to pick up the kids.

CHARLOTTE CLIMBED INTO the car with her usual greeting: "What's for dinner?"

"My love, it's polite to say hello."

"Hi, Daddy. How are you?"

"I'm good, thanks. How was camp?"

"Good."

"What did you do?"

"Nothing."

"Did you play with anyone?"

"I don't remember. What's for dinner?"

"I'll tell you once we're driving. Can you get buckled, please?"

"I'm buckled."

"Thank you. Chicken, rice, and green beans."

"Eww."

"Charlotte, it's not polite to say *eww* when someone cooks for you."

"I hate chicken."

"You loved it the last time I made it."

"No, I didn't."

"You told me, and I quote, 'Daddy, I love this, can you make it again?'"

Myles, facing backward, said, "Eww."

"See? He doesn't like it, either." Charlotte leaned over him. "Myles, can you say *eww chicken*?"

"Eww tit."

AT HOME I put her in the bath. The water turned gray.

"Do you just roll around in the dirt all day?"

"Not all day."

I heard the front door close; the double thump as Amy kicked off her boots.

"Smells yummy," she called.

She appeared in the doorway. "Hello, everyone."

"Hey," I said. "How was your day?"

She smiled tiredly. "There's only one kind."

Charlotte said, "Mommy, I had the best time at camp."

"That's wonderful." Amy bent to kiss me and take Myles. "I want to hear all about it."

Over dinner Charlotte announced that she'd played with Millicent, Ambrose, and Clementine. They had built a fort from sticks and eaten Popsicles for snack.

"Mine was blue raspberry," she said.

"Why do all your friends sound like they have consumption?" I asked.

"What's that?"

Amy suppressed laughter and kicked me under the table. "Blue raspberry sounds delicious, sweetie. This is delicious, too, Daddy."

"Thanks."

Charlotte said, "Daddy, I looove this chicken. Can you make it again?"

Myles said, "Eww tit."

CHAPTER 4

At my desk the next morning, I dove deep into Swann's Flat. Business registry records supported my initial impression: beyond sketchy.

For a tiny place, it was throbbing with commerce, home to a Finance Corporation, a Development Corporation, a Land Corporation, a Land Development Corporation, a plain old Corporation, a Company, LPs and LLPs and INCs, nonprofits and legacy corporations and stock corporations, and buried among them, the Swann's Flat Resort Area, LLC.

SFRA?

Formed on January 22, 1991; inactive as of 2007.

The initial filing consisted of a single typewritten page. There were no officers listed. The business address was 134 Monkeyflower Drive, Swann's Flat, CA 95536. The registered agent for service of process was ML Corporate Solutions, located next door at 136. The purpose of the limited liability company was *to engage in any lawful act or activity for which a limited liability company may be organized under the California Revised Uniform Limited Liability Company Act.*

Didn't get much vaguer than that.

No website. To be expected, given that they'd gone out of business almost two decades ago.

Why was Marisol still paying them?

Who was she paying?

A disgruntled person is a private investigator's best friend. If you want dirt on someone, talk to the folks they've pissed off.

I ran a docket search.

Since 1995, Swann's Flat Resort Area had been sued twenty-four times. The specifics varied from case to case, but the themes were consistent.

Land and lies.

Petitioners David and Mary Walsh purchased a lot at 17 Wildrose Run, paying installation and connection fees for water, power, and sewer lines. The complaint noted that this had to be done for every new home; the existing grid did not cover the peninsula but went in piecemeal. Four years later, the Walshes put their lot back up for sale without having broken ground, receiving one offer, well below their original purchase price. They accepted. During the inspection period, however, it emerged that the local utilities body was refusing to honor the previous connection fees, requiring the prospective buyers to pay an additional $27,825. The buyer subsequently dropped out. No more offers had been forthcoming. The Walshes sought $87,341 in damages from the utilities body, the Swann's Flat Board of Supervisors, Does I-XX, and Swann's Flat Resort Area ($12,980 in resort fees). After much wrangling, they'd settled for an undisclosed amount.

Petitioner Joseph Hui Lee purchased a lot located at 21 Elkhorn Court. After two years he had yet to receive title. He was suing the title company, the broker, and—for $7,767 in resort fees—Swann's Flat Resort Area. Years of motions and countermotions came to an abrupt halt with Lee's death in 2001. His heirs had elected not to continue the fight.

Every case led to five more, the number of search terms growing exponentially.

I spent the next few weeks tracking down plaintiffs. Many

were presently deceased. Those I managed to reach tended to fall into one of three categories: They were elderly, were military, or lived out of state—in some cases, overseas. All had bought their properties sight unseen, after reading an ad or receiving a cold call. They recounted a sales pitch that resembled uncannily the online listings.

An exclusive piece of the California coast at a bargain price, plus a low-cost, no-hassle loan.

Who could turn that down?

The nightmare began before the ink was dry.

Soaring HOA fees. Hidden resort fees. Assessments, twice a year or more.

Any attempt to begin construction ran into permit hiccups, materials holdups, labor shortages, problematic site conditions, inclement weather. Eventually the buyer would lose heart and try to sell, only to be informed by a real estate agent that they had little chance of recovering their full purchase price on the open market in any reasonable amount of time.

At that point, with the situation seemingly beyond salvage, they'd receive a call from a corporate buyer, offering to assume their debt in exchange for signing over the deed. Almost everyone agreed. A few refused, abandoning the property and ceasing to pay taxes. The county then repossessed the lot and auctioned it off to the very same corporations, who then relisted it for sale.

Same result either way. The buyer ended up with nothing and the cycle began anew.

ELVIRA DELA CRUZ said, "I was stupid and lost my money."

In 1998, she'd bought a lot in Swann's Flat that proved unusable. Acting as her own attorney, she filed suit against Swann's Flat Resort Area ($6,015 in resort fees) and the salesman, a man named William C. Arenhold. The case was dismissed in summary judgment.

Now she was in her late fifties, with microbladed eyebrows and Barbie-pink lipstick. For lunch she'd chosen a hot pot restaurant in the St. Francis Square shopping center, across the parking lot from the dental office where she worked as a hygienist.

"You're being a little unfair to yourself," I said.

"Oh no." She dunked a slice of pork into the bubbling broth. "I was stupid."

I'd asked to meet, prompted by the parallels to Marisol Santos Salvador. Both women lived in Daly City and belonged to the Filipino community. They'd bought their plots within eighteen months of each other. What really caught my eye, however, was the attorney representing Arenhold.

Rolando Pineda, Esquire.

Mr. Pineda. He's a family friend.

Elvira surprised me further by informing me that Pineda had started out as *her* lawyer.

"I had a slip and fall against the city. He got me thirty thousand dollars and took half. He asked me, 'What are you going to do with the rest of the money?' I said, 'Pay my bills.' He said, 'You need to think about the future. Let me introduce you to a man.'"

"William Arenhold."

She nodded. "He came to my apartment and showed me pictures. The beach, the sunset, dolphins jumping. It was so pretty. He said I can build my dream home for when I retire. 'I'm twenty-five, what do I need that?' He said, 'It's an investment. Wait a few years and sell, you make ten times the money. But you have to move fast or someone else will buy it.'"

"Slick."

"Oh yes. He was tall, like you. Very handsome. He wore a fancy suit. And he had nice teeth." She smiled. "I liked that."

"How much did the land cost?"

"Fifteen thousand."

"The same amount Pineda won for you."

"Pretty funny, huh? I told Bill, 'I can't spend everything, I need to save some.' 'Don't worry, you put in what you can, I'll get you a loan.' Every month I paid sixty dollars plus interest. They also charged for the water, for electricity, the sewer, maintenance, security. See? Drip, drip, drip."

"How long did this go on?"

"Four years. One day I decided to go see what it looked like."

"You hadn't seen it before?"

"Just pictures." She chortled. "You think I'm over-the-top stupid."

"I really don't."

"You're being nice," she said. "I am. I was. I didn't know what I was doing. I trusted Pineda. He was a lawyer."

"That seems like the worst reason to trust someone."

Elvira cackled. "I like *you.*"

"What happened when you got there?"

"Oh, it was terrible. That road—have you seen it?"

I shook my head.

She mimed puking. "Like a roller coaster. It took hours, my car was overheating. I get to the town and there's no houses. There's no buildings. It's just trees and trees and dirt and trees and dirt, and everywhere plastic signs sticking up, with numbers. I drove around in circles till I found it. Sea Otter Lane. Eighty-one, seventy-nine . . . Seventy-one, that's mine. But there's nothing."

"Was there supposed to be something? I thought it was an empty lot."

"Yeah. But this is *nothing.* It's a big hole. Like there was an earthquake."

Arenhold, in his deposition, had stated: *The disclosures explicitly indicate that heavy seasonal precipitation poses an erosion risk and that the buyer is therefore advised to conduct an independent soil survey.*

"It doesn't look like the pictures," she said.

I further made explicit to Ms. Dela Cruz that those images are meant to give a sense of the geology and biodiversity of the region as a whole, rather than referring to any plot in particular.

"I was in shock," she said.

"I bet."

"I had my camera with me. I brought it to take a picture to put on my wall at home. Instead," she said, giggling, "I took pictures of the hole."

"I'm amazed you can laugh about it."

"I wasn't laughing then, I was crying. When I finished taking pictures of the hole, I got in my car. It won't start."

"Oh no."

"Oh *yes,*" she said gleefully. "I didn't have a phone, either. So I walked."

"Where?"

"I don't know, I just started walking and crying. I got lost. I wanted to lie down and die. A truck comes by and a man rolls down the window. 'What's wrong, miss?' "

"Who was he?"

"He didn't say his name. But he was handsome, too. I told him there's a hole in my land and my car won't start. He smiled and said, 'Hop in.' It was stupid, to go with a strange man."

"You were stuck."

"Yup. He drove me to my car. He couldn't get it to start, either. He said he would take me to his friend who's a mechanic."

I said, "There are no houses but there was a mechanic."

"Well, when he started driving, then I saw some houses. They're in another part of town, close to the water. The mechanic tows my car to his garage, puts coolant in. Four hundred dollars."

"For a bottle of coolant."

"And to tow."

"That's crazy."

"Oh yes," she said. "But he had my keys, what was my choice?

I wrote him a check and drove away as fast as I could. When I got home I showed the pictures of the hole to my sister's husband. He's an engineer. He laughed at me. 'Elvira, you can't build here. They cheated you.' I went back to Pineda. 'You need to sue them and get my money.' He said he can't do that, he's Bill's lawyer, too. It's a conflict of interest. He told me he can't be my lawyer anymore."

"Did you try to find another one?"

"I couldn't afford it. Everyone I talked to told me to forget it. But it made me so mad. So I did it myself. More stupid. I lost and I had to pay Pineda even more."

"I'm so sorry you had to go through this."

She swirled a piece of bok choy in broth. "Boo-hoo."

"Ms. Dela Cruz, do you know a woman named Marisol Santos Salvador?"

"I don't think so."

"This is her," I said, showing a picture.

Elvira popped the bok choy into her mouth, chewed. "Okay, yes."

"You do know her?"

"She was a patient of Dr. Quinio," she said. "I remember her teeth."

CHAPTER 5

The Law Offices of Rolando Pineda and Associates occupied a second-floor suite above a bakery on Mission Street—the same bakery, perhaps, where Marisol used to buy her day-old bread. I climbed the steps through a heady aroma of butter and toasted coconut.

The door displayed Pineda's name in gilt. No word on who the associates were.

As I entered, the receptionist whirled around in her chair, as though I'd caught her napping. She was in her sixties, wearing a leopard-print blouse. Big-bodied, with a big blond bouffant.

"Can I help you?"

"My name is Clay Edison. I'm a private investigator. I'm here to speak with Mr. Pineda."

"Do you have an appointment?"

"No."

"What is this regarding?"

"Marisol Santos Salvador."

"Have a seat, please."

She went through an interior door, returned. "I'm sorry, Mr. Pineda isn't available."

"It'll only take a second."

"He's out of the office."

"Then who are you talking to back there?"

She tried to look authoritative but fell far short. "You'll have to make an appointment."

"How about tomorrow?"

"We don't have any openings."

"You're not even going to check the calendar?"

"It's a very busy day."

"What's the first available?"

"I'm afraid we're not taking new clients."

"I'm not a client." I shouted over her head: "Mr. Pineda, I need to talk to you."

"*Please* keep your voice down."

"Tell him it's about Swann's Flat. Tell him William C. Arenhold sent me."

She blanched and disappeared again. When she came back she didn't say anything, just held the door.

CHRIS HAD DESCRIBED Rolando Pineda as not totally with it. To me he appeared perfectly sharp: younger than his eighty-five years, with dyed-black hair and a pencil mustache, eyes set deep in a vaguely saurian face. Framed photos, taken over decades of evolving fashion, showcased his longevity.

Pineda, shaking hands with a mitered bishop.

Pineda, cutting the ribbon on a baseball field.

Receiving an award for civic leadership.

In full-dress uniform, waving from a Veterans Day float.

An enlarged copy of a check for $2.2 million hung beside diplomas from Loyola Law School and Cal State Fresno and his license from the State Bar of California.

"You gave my girl quite a turn." He folded his hands over a concave belly. "She has a heart condition. You should be more careful."

"My apologies."

"May I see your license, please?"

California PI licenses are embarrassing. They look like they were made on the teachers' lounge copy machine by an unambitious third grader, especially compared with the august license on Pineda's wall. He scanned briefly and returned the card as if doing me a favor.

I said, "Marisol Santos Salvador was your client."

"I can't comment on that. Privileged information."

"She owned a property in a town called Swann's Flat."

Like most lawyers, Pineda knew how to use dead air to his advantage. He said nothing, let me stand there, my statement deteriorating.

"For thirty years she's been making payments to an entity called Swann's Flat Resort Area," I said. "It adds up to around fifty thousand dollars."

"Who hired you?"

"In 2002 you represented William C. Arenhold in another suit over Swann's Flat land."

I slid him copies from the case file: letters on his professional stationery, signed by him.

He smiled but didn't look at the page. "My eyesight isn't what it once was."

"The petitioner's name was Elvira Dela Cruz. You were her lawyer, too."

"I've been in practice for fifty-six years. Do you know how many clients I've represented?"

"You introduced Ms. Dela Cruz to William Arenhold and encouraged her to invest with him. Is that what you did for Mrs. Salvador?"

"I'm not qualified to make such recommendations."

"You're not qualified to practice law, either, but that's not stopping you."

"I beg your pardon?"

"You were disbarred," I said. "Eight years ago."

Pineda laughed. "Chris is getting his money's worth with you, isn't he."

"What you're doing is punishable by a fine of up to a thousand dollars and up to one year in jail."

"Nobody goes to jail. They pay the fine."

"How do you think your other clients would feel if they found out?"

"They don't care. They only want me to write angry letters to Comcast."

"Should we start again?"

He sighed and gestured *go ahead*.

"Did you advise Marisol Santos Salvador to purchase property in Swann's Flat?"

"I am always concerned about my clients' welfare."

"Is that a yes?"

"I may have. It was a long time ago."

"Did you introduce her to William Arenhold?"

"I may have."

"How many other clients did you introduce to Arenhold?"

"I can't recall the specifics."

"When Mrs. Salvador bought her property, did you receive a finder's fee?"

"I worked for Bill on retainer."

"What about the monthly payments? Did you receive a cut of those?"

"Absolutely not."

"Were you aware that Mrs. Salvador was writing checks up until her death?"

"I urged her to sell. More than once."

"I thought you didn't give financial advice."

"I was speaking as a friend," he said.

"Is that how you'd characterize your relationship with her?"

"Young man, you watch your mouth, please."

"Why didn't she listen to you and sell?"

He shrugged. "The ways of women are inscrutable."

"What's Swann's Flat Resort Area?"

"As I said, it's been a long time, but I seem to recall they were in charge of maintaining the grounds. Grooming trails, things of that nature."

"That's what she was paying a hundred thirty-five bucks a month for? Trail grooming?"

"They don't groom themselves."

"What's at the address? Is it a house? Acreage?"

"I couldn't tell you. I've never been there."

"I'm going to ask you again. How many people did you introduce to Arenhold?"

"My answer is the same. I don't recall."

"How did you meet Arenhold?"

"He was an accountant. I hired him as an expert witness on a case and we got to be friendly. Eventually he required representation of his own."

"He had you on retainer," I said. "You must have been doing a lot of work for him."

"He was a busy man, with many business interests."

"Do you still work for him?"

A flicker in the eyes.

"Unfortunately not," he said.

You gave my girl quite a turn.

I'd taken Pineda to mean that I'd startled her by raising my voice. But it wasn't the shout she'd reacted to; it was the name. *William C. Arenhold sent me.*

"He's dead," I said.

"Unfortunately."

"Since when?"

"About twenty years ago."

"How?"

"He was crossing the street and got hit by a car."

"Any context you'd like to add? Before you answer, I was a sheriff-coroner. I can look it up. But you'd be saving me some time."

"You're a little young for an ex-cop, no?"

The door opened and the receptionist put her head in. "Mr. Abayon is here."

"I'll be right with him," Pineda said. He stood up. "My clients need me. Best of luck."

Out in the waiting room, an older Filipino man in orthotic shoes leaned on a four-footed cane, clutching papers in one trembling hand.

Pineda flashed teeth. "Manuel! Good to see you, my friend. Please."

The older man moved past me with a hopeful, easy smile.

BACK AT MY desk, I studied up on the late William Collins Arenhold.

Like Marisol Santos Salvador, he had possessed neither a watercraft nor pilot's license.

That was the extent of their overlap. His history included two bankruptcies, two DUIs, and a drunk in public. He'd spent most of his adult life in San Francisco and at the time of his death was residing in Potrero Hill with his wife, Pamela, and their teenage daughter.

A friend at the San Francisco Medical Examiner's office emailed me a copy of their report. On the afternoon of September 6, 2007, Arenhold left his apartment for a business meeting at the Sir Francis Drake Hotel. Pamela told the investigator that she didn't know who the meeting was with or what it concerned. A server at the hotel bar recalled waiting on Arenhold and another gentleman of about the same age; they ordered a screwdriver and a glass of bourbon, respectively. The server did not recall hearing them argue, but when she came to the table to check on them, she found both men gone and a pair of twenties trapped under a glass.

After leaving the hotel, Arenhold had stopped at a Starbucks on the corner of Powell and O'Farrell to purchase a cup of coffee. He then walked two and a half blocks south to Market Street, where he stepped off the curb and into the path of an oncoming Muni bus.

His death was ruled an accident.

Having read—and written—thousands of similar reports, I sensed the ambiguity hiding in a plainspoken narrative. The investigator noted that Arenhold was under considerable strain, facing multiple lawsuits and the possibility of a third bankruptcy.

But the stigma of suicide is so severe and scarring for next of kin—as one of my former colleagues says, it taints the family tree—that some coroners will do everything they can to avoid the ruling, absent conclusive physical evidence or clear indication of intent.

Arenhold had not left a note.

He was struck while crossing a busy street.

The bus driver stated that he had no time to honk.

It happened so fast.

For her part, Pam Arenhold was adamant her husband would not have taken his own life.

Why would he buy coffee if he meant to . . . That doesn't make any sense. That's silly.

I looked her up. She was sixty-seven years old, currently residing in La Jolla.

I called her.

Someone answered on the first ring but didn't speak.

"Hello?" I said.

"Yes?"

"Hi, I'm looking for Pamela Arenhold."

"Yes?"

"Is this Mrs. Arenhold?"

"Yes, it is."

"Mrs. Arenhold, sorry to disturb you like this—"

"No, it's *wonderful* to hear your voice."

"Um . . . thank you. Would you be willing to talk to me about your late husband William?"

"Who?"

"William Arenhold."

"He's my Billy boy," she said.

"Pam, what do you remember about Billy's job?"

"He's a rascal. My Billy boy."

"Did he ever mention people he worked with, or things he was working on?"

"He brings me flowers," she said.

In the distance I heard a different voice, younger, female. *Mom? Who are you talking to?*

"What about Swann's Flat?" I asked. "Pam? Did he tell you about that? Can you try to remember?"

"I . . . What?"

"Swann's Flat."

Mom. Give that to me.

The younger woman came on the line. "Who is this?"

"Sorry," I said, "can you just put her back on for one second?"

"Don't call here again."

"Ma'am, I'm not trying to—"

"Did you hear me? Don't ever fucking call here, *ever again.*"

If getting hung up on was an Olympic sport, all the competitors would be PIs.

CHAPTER 6

I invited Chris in to discuss my findings, outlining some of the other cases and using them as a framework to understand Marisol's.

"Your grandfather passed in 1995," I said. "She bought the property the following year. My guess is Pineda approached her right after she'd collected the life insurance. He's uniquely positioned to know who's come into money, who's emotionally vulnerable."

"Piece of shit. What does he have to say for himself?"

"I think that's about as much as I'm going to get. I went back and his receptionist threatened to call the cops on me."

"Give me ten minutes alone with him. I'll make him talk."

"I'd like to state for the record that I don't recommend that."

He snorted a laugh. "All right. What do you recommend?"

"I'm not an attorney. Unlike Pineda, I'm going to stay in my lane."

"I'm not asking for legal advice. I just want to know what you think."

"I agree that he's unethical. That doesn't necessarily make him liable."

"Who knows what guarantees he made to her?"

"She's not around to testify. Neither is Arenhold. That gives Pineda the last word."

"We have this other woman. Elvira."

"Her case was dismissed with prejudice. A competent attorney would eat her for lunch."

"Pineda's not even supposed to be practicing."

"We could try holding his feet to the fire," I said. "But I don't recommend that, either."

"Why not?"

"The guy's eighty-five, with a history of public service. I'd bet he golfs with half the judges in the county. Now picture him getting up on the stand and doing the feeble-old-guy act. What jury is going to bring down the ax?"

"Criminal charges?"

"The standard of proof is higher, and fraud is notoriously tough because there's a fine line between that and salesmanship. That's assuming you can get the cops to care, let alone the DA. For fifty grand? Nobody's getting a headline out of that."

"It's more than fifty," he said. "The principal's sixty thousand alone. Plus property tax."

"Property tax you're never going to get back. Take my word for it: Anything less than millions and millions of dollars, they're gonna feel the juice isn't worth the squeeze."

"But if what you're telling me is true, it's not one case, it's dozens."

"At least. Figure that for every person who wakes up and sues, there's many more like your grandma, who keep writing checks, not realizing that the land is worthless. But in my opinion it's unlikely that Pineda's calling the shots. Aside from a few transactions, his name doesn't come up. My gut is he's a middleman. Arenhold, too."

"For who?"

"That's the question. I pulled the deed of conveyance for your grandmother's property, trying to find out who she bought it from. It's not a person. It's an LLC called Pacific Partners. They're a shell company in New Mexico, owned by something called Diversified Interests, in Nevada. Which is owned by Western Enterprises, in Wyoming. Confused yet?"

He said, "That's the point."

I took him on a tour of websites offering property for sale in Swann's Flat.

"This is all autogenerated," he said.

"For sure. Cut-and-paste copy, reused photos. The problem is it's decentralized. There's no contact person, just a bunch of corporations with bland names like Diamond Capital or Golden State Ventures. Trace the corporations, they end up in one of four places: Delaware, Nevada, Wyoming, and New Mexico. Those are the states that allow anonymous LLCs, and they're using multiple layers. I submitted an inquiry, hoping I'd hear from someone, but all I got was a link to a form wanting my address, Social Security number, income, et cetera."

He scrolled. Cursed quietly. "How is anyone falling for this?"

"I'm not and you're not," I said. "But we're not who they're targeting. The folks I spoke to had no investing experience. They lived far away and couldn't easily make the trip. A lot of them don't speak English very well. All they had to go on were pictures. You see the ocean and the price and imagine yourself in a beach house. Check this out."

I opened up a popular real estate site and typed in *Swann's Flat*.

A single result came back: 22 Black Sand Court.

Chris frowned. "Where's the rest?"

"This is a private listing. Whoever is running the scam has opted out of MLS, so the properties don't show up on the aggregators. For an ordinary seller, that's a bad thing. You want to reach as many buyers as possible, to get a quick sale for the most money. That's not the goal here. It's about scale: Set out four thousand fishing poles. Use bait search terms: *cheap California real estate* or whatever. The form weeds out anyone savvy enough not to give out their personal information. Meanwhile they can wait for someone more naïve to come along and bite."

"Like *lola*."

"I wouldn't be too harsh on her, Chris. I'm sure they gave her the hard sell. They had to, in those days, because everyone had to be sought out and pitched individually. Now it's streamlined. Sit back and let the suckers flock to you."

He pounded the desk lightly. "Oh man. It's so messed up."

"Yup. They're making money at every stage. On the sale, on the fees, assessments, loans, interest. Another advantage they have is time. If I've sunk my life savings into this place and debt is piling up, I can't wait around for years and years. I need to get out now. That's where the deed transfer comes in. They get the property back for next to nothing and sell it all over again."

"I just don't understand why she kept paying them."

"She had a dream. It's hard to let that go. Or she was hoping for the price to rebound. Or she realized she made a mistake and was too embarrassed to tell anyone. It might not have occurred to her that she had the option to *not* pay. When honest people get bills, they pay them."

He exhaled. "Okay. So what do we do?"

"I'll tell you what I told you before: It depends on what you expect to get out of it."

"You want me to let go of *my* dream."

"I want you to sleep easy."

"A name," he said. "Can you at least get me that?"

"There's one thread I'd like to pull. I have to warn you, it could start to get expensive."

"I'm warned. What is it?"

"ML Corporate Solutions. By law, anyone doing business in California has to be reachable. If you want to hide your address, you can hire a registered agent, and they become you, for the purpose of serving process. Every one of these corporations selling property lists ML, or something close. The name keeps changing. It's M-hyphen-L, or M-slash-L, or M-ampersand-L. Corporate Services or Corporate Agents or Business Solutions. The address is always in Swann's Flat, but there's a ton of them. I tried to figure out who owns them, and it's another giant maze of bullshit. Which is strange: They've obviously gone to the trouble of covering their tracks. But they use the same signature. It's almost like they're bragging."

"What's your next step?"

"Head up there in person. Check out the addresses. See if I can get someone to talk to me. Like I said, it could get expensive. And I can't promise anything."

"You found Peter's sister."

"Every case is different."

"You don't want to do it?"

"I want to be up-front with you."

"I wonder what it's like," he said. "Her land."

"Like dirt, probably."

He laughed despite himself. "Go for it. Pull the thread."

HIS WASN'T THE main authorization I needed.

Amy said, "How long will you be gone for?"

"I'm thinking two to three days. My mom can do drop-offs and pickup."

"What about gymnastics?"

"Isn't it Becca's turn for carpool?"

"They're away this week. We switched."

"Shit. I forgot."

"Do you want me to ask my mom?"

"Please. Thank you."

Shopping, cooking, bills; the everyday give-and-take of a two-income household.

The next series of exchanges went beyond that.

Amy said, "Will you be careful?"

"Yes."

"Will you communicate honestly with me, before, during, and after?"

"Yes."

"Are you going to carry a gun?"

"I'll bring it, although there may be times I don't have it on me."

"Worst-case scenario."

"I ask the wrong person the wrong question. They don't like me poking around in their business. But I want to avoid spooking anyone, if for no other reason than I'll get more information that way."

"What do you do if you no longer feel safe?"

"I leave."

The conversation had a practiced rhythm, having been hammered out over hours in couples therapy. And while it felt artificial, I understood the need for it.

I hadn't always been careful.

Sometimes I'd lied.

Sitting on the couch, holding my wife's hands, I tried to answer each question as if it were the first time she'd asked.

"One to ten," she said, "how much do I have to worry?"

"I'm going to call it a two."

She arched an eyebrow. "Two is a trip to the grocery store."

"What's one?"

"Sitting on the couch with me."

"Three . . . point five?"

She looked me in the eye for a few moments. Finally she said, "I can handle that."

"Thank you. I love you."

"I love you, too. Can you refill my water, please?"

"It would be my honor and pleasure."

When I returned she'd put on *House Hunters International*. She draped her legs across my lap and I began massaging her feet.

"Where are we tonight?" I asked.

"Madrid."

"What's our budget?"

"Eight hundred thousand."

"You can't get anything halfway decent for that."

"Not if you want to be in the city center."

"Otherwise what's even the point?"

Amy smiled.

We watched to the end and she made her prediction: "Number three, 'The Flat with Old-World Appeal.'"

On-screen, the couple said, "The Flat with Old-World Appeal."

"How do you do that?" I asked.

"There's always clues. You just have to pay attention." She put down her drink. "Kiss me, please."

"Yes, ma'am."

CHAPTER 7

On GPS the land around me was two pale green blocks, with Highway 101 wriggling between them like a poorly laid seam. I'd skipped the scenic coastal drive in favor of a more direct inland route through Sonoma and Mendocino.

Blackened trees haunted meadows vivid with post-wildfire regrowth; grassy fields gave way to tall coniferous forest; tourist traffic sloughed off till I was alone, tracing the bends of the Eel River, its banks high and dry in the stifling heat.

Most people—most Californians—forget about the top third of the state. In their minds the map stops at San Francisco. Tahoe, if you ski.

Dr. Dre said it best: *It's all good from Diego to the Bay.*

Anywhere farther north might as well be Oregon. Naked hippies chanting Willie Nelson songs while tending fields of marijuana.

Entering Humboldt County I passed a string of borderless towns more name than place. Green light filtered through the redwoods, dappling the windshield as I weaved by derelict company housing and rusting mechanical hulls. Remnants of a timber industry come and gone.

Farmstands: raw milk, homemade cheese, organic CBD oil.

For over an hour I didn't see another vehicle. Then a southbound oil truck blew past, rocking me in its wake.

The town of Millburg marked my turnoff, last call for fuel, food, and lodging. Retailers of all three occupied a single dusty block alongside other faded establishments. The elementary school, post office, fire station, and sheriff's substation shared a parking lot. One-stop shopping.

Needing to stretch my legs, I gassed up and left the car parked at the Union 76 station, walking half a block to Fanny's Market. A sign boasted HOT COFFEE—COLD BEER—ICE CREAM—SODA— SANDWICHES. The air was woolen and smelled like a campfire.

An enormous bulletin board monopolized the market's exterior wall.

HELP WANTED. FOR SALE. COMMUNITY EVENTS.

The largest section was labeled HAVE YOU SEEN ME?

Not cats and dogs and the odd escapee gerbil, but people, their pictures and vital information. The relevant authority; the number to call. Reward, if any.

Hailey Ray. 2-24-23. Hailey left her mother's house in San Luis Obispo to drive to Portland, Oregon. She was last seen walking along Highway 3 south of Weaverville. Her red Kia was found on the bridge over Little Browns Creek. Her wallet and keys were in the car. Hailey has a history of mental illness.

Sam Rosenthal. Missing from vicinity of Orleans since 07/3/2021. Sam and a friend went camping in Six Rivers National Forest. On Sat July 3 he went for a hike. He has not been seen since. He was wearing blue jeans, a purple sweatshirt, and hiking boots. He has a tattoo of an eagle on his left shoulder.

MISSING BECKA CANDITO. Blonde hair Brown eyes Ht 5-5 Wt 120 Last known contact April 2024 If you have any information

regarding Becka's disappearance or related criminal activity
please call the Trinity County Sheriff's Office tipline. Reward!!!

The flyers were tacked up two and three deep, battered by heat
and cold and sun, sagging inside protective plastic sleeves, the sub-
jects' facial features dissolving, as though their souls were leaching
out. Californians, but also travelers from Arizona and Colorado,
from New Jersey, even one from Germany. Several of the cases appeared to belong to other jurisdictions, and I wondered why they'd
been posted here.

I pushed through the screen door.

The market was stuffy and dim. A fan purred uselessly behind
the register, overseen by a paunchy middle-aged man wearing a
Phish concert tee and working a crossword.

I dispensed coffee from a self-serve urn and filled a basket with
snacks, taking care to avoid the rack of cannabis-infused baked
goods.

The clerk laid his puzzle aside to ring me up.

"That's an interesting bulletin board you got," I said.

He nodded.

"Maybe I should leave a note with you for my loved ones," I
said. "Just in case."

"Where you headed."

"Swann's Flat."

"That so. Thirty-eight-sixty."

I handed him cash. "I need a receipt, please."

"Yuh. Can I ask what you're driving?"

"It's a RAV4."

"Four-wheel drive?"

"No."

"Uh-huh. Well. Keep it in low and take your time. Once you
start, you're committed."

"I have to get there, one way or the other."

He slapped down my change. "Let's hope it's not the other."

FIVE MINUTES FROM town I was alone again, cruising west along two twisty lanes relieved by the occasional turnout or gravel spur. Ahead towered the broad back of the King Range. GPS predicted two hours to cover the final twenty-four miles. For the first nine of those I couldn't understand what the big deal was.

At Blackberry Junction, Swann's Flat Road splintered from the main highway, and a pockmarked sign issued from a thicket of manzanitas to admonish me.

WARNING
ROUGH ROAD NEXT 13 MI.
NOT ADVISABLE FOR LARGE
TRAILERS OR RVS
OR IN WET WEATHER
PROCEED AT YOUR OWN RISK

I downshifted and trundled forward.

The paving contracted to a single lane before petering out into cratered dirt. The grade pitched up violently, the forest closed in, oaks and madrones and Douglas firs mobbing the roadside like bloodthirsty spectators. Branches knitted. Shadows spread. My tires spun in the soil and loose stones. I lost the horizon, then the sky. With them went any sense of orientation, leaving me switchbacking blindly through billowing khaki clouds, jouncing in my seat, mashing the horn at every turn to alert oncoming vehicles. I wasn't sure what I'd do if I did run up against someone. Back up? Move over? How? I had six inches of clearance to either side. On my left the earth formed a sheer wall bristling with roots thick as baseball bats. On my right it collapsed into a tangled gulch.

I climbed slowly, watching the temperature gauge tick upward. GPS had frozen, as if I'd driven off the planet.

I was pouring sweat. I'd turned off the air conditioner to avoid overheating the engine, but when I cracked the windows dust flooded in, and I rushed to close them, steering with one hand as I hacked and sneezed and blinked tears down my cheeks.

Cresting a ridge into dazzling light, I glimpsed bright, turbulent water.

Then the grade plummeted and I plunged downhill, picking up unwanted speed, braking, skidding, struggling to correct, gravity taking over and the car a two-ton anchor to which I was strapped. I'd given up honking. I couldn't stop even if I wanted to. I simply had to ride it out.

Ten terrifying helpless minutes ended in a trough with a bone-rattling bang.

I jammed into park and threw off my seatbelt, sucking air.

When my head cleared I saw that I was at the bottom of a valley. A log bridge spanned the dry creek bed. Redwoods blotted out the sun. The foliage beneath grew stunted and waxy, a vast, rumpled carpet of wood sorrel and ferns, bark and leaves and needles and dirt and stone.

Across the bridge the grade spiked again. I shifted into gear, my heart pounding in dread. I had eleven more miles of this; eleven nauseating yo-yo miles of basin and range.

Up, up, up.

And down.

I'd traveled to other forbidding places—the Utah desert, the remote reaches of Yosemite Valley, where tourists never venture—and the same thought always occurred to me.

How did anyone ever find this?

Two hours was starting to feel awfully optimistic.

At mile eight, crawling around a particularly gnarly hairpin, I came to a roadside cross.

I stopped, grateful for the break, and got out.

Wooden crucifix, the inscription burned in.

KURT SWANN

1969–2009

A Jack Daniel's bottle stood nearby, neck sawn off to form a vase stuffed with dead flowers. The bottom was scummy and crawling with insects.

The memorial had been set perilously close to the edge. No choice. Otherwise it would obstruct traffic. At the same time, the placement seemed like an invitation to tempt fate. The cliffside was uneven, bitten by wind and rain. Craning, I saw a vicious slope of exposed sedimentary rock with nothing to break a fall.

I tossed a stone. It bounced, spun off into space, and sank into the void far below. I couldn't hear it land.

AT MILE ELEVEN, I reached the last and highest ridgeline.

The world tore open.

To the north, to the south, the coast stretched in a jagged ribbon. Whitecaps detonated against crags of black rock. The Pacific Coast baring its teeth.

It was a crude, ax-hewn land, bunched like the front end of a head-on collision, steep and inhospitable but for a squarish peninsula knuckling into the sea.

Swann's Flat.

I'd spent so much time studying it on a computer screen that it looked fake in real life.

Four miles wide, two miles deep, crisscrossed by black-green belts and hemmed in by soaring granite bluffs. The highly touted beach was a slender cove at the southwest corner. Adjacent was the marina, where the inn and boat launch were located.

Modest progress had occurred since Elvira Dela Cruz's time.

From my vantage I could pick out twenty-five or thirty structures, spaced far apart, lurking through the trees or plonked down in the open. The largest were situated along a prominent boulevard that ran parallel to the waterfront. Other than that, the street plan was scribbly and erratic, as if it had been laid out in crayon by a toddler.

I began my descent.

The grade relaxed and the canopy thinned, redwoods giving way to alders and pines, chokecherry and incense cedar. Trails periodically broke off into the woods. They didn't look especially well groomed. I'd have to take it up with the Swann's Flat Resort Area.

Paving reappeared. Power lines came loping out of nowhere.

I crossed another bridge, wider and better maintained.

SWANN'S FLAT

POP 10 ELEV 33

"HEART OF THE LOST COAST"

Wikipedia had given the number of residents as thirteen. Evidently there had been some attrition, but no one had gotten around to updating the entry. At ground level, I could no longer see clear to the ocean, though I could read its influence in the back-slanting tree trunks, blasted by relentless onshore winds. Lowering the window, I gulped a mouthful of salt.

My intention had been to start by running down addresses. GPS was still paralyzed and my cell showed no bars. I meandered at five miles per hour through a warren of streets named quaintly for local flora and fauna. Pepperwood Way. Screech Owl Court.

Block after empty block.

There was plenty of movement—the agitated thrashing of the pines, the furtive sorties of rodents, rabbits, quail.

Yet it felt barren.

Hostile.

Plastic lot markers sprouted in the weeds, heedless of reality.

Mocking it.

Numerous dead ends and wrong turns delivered me to the western edge of the peninsula, Beachcomber Boulevard. Misnomer: There wasn't any beach to comb, just a tarnished railing and a sheer drop to the rocks. Waves boiled in the hollows, gulls plunged screeching into ruffled blue silk.

I would have expected the lots closest to the water to be intensively developed, but the area remained largely raw, a battleground for native and invasive species: reed grasses and fescue, bright California poppies. Seaside woolly sunflowers, the zombie creep of ice plant.

Half a mile south I came to the first house.

What a house it was.

Three stories of white clapboard and storm shutters, fronted by a veranda and topped by a satellite dish, enjoying an unobstructed ocean view and occupying its own territorial ocean: forest, fields, a sheep pen, a barn, light farm machinery.

I was ogling, foot on the brake, when something tickled my peripheral vision.

A figure wearing a unisuit, helmet, and sunglasses zipped past on a bicycle, hand raised in greeting.

I started to return the gesture but the person was already a dot in my rearview.

I drove on, coming to another mansion, even grander. Then a third, more like the first.

One mile later Beachcomber terminated at a sad, cracked plaza.

The marina, such as it was.

Something had run out. Money, faith, or both.

Four boats sat on trailers in a rippling asphalt lot overlooking the water. A concrete strip wrapped down to the cove and widened out to become the launch. The bait kiosk was shuttered.

The inn, a weather-beaten Victorian, bore the curious name of Counts Hotel.

I slotted in beside the only two vehicles parked out front: a black, mud-spattered Range Rover and a red Ford F-150. The truck had a wheel lift mounted in the bed. Stenciled on the door WAS PELMAN AUTO SERVICE.

Grabbing my bag, I hurried up the steps through a stinging wind.

A bell jangled as I entered. The theme was nautical: navigational instruments, charts, fish trophies. A chandelier fashioned from rope and ship's lanterns drooled weak light over the unoccupied dining room. Black-and-white photos tiled the splintery walls.

Two scruffy guys in their mid-thirties sat at the bar drinking beer. They stopped talking to peer at me. A third man, older and grizzled, gripped a tumbler of ice and gazed lovingly at the sticky mahogany.

Scruffy Guy One lifted his mug to me.

I nodded, and he resumed the conversation with his buddy. I picked up enough to get the gist. Virtues of the .338 Winchester Mag versus a .30-06 for elk.

Behind the bar, saloon doors led to the kitchen. A woman in her fifties bustled through, drying her hands on her apron. She had flushed cheeks and a gin blossom nose and was built like a Viking queen.

She took a stubby pencil from over her ear. "Name your poison."

"I wanted to ask about a room."

"How many nights?"

"Can I see it first?"

She replaced the pencil, raised the hinged bar top, and led me upstairs to a mildewy room lacking a TV. Ticking puffed from the bedspread. The nightstand listed. A bookcase held a motley collection of casual reads: coffee-table books, cookbooks, thrillers.

Shabby without the chic.

By far the best feature was a bay window, its panes smeared with salt, giving a view of the cove and roiling waters along the southern coast. A bistro table and two chairs conjured romantic visions of honeymooners in terry-cloth robes, holding hands and sipping coffee as the day dawned. All that was missing was the robes, the coffee, the couple, and the romance.

"Bathroom?" I asked.

"End of the hall," she said.

"Wi-Fi?"

"You want that, go to Millburg."

"What counts about the hotel?"

"It's my name," she said. "Jenelle Counts. It comes from German. Kuntz. Art."

I picked up the landline. A dial tone, praise the Lord. "How much?"

"Six hundred a night. Comes with breakfast."

I managed to keep my poker face. "Works for me."

She smiled sourly. "Welcome to Swann's Flat."

CHAPTER 8

Downstairs, Jenelle Counts and I traded cash for a key.

I said, "Do you have a map I could look at?"

She pointed into the dining room, toward the gallery wall.

The photographs documented the evolution of the peninsula over the last hundred thirty years. Pure ranchland. A logging camp. The marina and cove during a more prosperous era, complete with an intact pier, ships bobbing as they waited to take on cargo.

A yellowing developer's brochure, unfolded and staples removed, depicted the street plan.

Be a Part
of the ♥
of the Lost Coast!

The brochure's styling placed it from the sixties. The street names were tiny and hard to read. I squinted at countless neighborhood blocks, as well as features that had never come to fruition: a golf course, an airstrip, playgrounds.

Behind me a voice said, "A stranger comes to town."

Scruffy Guy One had sauntered over. Flannel shirt, Bass Pro Shops cap with a fringe of dirty-blond hair poking out. Nice-looking in a rough-hewn way.

He straightened a grainy photo of a horse: muscular and proud, mane whipped up by wind, so that it seemed to be flying.

"General Sherman. He was the mail horse for twenty-five years. They'd load him up and he'd run riderless to Millburg and back."

He smiled. Strong white teeth. A small chip in his left lateral incisor gave him an *aw-shucks* quality—not *Deliverance* so much as Will Rogers.

I smiled back. "True story, huh."

"I mean, who's gonna argue?"

"Not the horse."

He chuckled. "No, sir."

I pointed to the photo of the marina. "What happened to the pier?"

"Washed away. We get some pretty hellacious storms come winter. Matter of fact, there's more than a couple wrecks out there. They say if you listen late at night, you can hear the sailors crying out for help."

He winked and extended a hand. "Beau Bergstrom."

"Clay Gardner."

"Pleased to meetcha, Mr. Gardner. What brings you to our neck of the woods?"

"Passing through."

"Where from?"

"Bay Area."

"Terrific. Where to?"

"Not sure. Just getting away from it all."

"Well." Beau grinned. "You're away now."

"No kidding. Nobody warned me about that road."

Scruffy Guy Two piped up: "She's a doozy."

Roundish face, sloped shoulders, hairline in early retreat. He read as a little younger, a lot less poised, than his compatriot.

"I might be stuck here permanently," I said.

Beau said, "I can think of worse places." He waved at the brochure. "Looking for something in particular?"

"I was planning to explore a little."

"I'd be happy to show you around, if you're interested."

"I wouldn't want to inconvenience you."

"No inconvenience."

Scruffy Guy Two said, "Beau's the head of the welcome committee."

Beau jerked a thumb. "And DJ's the village idiot."

DJ said, "Can't have a village without one."

"All kidding aside, I do some guiding," Beau said.

"Oh yeah?" I asked. "Like what?"

"Hunting, fishing, bird-watching, hiking."

"He's writing a book," DJ said.

"Nice," I said. "Like a guidebook?"

"More local history," Beau said. "And I don't know I'd call it a *book*. Right now it's just a big mess of notes. Don't ask when it'll be done."

"When'll it be done, Beau?" DJ hollered.

The solitary older man at the bar cleared his throat, the first sign that he was fully conscious.

Beau said, "And what is it you do, Mr. Gardner, down in the great Bay Area, that you need to get away from?"

"I'm in finance."

"Hence the need to get away."

"You guys grew up around here," I said.

"Born and raised," DJ said.

"They'll have to take me out feetfirst," Beau said.

The older man set down his glass with a *clack*. "Let's go."

I thought he was talking to himself. But DJ shotgunned his beer and followed the older man toward the exit. I noticed then the family resemblance.

"See ya, Beau," DJ said.

"Take it easy, gents."

They left, jangling the bell.

"Anyway," Beau said to me, "I should get a move on, myself. I'll leave you my number."

He motioned to Jenelle. There was something patronizing about the gesture—as if she were a hired hand. She looked none too pleased, but she complied, setting out a napkin and giving him the pencil.

"You need anything," Beau said, scribbling, "don't hesitate."

"Appreciate it."

"You have yourself a delightful day. Jenelle."

She nodded, and he went out.

I pocketed the napkin and started for the stairs.

She said, "Hungry?"

"Maybe later, thanks."

"Kitchen closes at seven."

"Okay. Can I ask you something? How's Beau, as a tour guide?"

She dumped ice into the sink. "He's the only show in town."

I USED THE landline to leave Amy a voicemail, letting her know that I'd arrived safely.

"There's no cell service," I said, reciting the number taped to the phone. "I'm stepping out soon but I'll try again later. Love you."

I put my bag on the bed and unlocked it.

Clothes for four days. Laptop. My fieldwork camera, a Canon EOS. Ballistic vest.

Gun case with two firearms: my SIG Sauer P320 and a smaller model, the P365, that I prefer for concealed carry.

After a moment's contemplation, I took the Canon and left the rest.

Downstairs Jenelle Counts was clattering around in the

kitchen. I photographed the developer's map, checking it against my list of addresses and plotting a route.

First stop: Swann's Flat Resort Area and ML Corporate Solutions.

Monkeyflower Drive was way over on the northeast side of the peninsula, catercorner to the marina. Even so, at a total distance of less than five miles, it shouldn't have taken me more than ten minutes to get there. It took twenty-five.

The map, it turned out, was a fantasy. At least half the lots and streets had been redrawn or renamed. Other streets were unfinished and died without warning. The missing amenities had been filled in with *other* lots and *other* streets, and the sadist who'd done the urban planning had an unhealthy fondness for claustrophobic cul-de-sacs. I had to keep switching my attention from the road to the camera. Once I almost drove into a culvert.

I was already feeling put out as I turned onto Monkeyflower Drive and began counting lot markers. Toward the end of the block, genuine anger began to curdle.

Number 134—home to Swann's Flat Resort Area, the entity responsible for trail grooming, that had accepted fifty thousand dollars from Marisol Santos Salvador and six thousand dollars from Elvira Dela Cruz and God knew how much else from God knew how many other people—was an empty lot.

Number 136, home to ML Corporate Solutions, was almost as empty. But not quite.

There was a mailbox.

In the middle of a field of waist-high grass.

Surrounded by a chain-link fence.

Padlocked.

I walked the length and breadth of both properties, shooting photos and video. This far inland, wind was less of a presence, and the dominant sound came from cicadas.

Ordinarily I would have canvassed the neighbors. There weren't any.

While it felt a bit absurd to be documenting nothing and nobody, the absence was itself evidence. It's a peculiar feature of our legal system that you have to hand someone a document in order to serve them.

There was no one here to accept papers.

What process server in his right mind would drive out here to begin with?

I hopped the fence at 136 and waded through the grass, swinging at gnats. The earth was pitted with gopher holes, and I went carefully, leery of stepping on a snake or tripping and injuring my bum knee.

The mailbox was a standard-issue size, made of galvanized steel and affixed to a wooden post. Peel-and-stick lettering read 136 MLCS. They hadn't bothered to sink the post into the ground; it stood crookedly in a plastic bucket filled with cement.

I opened the box. Spiders.

Footsteps behind me.

I spun, reaching for the gun I'd left behind.

In the road stood a mule deer and two fawns.

I raised the camera to take a photo for Charlotte, but the animals bounded into the brush and vanished.

NEXT STOP WAS Elvira Dela Cruz's lot at 71 Sea Otter Lane.

It was a disaster. Worse than she'd described. The hole was more like a ravine, crumbling and filled with boulders.

I further made explicit to Ms. Dela Cruz that those images are meant to give a sense of the geology and biodiversity of the region as a whole, rather than referring to any plot in particular.

I couldn't see the ocean. I couldn't see a sunset or any jumping dolphins, either.

———

ABALONE COURT LAY near the middle of the peninsula, and Marisol Santos Salvador's lot at number 8 was wooded but flattish, with a partial view of the bluffs. Far better than Elvira's. Marisol might never have realized her dream, but she hadn't been a complete sucker.

I doubted Chris Villareal would find any comfort in that.

I SPENT THE afternoon zigzagging to addresses associated with ML. At every one I found the same setup: mailbox on a post, chain link prohibiting access. The pattern of flagrant disregard gave me hope that I could build a case, and I recorded each location dutifully in images and words.

Occasionally I passed a house. Cupping my eyes to windows, I saw unlit rooms with scant or no furniture.

A CAR WAS parked outside 31 Quail Lane.

Acura MDX. Arizona plates.

I knocked.

The curtains stirred, and a woman peered out.

I smiled and waved.

She withdrew. Moments later, a man opened the door. The woman stood behind him, looking tense. They were both Asian, in their late twenties, dressed in outdoors gear.

"Yes?" the man said.

"Sorry to bother you," I said. "I just got to town. Do you live here?"

"Airbnb," the woman said.

"Any chance I can get contact info for the person you're renting from? I need a place to stay."

"I don't have it on hand," the man said.

"Would you mind checking the reservation?"

"Sorry," the man said. "We have to go."

He shut the door.

THE SUN WAS low as I headed toward my final stop. I felt ready to throw in the towel. I'd been up since four, was tired and hungry, and I wanted to speak to Amy before she got sucked into the chaos of evening routine.

Number 22 Black Sand Court, located in the peninsula's heavily forested southeastern quadrant, had the distinction of being the one and only finished home for sale in Swann's Flat. It was also unique in that the seller was an individual rather than a corporation. His name was Albert Bock, and I figured that he might be able to provide an insider's perspective on what it was like to buy, build, live, and sell in Swann's Flat.

I turned onto his block.

The place was a fortress.

To the extent that I could see it. Which wasn't much. The sharp peak of a roofline rose behind a solid wooden fence, ten feet high and topped by two more feet of lattice densely woven with vines. Crowning that, rusty razor wire. And behind it all, even higher bamboo.

<u>PRIVATE PROPERTY</u>
<u>NO TRESPASSING</u>
VIOLATORS WILL BE SHOT
SURVIVORS WILL BE SHOT AGAIN

I approached the front gate. Behind it a dog began barking madly. A security camera cast its blank eye on me.

I rang the buzzer and knocked. The barking got louder.

I rang again, waved to the camera. "Mr. Bock? Anyone home?"

The gate shook as the dog snarled and clawed and hurled itself against the wood.

I followed the fence toward a gravel driveway. I could hear the dog snuffling, tracking me.

Tall swinging doors blocked the driveway. They were bolted from the inside and gave about an inch. Close-packed cedars and pines eliminated any sightline to the house. Though I did get a good close-up of a black snout and gnashing teeth.

I jogged to my car for pen and paper, writing that I was interested in Mr. Bock's property and would be in town for a few days, staying at the hotel. I signed *Clay Gardner* and added the email address I'd created as part of my cover.

I didn't see a mailbox or slot. I wedged the note between the gate door and the frame.

A loud *pop* rang out.

Initially I didn't perceive the sound as a gunshot. My mind read it as a snapping branch.

The second shot cleared up any confusion, decapitating my passenger-side mirror.

I ran, diving into the driver's seat and punching the START button. Pressed flat against the console, I shifted into reverse and gunned it down the block; swung around, hit DRIVE, and stomped the gas.

In the rearview I saw a man emerge from the woods, a long gun propped on his shoulder, his features effaced by glare.

CHAPTER 9

I put a healthy distance between him and me and pulled over to assess the damage.

The mirror dangled on wires, its plastic neck shattered. Examining the side of the car, I couldn't find the scrape left by a passing bullet, which meant that he'd been shooting straight-on, from somewhere in the trees to the left of the front gate.

If he'd hit what he was aiming for, it was a hell of a shot.

What do you do if you no longer feel safe?

I leave.

The sun was dropping fast. I doubted I could make it to the main highway before nightfall, and driving that dirt road in the dark was suicidal.

I rationalized.

He could've fired at me as I was getting away. He hadn't.

He wanted me off his property. That was all.

But what if?

My note told him where to find me.

Visions of a lunatic, kicking open the hotel door and blasting away like some deranged parody of a Western movie.

My gut tightened.

I disconnected the wires, stashed the mirror in the footwell, and drove to the marina, parking at the hotel and crossing the plaza toward the boat lot.

I'd give it some time, see if he showed up.

The wind had slackened as evening came on. I jogged down the ramp to the cove. The concrete was steep and slick with sand. Low tide revealed remnants of the pier, rotted pilings that gasped to the surface between waves.

A woman stood on the beach. She was heavyset, with a blunt gray bob, clad in a matronly skirt and a fisherman's sweater. She smiled at me and went back to watching the sunset.

I gave her a respectful margin.

The sky had separated into layers, a band of molten brass at the horizon and above it steel wool shot through with iridescent fuchsia. Blood-red water lapped at the rocks. Into this luminous scrim were cut the silhouettes of landforms, cliffs and trees, coal-black lumps of coastline.

The world as negative space.

The woman humped over to join me, natural as can be.

"Never gets old," she said.

"How could it?"

"Most folks take things for granted."

"That's why most folks are unhappy," I said.

She nodded. Pointed west. "See that?"

"What am I seeing?"

She cackled. "Japan."

I laughed.

"Maggie Penrose," she said.

"Clay Gardner."

"Where from?"

"Bay Area."

"How long are you in for?"

Seeing me hesitate, she tilted her head. "Everything all right?"

"Sort of. I was out for a drive and someone shot at me."

"Oh jeez. Are you okay?"

"I'm fine. But he knocked the mirror off my car."

"How awful," she said. "Did you see who it was?"

"I was looking at a house on Black Sand Court."

"Ah. That'd be Al."

"You know him."

"I know everyone and they know me. Nature of the beast."

"I'm trying to decide whether to call the police."

The idea appeared to amuse her. "Feel free. Don't expect them anytime soon, though."

"That's unnerving."

She shrugged. "We don't need them. We look out for each other. It wouldn't work any other way."

"Sounds nice."

"It is. I grew up looking over my shoulder. Now I keep my door unlocked and my keys in the ignition. It's that kind of town."

"Al's door is most definitely locked," I said.

"I'll have a word with him."

"You don't have to do that."

"Well and good, but we can't have him going around scaring the pants off the tourists."

"Really," I said. "I don't want to upset him worse."

"Al? He's harmless."

I looked at her.

"In a manner of speaking," she said. "He just likes his privacy. But as you wish."

The sun had sunk into the water. From her skirt pocket she withdrew an LED headlamp.

She tightened it on her forehead phylacteryishly and switched it on. "Good night."

"Good night."

She humped up the ramp, headlamp bobbing.

I WAITED FOR the brass band to cool before heading up to the plaza.

All quiet on the western front.

In my hotel room I phoned Amy from the landline.

She was fine, the kids were fine, my mom was being a *huge* help.

"She's with you right now, isn't she," I said.

"Mm-hm."

"Can I talk to them?"

"Hang on, I'll put you on speaker . . . Say hello to Daddy."

"Hi everyone," I said.

"Daddy, I can't see you," Charlotte said.

"It's a phone call, not a video," Amy said. "You can talk to him."

"Daddy, I had a great day."

"That's great," I said. "Tell me about it."

"I made Foodland."

"Wow. That sounds amazing. What's Foodland?"

"Daddy," she said patiently. "It's a *land* for *food*."

"Right, how silly of me. Is Myles there? Buddy?"

"He's smiling at the phone," Amy said.

"Hi, Clay," my mother said.

"Hi, Mom. Thanks for taking care of everyone."

"You're welcome. Are you having fun?"

"Sure am. Honey, do you have a second?"

"Let me call you once they're in bed," Amy said.

"You have the number?"

"I wrote it down. Say good night to Daddy, everyone."

"Good night, Daddy."

"I love you," I said.

"Talk soon," Amy said and hung up.

I took a towel down the hall to shower. I was dusty and grubby and sore from hours of driving. Running my hands over my scalp

I became aware of the seam of scar tissue. Another scar—shorter, thicker, and uglier—bunched atop my right thigh, the flesh like eraser rubber. I had ceased to see or feel them, and I'd buried the memory of the night I got them: the last time someone had taken a shot at me.

When I got to the room the phone was ringing.

I picked up. "That was fast."

"Your mom's dealing with them," Amy said. "What's wrong?"

She knew. She always did.

I told her.

She said, "You're not hurt."

"The mirror's fucked, but I'm fine."

"Okay. First, thank you for being honest with me."

"Of course."

"You're sure you can't leave tonight?"

"I'm telling you. Even in daylight, this road is an accident waiting to happen."

"How soon can you go?"

"Dawn."

"Can you call the police?"

"I've been told they don't show up."

"How is that possible? You call and they just ignore you?"

"Honey," I said. "You work in Oakland."

She let out a nervous titter. "I'm a little upset that you weren't wearing your vest."

"I'm sorry. For what it's worth, I was mostly in the car, and there's next to no one out on the streets. But you're right."

She didn't answer.

"Amy? Did I lose you?"

"I'm here," she said. "You don't want to leave. Is that what you're trying to say?"

"I told you I would and I will."

"I'm asking what *you* want."

"I could use more time. But I don't want you to worry."

"I'm already worried." She sighed. "How much longer do you think you'll need?"

"It's hard to tell. I've only been here a few hours."

"And people are already shooting at you. What if this maniac decides to come after you?"

"I don't think that's likely."

"Based on what?"

"He had a clear shot at me as I was driving away," I said. "He didn't take it."

"So what? He could change his mind."

"He doesn't have a reason to."

"Did he have a reason the first time?"

"I was snooping around his property. He was scaring me away. Another person I spoke to told me he's harmless."

"Oh well, that's extremely reassuring."

I laughed. She started laughing, too.

"I can't believe we're having this conversation," she said.

"Me neither."

"What *is* this place?"

"I don't know," I said. "It's super weird. The whole town's like a stage set. This guy at the bar struck up a conversation with me and next thing I know he's volunteering to be my tour guide. Would you do that for someone you'd just met?"

"I wouldn't do it for someone I dearly loved. Does he want money?"

"Probably. I don't imagine they get too many outsiders."

"I'm sure they don't, if they reach for a gun every time someone rings a doorbell." She sighed again. "Okay. You can stay. With certain conditions. First, you cannot go near that guy."

"No desire."

"You have to wear your vest, too. That's non-negotiable."

"I will."

"I want you to check in with me every hour."

"That limits me pretty severely. I can only call from the room."

"Then you have to tell me where you're going and how long you'll be out of contact."

"I can do that. Thank you."

"You're welcome. And there's one more condition. You owe me a massage when you get back."

"As many as you want. It is beautiful here, I'll give it that. I wish you were with me."

"I'm sure you do," she said. "With another target you'd be splitting the risk."

"Amy—"

"Hey," she said. "This is me coping with stress."

"Okay."

"I'll order a vest in my size," she said.

I laughed. "I love you."

"I love you, too. Good night."

I pressed the hookswitch, fished out the napkin with Beau Bergstrom's number, dialed.

"Yeeellow."

"Beau, it's Clay Gardner. We met earlier."

"Hey hey. What's the good word?"

"If you're free tomorrow, I'll take you up on that tour."

"For you, sir, I am free as a bird. What's your fancy?"

"You mentioned a hike."

"There's a beauty, runs up along the railroad tracks."

"How long is it?"

"Eight miles, out and back."

"About how long will that take?"

I'd asked because I needed to tell Amy when to expect my call. But Beau seemed to interpret the question as a sign of weakness. In a tone half needling, half encouraging, he said, "You're a fit guy, you'll be fine."

"I just want to know how much water to bring."

"Figure five hours, plus time for lunch. What do you say?"

"Sounds good."

"It's a date, then," Beau said. "We should start before it gets too hot. Seven o'clock?"

"I'll be ready."

"And don't worry about water or food or nothing, I'll take care of that."

"Thanks very much."

"You, sir, are very welcome. See you in the morning."

It was nine thirty p.m. I'd missed the window for kitchen service.

I unknotted the bag of snacks I'd bought at Fanny's Market.

Chips, pretzels, mixed nuts, beef jerky.

PI health food.

I downed a couple of protein bars, typed up the day's notes, and got ready for bed.

Lying in the dark with the curtains drawn, I listened to the wind howl and the shutters groan, rocks colliding in the surf, like the bones of a sinking ship, the screams of drowning men.

CHAPTER 10

Despite my exhaustion, I slept poorly, waking often to imaginary gunfire. Each time, I stumbled to the bay window, parted the curtain a few inches, and peered out at the deserted, moonlit plaza. By five a.m. sleep was a lost cause.

It was too early to call Amy. I put on sweats.

The hallway smelled of coffee, and when I went downstairs, I heard Jenelle puttering around the kitchen, country music playing softly.

"Hello?" she called.

"Morning."

She emerged. "You're up early. Did you sleep all right?"

"Fine, thanks."

"Coffee?"

"Please."

"Milk and sugar?"

"Please."

She brought a mug. "Breakfast won't be ready for a little while. If I'da known I would've had it waiting for you."

"It's not a problem. Do you have any duct tape? I need to fix something."

"If it's the towel rod, just shove it into the socket."

"Not that."

She looked at me curiously. "Gimme a minute."

She disappeared through the saloon doors, returning with a roll of tape. "Here you go."

"Thanks."

"Will you need the room again tonight?"

"I'm not sure."

"Checkout is noon. After that I'll have to charge you for another day."

"I'm meeting Beau. I think we'll be back by about one. Can I let you know then?"

She nodded, and I thanked her and took the tape outside.

Fog smothered the plaza. Cormorants wheeled against a leaden sky.

I retrieved the mirror unit from the footwell and set to reattaching it.

The bell jangled. Jenelle Counts appeared on the porch. "You hit a deer or something?"

"Something like that."

She watched me for a minute, arms crossed, then went inside.

BREAKFAST WASN'T A six-hundred-dollar room perk, but it was ample: eggs, bacon, biscuits and gravy. I was starving, and Jenelle kept refilling my plate till I waved the white flag and went to dress.

Cargo pants, trail shoes; a lightweight shirt, cut baggy to hide the ballistic vest and the P365 in an IWB holster. False buttons and a magnetic closure allowed for quick access. In the mirror I saw a suburban dad who had never stalked anything deadlier than the aisles at Home Depot. The look didn't quite square with Clay Gardner's mover-and-shaker money-guy persona. But it would have to do.

At six thirty I called Amy. Wails filled the line.

"Please, Charlotte," she said. "He was playing with that."

"But it's mine."

"You weren't using it, and in this house we share our toys. Please give it to him."

"He doesn't share with me."

"I hear that you're upset, and I'm happy to talk to you about it once I've had a chance to speak to Daddy. Right now, please give the truck back to Myles."

"No."

"One. Two."

"*Fine.*"

A crash. Stomps. The wailing got louder as Amy picked Myles up.

"Good morning," she said.

I said, "What happens if you get to three?"

"You don't want to find out. How are you? Has anyone shot at you yet?"

"No, but it's early," I said. "What about you? Get any sleep?"

"Not enough."

I heard a tinny *beep beep beep.*

"Ba," Myles said.

"That's right, cookie," Amy said. "The truck says beep . . . What's on tap for today?"

"I'm hiking with my friend the tour guide. I have the vest on and I'm carrying. I should be back in the room by early afternoon."

"Thank you. Please call me when you are."

"I will. I love you. Have a good day."

"You too. Stay safe."

AT FIVE TO seven I came down to find Beau seated at the bar in hiking shorts and a faded purple T-shirt.

"Top of the morning," he said. "Heck happened to your car?"

"The mirror came loose."

"Oof. You want, I can call DJ for you. He'll fix it right up."

I thought about Elvira Dela Cruz, dunned four hundred dollars for coolant. "It's a rental."

"You get the extra insurance?"

"I'm covered under my regular policy."

"Smart. Those things are a rip-off. Okey doke," he said, clapping. "Since you're a man of culture, I thought we'd start here."

He led me to the gallery wall, gave a magician's flourish, and launched into a monologue, using the photos for illustration. Sheep grazing in the meadows. Grimy, hollow-eyed men in overalls, brandishing saws beside a vanquished redwood whose width exceeded their combined height. A pygmy steam engine dragging a wagonload of logs.

"Tracks used to run to the pier. Cove's too tight for ships to pull up, so there was a lumber chute off the end. They call it a doghole port, 'cause it's so small only a dog could turn around in it."

Next: the Reverend Dr. Everett Swann, town namesake and mill owner, godly white beard, undertaker's suit.

A volunteer spotter with binoculars patrolled the beach for Japanese aircraft or submarines.

That this spiel was so clearly canned didn't make it any less entertaining. Beau narrated with gusto, winking and nudging and peppering in ironic jokes.

"Miss Vicki Jo Pelman, Queen of the Salmon, 1975. Yes, indeedy: DJ's grandma; Dave's mom. Seeing them two baboons, you'd never guess what a looker she was . . .'Course she didn't have much in the way of competition. Anyone who comes to Swann's Flat in search of single women is barking up the wrong redwood."

A showman, through and through.

"What's the deal with the map?" I asked. "I was driving around and kept getting lost."

"Now there's one to break your heart. Mill shut down in the

mid-fifties. After that everyone cleared out. For about ten, fifteen years it was more or less a ghost town. Everett's son, Charlie, he dreamed up the idea to turn it into a vacation spot. He starts the pageant, buys ads, lines up investors, the whole nine. Even got the county to chip in for improvements. Then the Coastal Commission comes hollering about this dang limpet, only grows between here and Point Delgada. They sued to block. Charlie was fighting them for years, getting bled dry. One day he wakes up, takes his rifle to the cove, and blows his brains out."

"Oh my God."

Beau nodded somberly. "And on that note."

He smiled and gestured to the door. "Shall we?"

THE RANGE ROVER was a stick shift, and as we reached the outskirts of town and hit the entry road, I braced for a wild ride. But Beau was graceful on the clutch, shifting and banking through gusts of white fog, anticipating potholes and rocks. He could have had his eyes closed.

A mile up he pulled to the shoulder and set the parking brake. Sword ferns nodded. I didn't see any trail, groomed or otherwise.

While I doused myself in bug spray, he opened the trunk, taking a stout-barreled revolver from a gun safe. He strapped it on, handed me a canteen, and shouldered his backpack.

"*Vamanos,*" he said and marched into the woods.

Over the next hour, we hiked uphill, straddling mossed logs, stepping over roots and scat piles, while Beau delivered an unbroken stream of homespun patter.

Legends from before the white man. Colorful local lore.

Interspersed were episodes from his own free and easy childhood. He'd shot a mountain lion once.

"You tend to see them early in the morning or close to dusk. They're skittish. They hear you coming and take off. This time, it's the middle of the day, I'm strolling along, minding my own business. Bam, there she is."

"That is terrifying."

"*Oh* yeah. I was pissing my pants."

"How old were you?"

"Ten or eleven."

"Holy shit."

"I basically lived out here as a kid," he said. "Nothing really scared me. But man, I tell you . . . She musta been starving to be out in the open at that hour. She was crouching on a rock, and I can see her eyes narrowing. You don't want to run, 'cause that sets off the predatory instinct. What you're supposed to do is stand your ground, wave your arms, yell, get big, throw rocks. She didn't give two farts. She hops down and starts creeping toward me. I sure as heck wasn't going to outrun her. So I did what I had to do." He clucked his tongue. "Right between the eyes."

"You hit her the first time?"

"I was a pretty good shot, even then. I used to carry this itty-bitty Glock 26."

"What about now?"

Bergstrom stopped to unholster the revolver. "S&W500."

"Beast."

"Oh yeah. Stop a bear. The recoil's a bitch. Take your arm off, you aren't ready for it." He glanced at me. "Wanna try?"

". . . Me?"

"I don't see anyone else around."

"I mean. Is that allowed?"

"Why not? It's not like you're gonna hit anyone." He paused. "'Less you're one of those gun control guys."

"No. Not . . . It's a complicated issue. No offense."

"None taken. So let's carpe diem."

I said, "Okay."

Kindly smile. "You never shot a gun before."

"Not really."

"All righty. Lesson one. Go on. She won't bite."

I accepted the revolver, aware of the other gun strapped to my body.

"See that alder over there? With the knot? That's your target. Line it up and take a couple of deep breaths. You're waiting for the space between one breath and the next. And you're not going to pull, you're going to squeeze. Got it? Safety off. When you're ready."

The report was deafening, like a bomb going off. Crows exploded from the treetops.

Bergstrom reached over and thumbed on the safety.

"Did I hit it?" I said.

"Close. You want to try again?"

"That's okay."

He took back the gun. "Feels good, right?"

"Yeah. It does."

"Can't do that in the great Bay Area."

"You'd be surprised."

He laughed. "All right, soldier. Move out."

BY HOUR TWO the fog had burned off. A pair of corroded iron rails surfaced through the soil: the abandoned logging tracks. We followed them as they snaked alongside a gully. Beneath my shirt, the holster was chafing, the vest clammy. Beau apologized for talking my ear off, switching from boosterism to male chitchat. Work, family, sports, hobbies, cars, travel.

I drew on Clay Gardner's backstory.

Married, no kids, Berkeley graduate, MBA.

Tennis. Skiing. Hawaii and Cabo and Tahoe.

"What do you drive, when you're not driving a rental?"

"Tesla."

"Model?"

"S."

"Happy with it?"

"Point A to point B," I said. "Lease is up in a year, got my eye on a Porsche Taycan."

My answers appeared to satisfy him: He expected no less from a man like me. On the off chance he double-checked, he'd find corroboration on Clay Gardner's fictitious LinkedIn, Instagram, and Facebook accounts.

Gradually we began to diverge from the tracks. Keep with them, Beau said, and you'd come to the abandoned mill—a site worth visiting in its own right, but best kept for another day. He had something else in mind.

"Not long now," he said.

Whatever landmark he was using was invisible to me. He veered through the trees, and we arrived at a clearing, where I beheld one of the most astonishing sights I'd ever seen: a grove of redwoods shaped like giant candelabras. Each tree started as a single thick trunk before forking into two, four, ten separate arms, growing sideways, backward, up, down; whirling like dancers, writhing like flames. Shafts of light pierced the gloom.

Beau beamed, a collector showing off his prize piece. "The Cathedral."

I drifted forward, mesmerized, listening with half an ear as he explained the conditions that had caused the trunks to split, a combination of harsh salt air and fierce wind. Thankfully, the loggers had left the trees standing—not out of reverence, but because their warped forms rendered them useless as lumber.

"'Course there's rumors, too," he said.

"What's that?"

"Indian burial ground. Haunted."

He winked and reached around for the backpack. "I got ham and Swiss, or turkey and cheddar."

"Turkey, thanks."

We sat cross-legged and ate. Sound carried in the syrupy heat: birds and small animals, needles snowing to the forest floor.

"I can't get over how peaceful it is," I said.

"Yes, sir."

"I'm glad they didn't turn it into Disneyland."

"Amen."

I finished my sandwich, crumpled the foil into a ball. "You know, when I was out yesterday I saw tons of lot markers. But you're saying they're not for sale."

"Oh, you can *sell*. You just can't build within twenty-five hundred yards of the shore."

"What about the houses on Beachcomber?"

"Grandfathered in. Truth is, us full-timers like it just fine this way. It takes a special kind of person to fit in here. You gotta be willing to do things the hard way. Gets lonesome, too."

"What you call lonesome, I call private."

"Yes, sir. God knows, privacy, they aren't making any more of it."

"Cheers to that."

We clicked canteens. Mine was dry.

Beau swigged and wiped his mouth on his wrist. "'Scuse me while I drain the main vein."

Once he was gone, I undid the top two magnets on my shirt. The vest was soaked through.

I reclosed the shirtfront.

"Psst."

Across the clearing, Beau put a finger to his lips. He mimed taking a photo.

I tiptoed over, camera in hand, and followed his gaze.

A bear was nosing through the underbrush.

It was small. A cub. The mother couldn't be far behind.

Beau's hand rested on the revolver. He nodded urgently. *Now or never, chief.*

I lifted the camera, focused, snapped.

The bear sat up on its hind legs, staring in our direction.

"Shit," Beau muttered.

He drew me back into the clearing. We gathered our supplies and started downhill.

CHAPTER 11

Nearing the trailhead, he said, "There's a few lots left."

He held back a blackberry vine. "Also grandfathered."

I knew what he was doing.

Private tour of his wilderness Eden. Tales of the Old West.

Instant bromance, just add ammo.

Fire away, city boy.

Friendly questions about my lifestyle, calibrated to gauge disposable income. He already knew I could blow six hundred bucks on a crappy hotel room. That had to be promising.

The halo of scarcity. The allure of exclusivity.

Takes a special kind of person.

Tell me, soldier: Are you that guy?

If I didn't know any better I'd guess he'd hired the bear, too.

Altogether it made for a damn fine sales pitch. On some level I admired it.

I said, "Are they on the market?"

"Not officially."

I nodded but didn't say more, and he didn't raise the topic again, not for the rest of the hike or on the drive into town.

At the hotel I dug out my wallet, peeling off three hundreds.

He grimaced. "Clay."

"Token of gratitude. I insist."

"Really. It's my pleasure."

"And this is mine."

A beat. He tucked the money in his breast pocket. "Good man."

"I'm gonna get cleaned up," I said. "Maybe afterward you can take me around, show me what's available."

For a moment he seemed not to understand. Then he mugged pleasant surprise. "Yeah, we could do that. Sure thing."

"Great. Thanks."

"I'll need to make a couple calls first, run it by the owners."

"Will that be a problem?"

"No, no. Just a formality," he said. "Pick you up in—an hour?"

"Better make it an hour and a half."

"You got it, brother."

I PAID JENELLE Counts for another night and left Amy a voicemail that I was alive and well.

The holster had left a rashy red band around my waist. I draped the vest over a chairback to air out. It was still sopping when I returned from the shower. The thought of putting it on again made me shudder.

I sat on the bed in my towel, typing up notes.

A high-pitched squeal cut through the thrum of the tide.

Brakes.

Beau wasn't due for another twenty minutes.

Setting the laptop aside, I went to the bay window and peeked out.

Not the Range Rover. Not Pelman Auto Service, either.

A compact Chevy truck, mottled orange and primer, idled in the plaza. The driver had gotten out and was standing by my car, inspecting the taped-up mirror.

He gave it a wiggle.

I shrank back.

I didn't think he'd seen me. I'd barely seen him.

I recognized his shape nevertheless.

Al Bock.

I crossed the room in two steps and set the chain.

Threw on the damp vest.

Grabbing the gun from the nightstand, I sank to the floor, keeping the bed between me and the window, back pressed to the wall.

Waves rolled in and out.

Wind pulsed against the window glass.

Another squeal.

I counted to sixty and crawled to the bay window.

The Chevy was gone.

THE FIRST PROPERTY Beau brought me to was on Mink Road, a gently rolling 1.1-acre parcel with pristine mountain views. Importantly, the site had existing lines for water, power, and sewer, plus pre-approved architect's plans. The current owner hated to sell. But he'd taken a hit in the most recent down market.

Asking price was $705,000, nearly twice as high as the most expensive online listing.

"Bet you could make him an offer, though," Beau said.

Amy and I had watched enough HGTV for me to know that the first property is never The Property. He was testing the waters. It was on me to play the part of the disinterested buyer while keeping him hooked on the belief that I was hooked.

I strolled around—snapping pictures, hashing out where to put the pool, the guesthouse—before concluding, "It's a good start."

He smiled. "Should we move on?"

"I think so."

The scenario repeated itself, with larger parcels and higher prices, at the next two stops, on Grouse Way and Coyote Court. They were nice, I allowed, but at the end of the day I preferred to be closer to the beach. There wasn't anything like that available, was there?

There was.

Number 11 Sea Star Court was 2.3 acres. The entire ocean-facing side of the property had been razed. I could see the hulking outlines of the mansions along Beachcomber.

Asking price was $1,875,000.

I let him finish extolling the lot's virtues. "What about on Beachcomber itself?"

He gave me a look. The Look. Another HGTV staple.

What I was asking for was impossible—the real estate equivalent of cold fusion.

Didn't I realize that I was going to have to compromise?

He wasn't going to be able to pull this off.

If he did, it would take a tremendous amount of hard work.

"Let me put this in context for you," I said. "It's not necessarily about building or not building. Obviously it's good to have the option. But it's as important to me to preserve and hold value. I work in a highly volatile sector. I'm always hunting for opportunities to shave off risk."

I thought if Peter Franchette could hear the bullshit streaming from my mouth, he'd take me on as a mentee.

Beau rubbed his chin. "Okay, here's what I can do for you. There's someone I want you to meet. You'll be around tomorrow?"

"Not for very long. I have an appointment in the city. I need to leave first thing."

"Let me see if I can set it up for tonight. That work for you?"

"It does. Thank you, Beau."

"Glad we could make it work. You'll like him," he said. "You guys speak the same language."

———

AMY, CALLING FROM her homeward commute, said, "I'll be glad to have you back."

"I'll be glad to be back. Listen, I need to tell you something."

". . . Okay."

"I saw the guy."

"Which—the gun guy?"

"He came to the hotel."

"Oh my God."

"He didn't come inside. He was checking out my car. I saw him from my window."

"Did he see you?"

"I don't think so. I can leave if you want me to."

"But?"

"I was really hoping to talk to Beau's person."

"When's that happening?"

"Soon, I hope. I'm not sure how long the conversation will take. But it's almost six thirty. If I'm not out of here pretty soon, it's going to start getting dark, and I'm stuck."

"Can you move somewhere for the night?"

"I could find a quiet street and sleep in the car."

"I don't want you to have to do that."

"I can ask the innkeeper to lock the front door," I said. "Keep the chain on and my gun within reach. Or leave now. It's your call."

"I don't like this, Clay."

"I know. I don't, either. In my opinion, it's still unlikely the guy tries anything. It's the second chance he's had to get at me, and the second time he passed."

"He could be planning," she said. "That's why he's hanging around."

"You're right."

"Is this person you're meeting even going to give you what you need?"

"I feel close. But that's a guess."

She sighed. "I'm not going to sleep tonight. Don't bother to say it, I know you're sorry."

"Okay."

"Do you have any idea how many massages you're going to owe me?"

"As many as you want."

"As many as I want."

CHAPTER 12

I paced, occasionally stopping to part the curtains.

A creak in the hall, a knock at the door.

Drawing the P320, I called, "Yes?"

"Kitchen's closing," Jenelle Counts said.

"Okay."

"Do you want dinner?"

"All set, thanks."

She left.

At seven forty-nine, I saw Maggie Penrose, the woman from the beach, disappear down the boat ramp to the cove, awash in pinks and golds.

At eight eleven, I saw her return, headlight bobbing.

Eight thirty came and I still hadn't heard from Beau. He wasn't answering my calls, either. The silence felt calculated, and I was debating whether to try him again when the Range Rover pulled up. I watched him hop out and hurry around to open the door for the passenger, reduced by the dim to a squat shape wearing a cowboy hat.

They disappeared beneath the porch overhang.

I checked my watch: eight fifty-three p.m.

The room phone rang.

Jenelle said, "You have visitors."

"Thanks. I'll be down in a sec."

I swapped the P320 for the P365 and put on my second magnet-front shirt. I didn't have a third.

It felt prudent to keep them waiting, just as they'd done to me. Right up to the edge of discomfort, but not beyond.

At nine oh seven I came downstairs.

The bar was unattended, the kitchen lights off.

"Mr. Gardner."

In the dining room, Beau Bergstrom stood at a table, smiling. The other man was smiling, too, behind a bristling white goatee. His upper and lower halves were comically mismatched: scrawny legs in tight Levi's, black western shirt straining at the gut and spilling over an ornate brass belt buckle. He resembled nothing so much as a golf ball on a tee.

"Clay, I'd like to introduce you to my dad," Beau said.

The hat was a camel Stetson with a beaded hatband in a Navajo pattern. The man tipped it to me. "Emil Bergstrom."

A pronounced twang shortened the vowels of his first name. *ML.*

I shook their hands. "Great to meet you."

"Better to meet *you*." Emil fired finger guns at me. "Bourbon man?"

"Scotch. Neat."

"Shoot. I was close. Coming right up."

Beau fetched a bottle of Glenfiddich from the bar, placing it in front of his father along with two tumblers.

Emil uncorked and poured. "How'd you like that hike?"

"Great, thanks to Beau."

"Been too long since I made it out to the Cathedral. Something else, huh?"

"Spectacular."

He slid me a tumbler. "'Tween you and me, I'm not sure I'll ever see it again. I got this arthritis in one hip and both knees."

"Sorry to hear it."

"Aw, never mind. It's a good excuse not to go frolicking in the woods. Nature's always been more the boy's thing than mine. He takes after his mama. She was a child of the land, and a child of the land she begat."

He pinched Beau's cheek. Hoisted his glass. "Slainte."

We clinked and drank.

"So," Emil said. "My son tells me you're smitten with our tiny slice of paradise."

"Guilty as charged."

"How'd you find us?"

"Google."

"I think I've heard of that." He winked. "Can't say I blame you. Stressful job, finance."

"It can be."

"What sort of finance?"

"Private equity."

"Buy low, sell high, so forth."

"That's it in a nutshell."

"Your interest is in an investment property."

"Primarily."

"Gotcha," he said. "Hate to pry, but we've had some unfortunate instances where people fall behind on payments, or they can't afford the upkeep. It can turn into a real hassle."

"It won't be an issue."

"I didn't mean to suggest it would. We do the same for everyone. Only fair. It's a tight-knit community, y'know. We depend on each other."

"Maggie Penrose said something along those lines."

Emil smiled. "You met Maggie."

"Yesterday evening, down by the beach."

"You can set your watch by her," Beau said.

"She's a pearl," Emil said. "We're lucky to have her. Anyhoo. Ours is a delicate ecosystem. You understand."

"I do."

"Glad we're on the same page. From our end, there's a brief application process. We ask to see three years' worth of tax returns. Would you be comfortable with that?"

"Can I ask who's 'we'?"

"The Board of Supervisors," Beau said.

"I can get that for you," I said. "I'd rather not go to the trouble before I know what it is I'm applying for."

"Of course," Emil said. "I'll have Beau draft a proposal for you."

"I'm here now."

"Well, I admire the pep in your step, but you're gonna have to get used to waiting." Emil smiled. "We don't move at city speed."

Push?

Or dance?

ML.

There must be a piece of paper somewhere with his signature on it.

Dance.

I smiled. "You know what, Mr. Bergstrom? You're right. And this is a pretty clear demonstration of why I really need to get away."

He chuckled. "We'll fix you yet."

THEY DEPARTED WITH Clay Gardner's email address. The proposal would be forthcoming.

Jenelle wasn't around to lock up.

I doubted she ever bothered. If anyone in Swann's Flat did.

Why would they?

It was that kind of town.

I bolted the front door and wedged a dining room chair under the handle.

In my room I locked the door, set the chain, and wedged a chair under the knob.

I laid out clothes for the following day and packed my bag.

I moved the mattress to the floor, out of line with the window.

I put the P320 on the floor nearby and got into bed.

IT WAS ANOTHER terrible night, about three hours of patchy sleep. This time it wasn't gunfire I was hearing in my dreams, it was squealing brakes. I resisted the urge to get up and check. Didn't want to stir the curtains and find him sighting up at me along the barrel of a rifle.

The phone shrilled me awake at four fifty-five.

I crawled over to it. "Yeah."

"Are you in your room?" Jenelle Counts said. "I can't get the front door to budge."

"Shit. One second."

I put on clothes, ran downstairs barefoot, and let her in.

"What the hell is all this about?" she said.

"I'm so sorry. I thought you lived here."

"I do. My entrance is around the back. That's where I called you from." She frowned at the chair. "What possessed you to do that?"

"I just— Al Bock shot at me. He's the one broke the mirror off my car."

Jenelle goggled.

Then she whooped laughter.

"That old goat? What'd you do to get on his bad side? Not that it takes a whole lot."

"Nothing. I went by his house. Yesterday I saw him poking around outside the hotel. I was concerned he'd show up and do something crazy."

"Why'd you go there to begin with?"

"It's for sale. I wanted to see it."

"It's been for sale for fifteen years," she said. "He's turned down every offer ever came his way. You seem like a nice enough guy, but I wouldn't hold my breath."

"Duly noted."

"Well. I'll need some time to get your breakfast ready."

"Thank you, but I have to hit the road."

"You don't want anything?"

"Just coffee, please."

"All right. I'm afraid I can't refund that portion of your money."

"I wouldn't ask you to."

The mug was waiting when I came down with my bag.

"Come back soon," Jenelle said.

"Thanks. Can I have a to-go cup, please?"

"You want that, go to Millburg."

A WHITE ENVELOPE flapped on my windshield, trapped beneath a wiper blade. Inside was a personal check, made out to Clay Gardner in the amount of two hundred dollars and signed by Albert Bock.

The memo line read

SORRY

DRIVING AWAY FROM the marina, I felt in the snack bag for the package of beef jerky, tearing it open with my teeth and shaking a piece into my mouth.

It tasted awful—funky and dry. I battled the first mouthful for ten minutes before giving up and spitting it out the window.

Chris Villareal had asked for a name. I'd gotten him two. Maybe he'd be content to stop.

I hoped not. I didn't want to stop. My mind was churning, and

I felt eager to get home and see what I could dig up on the Berg-stroms.

I crossed the bridge at the town limits.

The paving ended.

The road began to rise.

Away we go.

The broken side mirror rattled at every bump and rut. I kept expecting it to fall off, but it was somehow still attached as I passed the Cathedral trailhead. Never underestimate duct tape.

I rubbed my eyes, gave my head a hard shake. I'd only had time to guzzle down half a cup of coffee, and I felt droopy and dull.

Cornering sharply, I reached a straightaway and fed the gas.

I heard it before I saw it.

Rubber scraping earth, metal on metal, the guttural wheeze escaping me as I was thrown against the door, my bag tumbling around in the cargo space.

I heard her shriek, heard the shriek end, suddenly, sickeningly, as I struggled to make sense of her face.

A manic swirl of colors and shapes, oval eyes swollen, mouth a black cavern.

Her body, a bright-blue blur, wiped away.

CHAPTER 13

'd wrenched the wheel to my left, away from the cliffside and toward the forest, and when I came to rest and kicked open the door I saw that her reflex had been the same.

A single skinny tire track mirrored the fat pair left by me.

The lines almost kissed.

Then hers broke off.

I swooned, scanned the trees. Flies muddied the air. "Hello?"

Silence.

My head was pulsing. More pressure than pain. A punishing rhythmic whoosh.

I started forward unsteadily. "Hello? Are you there?"

A moan.

I stumbled toward it.

She lay fetal in a patch of ferns, about twelve feet from the road. Her eyes were clenched, her face streaked with grime. The cushioned landing had helped, but not enough: Scratches marred the surface of her helmet, abraded flesh wept, and she rocked, clutching her shin, blood oozing through her fingers.

I knelt. I didn't want to touch her. "Hey. I'm here . . . Hi. Can you hear me?"

She opened her eyes. Dirt speckled her eyelashes. She looked twentyish. Her unisuit was color-blocked, teal and black. Not the same suit she'd been wearing thirty-six hours prior, when she'd zoomed by me on Beachcomber. But the same person.

"Can you hear what I'm saying?" I asked. "Do you understand me?"

She nodded groggily.

"Okay. What's your name?"

She rose to her elbows.

"Hold on—whoa whoa whoa whoa whoa."

She was trying to stand up. Blood coursed down her shin.

"Hold still a second, please, okay? I'll be right back. Stay here."

I ran tripping to the car and pulled a T-shirt from my bag.

She was sitting up when I got back. I used the shirt to bind the gash on her shin.

She sucked air through her teeth.

"Too tight?"

She shook her head.

"Where's the nearest hospital?" I asked.

She unclipped the helmet, leaving a red line under her chin. "I don't need to go to the hospital."

"I really think—"

She looked around. "Where's my bike."

"Miss. Wait, please. Wait. Don't get up. I'll look for it. You sit."

I found it in a bramble. The frame was warped, rear wheel bent into a taco shell. I brought it to her and her face fell.

"Shit," she said.

She rolled onto her hands and knees.

"Stay there, miss. Please."

But she was determined to stand, with or without me, so I helped her up, and we shuffled to the car. She had an athlete's build, wide shoulders and wide back. One cycling cleat clicked on the dirt.

"I'm gonna mess up your seats," she said.

"Don't worry about it."

I tossed the snack bag into the rear and settled her.

"My bike," she said.

"I'll get it."

I dragged it back through the brush, loaded it into the cargo space, and got behind the wheel. She had taken off her helmet and was raking at a mass of curly auburn hair, shedding leaves and sticks. She was younger than I'd originally thought—more like sixteen or eighteen, with the straight nose and rosebud mouth of a classical carving.

I started the engine. "We need to get you looked at."

"Just—take me home."

We were roughly two hours from Millburg. The pounding in my head was worsening, and my memory of the crash felt disjointed, like a film missing frames. I couldn't accurately gauge how hard I'd hit her but the distance she'd traveled and the damage to the bicycle suggested a gruesome degree of force.

She might be concussed. She might be bleeding internally. If she were to go into shock, I would be stranded, with no service and no help.

A two-hour drive over tortuous road . . .

"Can we please go," she said.

"Where's home?"

"In town."

"Swann's Flat."

"Yes." She rested her head. "I'll tell you where to go."

I began turning the car around. With so little room to maneuver, I could only move a few inches at a time, dancing between the ditch in front of me and the nothingness at my back.

I tapped the gas. Too hard. She winced.

"Sorry," I said.

"Maybe I should drive."

"I'm not sure that's a good idea."

"I'm kidding."

"Right. Okay."

"You're hurt," she said.

"What?"

"Your forehead."

I didn't remember the impact but she was right: Looking in the rearview, I saw minor cuts and a goose egg at my hairline. "I'm fine."

"You're sure? 'Cause it would really suck if after this you drove me off a cliff."

I laughed.

She smiled. "I'm Shasta, by the way."

"Clay."

"Nice to meet you, I guess."

I was relieved to see her perking up but also wary.

My training had drilled it in. Assess the injury; stabilize the victim.

Now the adrenaline had begun to dissipate, and I could see her and myself more plainly. I was no longer a first responder. I was the one who'd made her a victim.

I finally managed to get the car facing Swann's Flat and started downhill. Shasta arched uncomfortably against her seatbelt, tugging on the unisuit zipper to expose the hollow of her throat. A second red line dented the flesh, like a ligature mark.

"You okay?" I asked.

"Yeah, I just feel hot."

"Do you want the air on?"

"Window's fine," she said, groping for the switch.

She looked flushed. Temperature dysregulation. Not a good sign.

"How's your leg?" I said.

"Hurts."

"I'm sorry."

"It's not your fault," Shasta said. She rubbed at her neck. "I get in the zone, and . . ."

Her eyes widened. "Stop the car."

"I—"

"Stop."

I braked. "What's wrong."

She unbuckled her seatbelt.

"Wait wait wait," I said.

She got out.

"Shasta." I cut the engine and went after her. "Hold on. *Shasta.*"

She was limping uphill toward the crash site.

"Where are you going?"

"My necklace."

"We can get it later."

She ignored me. I wasn't about to restrain her. I trailed her dizzily, ready to catch her if she fell.

She limped off the road and into the brush.

"Let me do this," I said.

"You don't know what it looks like."

"Describe it to me."

She didn't answer.

"Can you tell me what it looks like?" I said.

"White shells with a silver pendant."

We tramped around in overlapping circles, stooped over, combing through foliage.

My father, a retired science teacher, used to drag my brother and me on endless nature walks while quizzing us on species. The most common plant in the vicinity was redwood sorrel, a low-growing creeper with tiny white flowers. It hid perfectly the remains of the necklace: puka shells, scattered far and wide.

I held one up. "Is this it?"

Shasta came over. "Oh fuck."

She dropped to her knees and began clawing at the earth. *"Fuck."*

"Please sit. Please."

She gave in, sinking down gingerly and rubbing her eyes while I crawled around, collecting shells and putting them in my pocket. My head was going *whomp-whomp-whomp*.

"Is this yours?" I asked, holding up a wireless earbud.

"Shit. Yeah. Do you see the pendant?"

"Not yet. What does it look like?"

"It's a rooster."

"How big?"

She spaced her thumb and forefinger an inch and a half apart.

The broken necklace cord dangled in a patch of salal. It must have caught when she went tumbling.

I parted branches, swept my phone flashlight.

A glint.

The rooster strutted in profile, tall wavy comb and grooves for feathers. It looked like something you'd buy on a whim at a crafts fair, its charm a function of its imperfection.

I brought it to her. "The shells are all over the place. And I don't see the other earbud."

"Forget it, this is the main thing." She clasped her treasure to her chest. "Thank God."

"Stay here, I'll get the car."

"I can walk."

By then I knew better than to argue.

CHAPTER 14

Back in Swann's Flat, Shasta navigated me westward.

"Where were you riding from?" I asked.

"Blackberry Junction."

"Wow. That's no joke."

"The hills are murder. But it's great for conditioning."

"Are you training for something?"

"I race triathlon."

"Cool. Well. I hope you can get back to it soon."

"Thanks. I don't know." She rubbed the rooster pendant between her fingers. "Maybe this is the universe telling me I need a break. Next left."

With a jolt I grasped our destination.

Beachcomber Boulevard, and its mansions.

I glanced at her.

Who was this person?

More to the point, who were her parents?

Even more to the point, who was their *lawyer*?

We passed the first mansion and kept going.

At the second mansion, the biggest, she said, "This is me."

I pulled into the driveway and helped her out, and we headed up the walk between beds of salt-loving plants. The wind thumped at our backs. Her cycling cleat knocked on the porch steps, setting off a torrent of barks inside. Normal barks, not the bloodlust of Al Bock's monster.

The doormat read CLANCY.

"Do you have a key?" I asked.

"It's open."

Before I could try the door it swung inward. A woman swept over the threshold.

"Thought you went for a ri—*oh my God.*"

Her face recapitulated Shasta's in the instant prior to the crash: the same almond-shaped eyes rounding into terror, skin stretched taut over high cheekbones. Her hair had been dyed a deeper red. A long blue caftan dress trailed behind her like fire as she rushed forward.

"*Oh* my *God.*"

"I'm fine," Shasta said.

"You're not *fine,* look at you, you're *bleeding.*"

A huge hairy sheepdog burst through the doorway and ran berserk circles around us, jumping and pawing at my back.

Shasta said, "Down, Bowie."

"Get inside, now," the redheaded woman said to either Shasta or the dog.

"Bowie. *Down.*"

"*Jason,*" the woman shouted into the house. "*I need you.*"

"Mom, please," Shasta said. "Can you just . . . *Bowie.*"

Her mother dragged the dog by its collar while it leapt and yelped and strained. Shasta and I came through the foyer into a generous living room, done in mid-nineties green and apricot. To the east, sliding glass doors gave onto a patio with outdoor furniture. Perforated sunshades muted the ocean-facing windows. One doorway led to the kitchen, another to the dining room, a third to a back corridor. A glass-sided staircase corkscrewed up and out of sight.

"Jason. I need you *now."*

While her mother hauled the dog down the hall and out of sight, Shasta and I straggled into the kitchen. Generous, well-appointed, dated.

I eased her onto a banquette and brought a chair to prop her leg.

"Can you get me some ice, please? There's bags in that drawer."

I filled a baggie from the refrigerator ice maker, wrapped it in a dish towel. "What else?"

"Thank you," she said. "Maybe some—"

Shasta's mother entered. I could hear the dog's muffled howls.

"Let me see."

Reluctantly Shasta removed the ice pack.

Her mother untied the T-shirt binding and recoiled. The blood had slowed to a trickle.

"Uch."

"It looks worse than it is," Shasta said.

"How do you know that? Are you a doctor?"

"Leonie?" A man ambled in. Rangy and tan, with a close-cropped beard and a crew cut, wearing flip-flops, jeans, a rumpled navy polo shirt. "Were you ca—oh shit."

"Call Maggie," Leonie said.

"What happened?"

"Jason. Did you hear me?"

"Yeah. Yeah yeah yeah." He took a cordless phone from the counter and dialed.

Shasta said, "It was an accident."

"Hi, Maggie. It's Jason."

Leonie waved him into the living room. He went, saying *Sorry to disturb you so early* . . .

"Start again," Leonie said. "From the beginning."

"I went for a ride," Shasta said.

"Where."

"How I always go. I was on my way home. I had my music on and wasn't paying attention."

"I was coming around a bend, in the opposite direction," I said. "I didn't see her till it was too late."

Leonie blinked, bewildered, as if registering my existence for the first time. Oblique light etched the lines on her face. There weren't many; she didn't look much older than Shasta. You could take them for siblings, though Leonie was shorter, and slight, as if she might shatter upon impact.

"You *hit* her?"

"It wasn't his fault," Shasta said.

"I'm not asking you, I'm asking him."

"We both swerved," I said. "I clipped her rear wheel."

"It wasn't his fault," Shasta said again.

"Can you be quiet," Leonie said.

"I'm very sorry, ma'am," I said.

"You should be."

"Mom," Shasta said.

"The bike is in my car," I said.

"I don't care about that," Leonie said.

"Mom. You're not listening."

"What, what is it, *what?*"

"I need some Advil."

Leonie strode over to a cabinet by the microwave and grabbed a bottle.

"Ma'am," I said. "You shouldn't give her that."

Leonie stared at me. Her chin was trembling. "Why not."

"It can cause bleeding. Tylenol's okay."

She swapped bottles and filled a glass of water, twisting her fingers as Shasta swallowed the pills. "Does it hurt?"

"Not that bad," Shasta said.

"It's going to scar."

Shasta rolled her eyes.

Jason reappeared and set the phone in its cradle. "She's on her way."

"Thank God," Leonie said.

He crouched by Shasta. He, too, was on the young side. "How you feeling, kitten?"

"Fine. It's a scratch."

Leonie snorted.

Jason stood up and faced me uncertainly. "Hi."

I raised a hand.

"This is Clay," Shasta said. "He brought me home."

"After hitting her," Leonie said.

"It was an *accident*," Shasta said.

Leonie walked stiffly to a window and watched the street. Jason looked back and forth between the women, trying to decide whom to believe and how to regard me.

He settled on a tepid smile. "Thanks for bringing her."

"Did she say how long she'd be?" Leonie said.

Shasta said, "Mom. Relax. She's literally two minutes away."

Two long minutes.

A car pulled up outside.

"That's her," Leonie said and ran out.

I could hear her voice (*Take her to Eureka . . .*) as she reentered with Maggie Penrose, dressed in skirt and sweater and carrying an old-school black leather doctor's bag. No headlamp.

Seeing me, Maggie paused.

"You," she said, not unpleasantly.

"Me," I said.

"Go get the car ready," Leonie said to Jason.

"Hold your horses, please," Maggie said.

She pulled over another chair, smiling warmly at Shasta. "Hello, my lovely."

"Hey, Mags."

"Let's have a peek . . . Oh my. That's a *good* one."

Leonie chewed her thumbnail. "Is it bad?"

"I'm afraid we're going to have to amputate." Maggie opened her bag. "Shoo, all of you."

Jason turned to go. Leonie remained rooted in place.

"Lee," he said. "C'mon."

Leonie stormed out, brushing by him.

He and I followed her into the living room, and the three of us stood in awkward silence, Jason nodding indecipherably and Leonie refusing to make eye contact while I peered around, a dumb smile plastered to my face, feeling time slip away.

If not for the crash I'd be halfway to Millburg by now. Amy was expecting a call from me as soon as I regained service. Through the perforated shades, the sky glowed pewter. Fog drifted over high, violent surf. I felt desperate to escape, gripping at the carpet with my toes, through my shoes, to prevent myself from running.

In the kitchen, Maggie Penrose was performing a mini mental status exam. Shasta answered in an undertone.

The dog had quieted. Mournful yips emanated from down the hall.

Jason started toward it. "I'm gonna let him out."

"Leave it, please," Leonie said.

"I don't want him to have an accident."

"I said leave it."

He relented.

One two three bright light Dr. Penrose said.

"So . . . ," Jason said.

"Clay," I said.

"Clay. What brings you to our neck of the woods?"

"Just visiting."

"Where from?"

"Bay Area."

"Right on. Welcome to Swann's Flat."

"Thanks," I said.

Leonie stared resolutely at the carpet.

"How long you here for?" Jason asked.

"I came in Monday. I was actually on my way out of town."

"You were at the hotel?"

"Yeah."

"Enjoy your stay?"

I nodded.

"Awesome," he said.

Maggie Penrose said *Wiggle your toes.*

"Must be nice to have a doctor for a town this size," I said.

"One of everything you need," Jason said, smiling. "None of what you don't. Drink?"

"I, uh— I'm good. Thanks."

He crossed to a corner bar with a mini fridge. Popping open a bottle of Sierra Nevada, he flopped on the couch, patting the cushion for Leonie. She didn't move.

Wind roared, waves crashed, the dog continued to keen.

That's good Dr. Penrose was saying. *Deep breaths.*

Whomp-whomp went my head.

"You have a beautiful home," I said.

Leonie rotated toward me like a tank turret.

Maggie Penrose emerged from the kitchen, drying her hands on a paper towel.

"How is she?" Jason said.

"Good, all things considered. She's a toughie. How'd she seem, right after it happened?"

"Dazed," I said. "But not for long. She did complain of feeling hot."

"Mm." Maggie turned to Leonie. "I'd like to bring her to my place and take an X-ray."

"Is it broken?" Leonie said.

"Doesn't look that way, but I'd like to be sure. You, too," Maggie said to me. "I need to look at your head."

"Where am I going?" I asked.

"Oh no you don't," Leonie said. "You're not jumping in your car and running off."

"Honey," Jason said.

"It's okay," I said. "I can go with Dr. Penrose."

"I want a copy of your driver's license," Leonie said. "I want your phone number and your insurance and the name of your attorney."

I couldn't give her those without blowing my cover. I also didn't see how I could lie without committing a crime.

I was ready to reach for my wallet when Shasta hobbled into the doorway, her shin mummified in gauze and tape.

"Can we *please* go?" she said.

Jason got up from the couch. "You two go on ahead. Come on, kitten."

He accompanied Shasta through the kitchen toward the garage.

Maggie said, "We'll be back soon."

"Yes," Leonie said. She was speaking to me. "You will."

CHAPTER 15

I got into Maggie Penrose's green Subaru Outback and she started down Beachcomber.

"Quite the exciting vacation you're having," she said.

"That wasn't the goal."

"Do you have medical training?"

I'd tipped her off by mentioning Shasta's temperature.

"I took a first-aid class last year," I said. "We had a unit on concussion."

"Mm."

"I did offer to bring her to the hospital. She wouldn't let me."

"Well, that's Shasta for you."

"I would've just taken her but I don't know where it is."

"There's a clinic in Benbow, and a small site in Fortuna. Anything major, we go to Eureka."

"That must take—what? Three hours?"

"By car. Faster by boat, depending on the tide."

"Do you think Shasta will need that?"

The doctor eyed me.

Was I expressing sincere concern? Or fishing for an out?

"I'm going to reserve judgment," she said.

Short drive: Hers was the mansion closest to the marina, which explained how and why she walked to the cove every evening. The layout was identical to the Clancys'—central living room, patio, spiral staircase—but slightly smaller and with a dead-gray decorating scheme even more tired, as if both houses had been built from the same basic plan.

"I'll want to see her first before I get started on you," Maggie said.

On cue, Jason Clancy called out: "We're here."

He entered with Shasta leaning on his shoulder.

"Would it be possible for me to make a phone call?" I asked.

"In my office," Maggie said, pointing to the back hall. "Third door on the left."

"Thank you."

I found the right room and shut the door quietly. It was about seven forty-five a.m. With luck I could catch Amy before she left to drop off the kids and head to work.

I dialed from the desk phone. It rang once and went to voice-mail.

"Hi. Everything's fine. Call me on this number. I don't know if you can see it. It's . . ."

I checked the desktop for personalized stationery or a prescription pad, moving tchotchkes and photos but finding nothing. I balked at rifling drawers; that felt invasive.

"I'll call you again soon," I said and hung up.

I slumped in the desk chair. The goose egg was throbbing now, too, in addition to the *whomp-whomp*. Competing drummers playing out of sync. The furniture and walls seemed to be—not where they should be.

How hard had I hit my head?

I leapt up and took a lap around the room, flapping my limbs to restore a feeling of immediacy. Diplomas on the wall from Williams and Case Western Reserve School of Medicine. Shelving units with well-thumbed clinical texts on a wide range of topics, back issues of *JAMA,* smattering of psychology books. A small-town GP wore many hats.

The phone rang.

I lifted the receiver. Cartoons blared in the background. "Amy?"

"Where are you? I thought you left already."

"I tried to." I told her what had happened.

"Oh my God," Amy said. "Are you okay?"

"I have a pretty big bump on my forehead."

"You hit your head?"

"I'm at the local clinic. The doctor's going to look at me when she's done with her."

"Is *she* okay?"

"Banged up, for sure. Hopefully nothing serious. We should call our insurance."

"Do you need me to do that?"

"I'll see if I can get to it."

"What about a lawyer?" she asked.

"Probably, yeah."

"Let me ask my parents who they use."

"Okay. I'm still going to try and get out of here today, if possible."

"Do you think you can? Are you safe to drive?"

"I don't know. I'm pretty tired. I think that's why I didn't react faster. I was up most of the night, waiting for the gun guy. I should be fine once I get some more caffeine into me."

"At least he didn't show up."

"He did, actually."

"What?"

"No, it was okay. He left me money and an apology note."

"Saying what?"

" 'Sorry.' "

"That's it? 'Sorry'?"

"I mean, it's not a love poem. But I think we can assume he doesn't intend to shoot me."

"Can we?"

"I'm saying if I end up getting stuck here again for another night it'll be okay."

"Please, no."

"The minute I can leave, I will. I don't want to flee the scene and have them call the cops on me."

"I thought the cops didn't come."

"Maybe not here. But it's two hours to reach the highway. If someone calls ahead they could pick me off."

"I don't know what to say. This place is a curse."

"I'm sorry, Amy."

"I'm not mad at you," she said. "It's not your fault."

"Let's hope they see it the same way."

"Are you sure you're okay to drive?"

Whomp-whomp.

"Let me talk to the doctor," I said. "I'll check in when I have a plan."

"I have patients all day. Leave a message."

"Okay. Love you."

"You too."

I hung up and drew over one of the desk photos. It depicted Maggie Penrose in a moment of exultation: rising onto her toes, fists aloft, cheering at the finish line of a race. A girl of twelve or thirteen heaved through the tape.

Shasta.

The door opened. Jason Clancy leaned in. "Doc's ready for you."

THE GOOD NEWS for Shasta was no broken bones.

"The resilience of youth," Maggie Penrose said.

But there were bruised ribs and lots of scrapes and the gashed shin was nothing to sneeze at. The doctor had assigned a grade 2 concussion.

"If she starts acting very funny, passes out, seizes, vomits, anything that worries you, call me right away. Same if you can't rouse her. Keep the lights low, keep the house quiet. No screens, today or tomorrow. We're taking it easy, understand?"

"How will they be able to tell if I'm acting funny?" Shasta said.

Maggie smiled. "If you're agreeable all of a sudden."

She turned to Jason. "I'll bring Clay over to you when I'm done."

He nodded and put his arm out for Shasta.

"Batter up," Maggie said to me.

The exam room was a converted den, outfitted with a padded table, supply cabinets, mechanical scale, IV pole. All the equipment showed age and wear consistent with a rural practice. A notable exception was the X-ray machine—a sleek, compact unit.

I commented on it. Maggie shrugged.

"We get hikers during the summer. They turn an ankle. Or dehydration, that's another fan favorite. Let's start by having you walk to the end of the room and back."

She did a series of rapid neurological tests.

"Do you think I can drive?" I asked.

"Up to you. I won't say no. But you have to monitor yourself and pull over if you need to. Can you promise me that?"

"Yeah."

She began cleaning my forehead with iodine. "Where'd you get this nifty little guy?"

She meant my scar.

I gave my standard answer: "Work accident."

"What kind of work do you do that you're getting your head damn near chopped off?"

I'd slipped again, speaking as Clay Edison, not Clay Gardner.

"I'm in finance," I said.

"Did you get attacked by a quarterly report?"

I laughed. "When I was nineteen, I had a summer job at a warehouse. Construction supplies. I was carrying a big sheet of glass with this other guy. With suction cups? He didn't put his on correctly, and one of them came loose. The pane slips, hits the ground, and cracks in half. A huge shard kind of—"

I made a slicing motion. "Like a guillotine."

"Ouch," she said. "Nasty."

It really was, for the poor kid it had actually happened to. He was an old coroner's case of mine. The pane had severed his carotid and he'd bled out on the warehouse floor.

Maggie tore open a fresh gauze pad. "They did a good job sewing you up."

"I got lucky."

"Unfortunately," she said, applying tape, "you're stuck with me now."

She stepped back. "All better."

"Thanks. What do I owe you?"

A wry smile. "We'll call it even for getting shot at."

I nodded. "Thanks."

"Well," she said. "Time for you to face the music."

CHAPTER 16

She dropped me at the Clancy residence, waiting for Jason to admit me before driving away.

"My wife's getting Shasta set up," he said. "Come in."

In the kitchen he placed a mug by the burbling coffeepot. "Help yourself. Milk's in the fridge."

"Thank you."

The sheepdog bounded in and headed right to me, licking my hands.

"You making friends, Bowie?" Jason said.

The dog sprawled to show me his belly.

"He must like you," Jason said.

"I like him, too."

"I mean it, he's not like that with everyone."

"I'm flattered." I rubbed the dog's stomach. "Bowie as in the frontiersman or as in the singer?"

"Singer. His full name's Bowie Stardust."

"You're a fan."

"I didn't pick it."

Footsteps approached. I gave the dog a final pat and straightened up as Leonie entered.

She said, "How are you feeling?"

The shift in her demeanor was so drastic that at first I didn't think she was talking to me, assuming the question was meant for Jason. But she was studying me with a pinched expression. Not so much concern; there was some of that, although it was overlaid with anxiety.

As if I was the one who'd threatened her with a lawsuit instead of vice versa.

"All right. Thanks for asking," I said. "How's Shasta?"

"She's resting." A beat. "Thank you for taking care of her."

"I'm glad I could help. I just hope she's okay."

Leonie nodded.

I waited for her to once more demand my contact information. Lying outright opened me to criminal charges and jeopardized my license. I didn't think I had to volunteer anything, though.

"You got coffee," she said.

"I . . . Yeah. Yes. Thank you."

"Hungry?"

What was this? Some sort of psychological trap? Lure me in, get me talking, pull the rug?

"I'm good, thanks," I said. "I'm happy to stick around as long as you'd like. Otherwise I was planning to head out. My wife's expecting me."

Leonie looked at Jason, who shrugged.

"You can go," she said.

"Okay." I was mystified but grateful. "I'll just grab the bike from my car."

She nodded. To Jason: "Make her some eggs?"

He opened a drawer and took out a skillet.

I CARRIED THE bicycle up the front walk and propped it against the porch rail. Leonie stepped from the doorway to run her fingers over the warped frame, regarding it as though it was an extension of her daughter's body.

"I'll pay for it," I said.

She shook her head. "I apologize for how I spoke to you before."

"There's no need."

"I was upset."

I nodded.

"I mean," Leonie said, "she keeps insisting it wasn't your fault. So."

She sighed.

Hot, acrid breath washed over me.

She was drunk, I realized. At nine in the morning.

"Do you have children?" she asked.

It had felt cleaner and simpler to pare back Clay Gardner's attachments to the bare minimum. A wife, yes; he needed the gloss of stability and conventionality. A man of his socioeconomic status would be a catch. He might even be on his second marriage.

But kids?

In the city?

In these uncertain times?

No, thank you.

That was how I'd presented myself to Beau, at least.

Now I had other worries. Leonie might sober up and regret letting me off easy. I'd mentioned staying at the hotel. She could go to Jenelle Counts to track me down. Jenelle knew I'd met with Beau and Emil Bergstrom. And they had Clay Gardner's fake email address and burner phone number. If Leonie turned those over to an attorney, the whole façade would unravel.

The cynical side of me saw an advantage in establishing common ground.

"Two," I said. "Girl and a boy."

"So you understand, it's upsetting, to see your child like that."

"Of course."

"How old?" she asked.

"Four and fifteen months."

"That's a fun age."

"It can be."

"Trust me," she said. Her voice was hollow. Fingernails scraped idly at the doorpost. "Enjoy it while it lasts."

I CLIMBED BEHIND the wheel.

Whomp-whomp.

I leaned back and closed my eyes.

THREE HOURS LATER I sat up abruptly. My neck was damp, my stomach growled, and the windows were fogged. But the headache had subsided some, and the pulsing sensation was gone.

I lowered the windows to air out the car, feeling in the rear footwell for the snack bag. The jerky had spilled out: hard, shiny, greasy nuggets everywhere.

I stared at the torn packaging.

"Fuck me."

UNCLE HANK'S
QUIRKY JERKY

And below that, in much, *much* smaller letters:

ALL-NATURAL ORGANIC GRASS-FED CANNABIS-INFUSED BEEF

HI PROTEIN ☺ NITRATE FREE ☺ KETO FRIENDLY

I wasn't caffeine-deprived. I wasn't concussed.

I was high.

MOST EDIBLES WEAR off after three to four hours. I hadn't consumed that much jerky, and five hours had elapsed.

I gave it another thirty minutes and started the car.

I took it extra slow.

Creeping around the gnarly hairpin, the roadside memorial came into view.

I stopped.

The dead bouquet in the Jack Daniel's vase had been refreshed. Bright-yellow fists, a native coastal species, the seaside woolly sunflower.

ON THE OUTSKIRTS of Millburg, my phone flickered to life.

I left Amy a voicemail and dictated a text.

On my way home. Stopping for gas. Hopefully back by eight. Will keep you updated. Love you.

I pulled into the 76 station, started the pump, stuffed the old snack bag into the trash, and walked up the block to Fanny's Market.

The same clerk was at the register. He folded over his crossword. "Welcome b— Hey now. What happened to you?"

"Swann's Flat happened."

I dispensed coffee from the self-serve urn and filled a basket with non-infused snacks, paying close attention to the fine print.

While he rang me up, I said, "You might want to warn people about that jerky."

"Hm?"

"Uncle Hank's."

"Something wrong with it?"

"I didn't see it was laced. The packaging needs to be clearer. And you should have a sign up on the display."

"I'll convey the feedback."

"Are you Hank?"

"No. But he's married to Fanny. Twenty-eight fifty-seven."

Outside I examined myself in the selfie camera.

Maggie Penrose had done a neat job, trimming the gauze to keep it out of my eye. It hung askew in the corner of my forehead like a postage stamp, the goose egg beneath bulging.

Behind me was the giant bulletin board with its shriveled mosaic of faces.

Have you seen me.

Hailey Ray and Sam Rosenthal and Becka Candito shared space with others lost behind the Redwood Curtain.

Sixty-one-year-old Elise Verdirame with her red glasses. Thirty-two-year-old Serena Harper with a heart tattoo on her shoulder. Wally Muñoz who liked the 49ers so much that he wore both logo cap and logo shirt.

Nick Moore, twenty-one, big, toothy grin.

In two photos his hair was scraggly, his eyes red with flash. The third photo had been taken outdoors in bright light. He'd shaved his head and was shirtless, torso lean and sunburnt.

A silver pendant in the shape of a rooster gleamed against his chest.

A puka shell necklace cut a white line against his throat.

Shasta's necklace.

I could've been wrong. The picture quality wasn't great.

But . . .

I put my phone and snacks and coffee on the ground, untacked Nick Moore's flyer, and shook it out of its protective plastic sleeve.

Identifying features: Three-inch surgical scar on his right knee. Anchor tattoo on the upper right arm, the word F A S T across his left knuckles.

Date of last contact was June 2024. About one year ago.

No reward posted.

Anyone with information should please contact Tara Moore. Email; phone, area code 559.

I looked closely at the necklace. Hard to say if it matched Shasta's. A shell is a shell, and I'd never seen hers strung together, only picked the individual pieces out of the dirt.

I couldn't be sure about the rooster, either.

Fading. Pixilation.

A different rooster? Another bird altogether?

Maybe Nick and Shasta each had their very own puka shell rooster pendant necklace. Maybe everyone under twenty-five did. Maybe puka shell rooster pendant necklaces were on-trend. I think I'm well informed for a dude in his forties. But who could say what The Kids were into?

Maybe I was still stoned.

I took the flyer inside and laid it on the counter.

"Excuse me," I said. "Do you know anything about this person?"

The clerk folded over his puzzle. "Not more than what it says here. Why?"

"I thought I recognized him."

"Stare at that wall long enough, you're bound to start seeing things."

"The contact person is Tara Moore. Is that his wife, his mother?"

"I couldn't tell you. There's folks coming through here all the time. We let them use the board but I don't get involved."

"Can I get a copy of this?"

"That's all we have. Feel free to take a picture. Just put it back when you're done."

"Okay. Can I borrow your pencil for a sec?"

He gave it to me. I wrote my number on my receipt.

"If you hear from her," I said, sliding it to him, "please ask her to get in touch with me."

"I wouldn't count on it. You could always give her a call yourself, you're so concerned. Only, you know."

He took his pencil, flapped the crossword to stiffen it. "Try not to get her hopes up."

TWO

CHAPTER 17

Howdy Clay,

Great meeting you!

As per your request, please find the attached proposal, for 185 Beachcomber Boulevard. This is the last remaining waterfront parcel zoned and permitted for residential use. It's a real gem! The property includes 4.7 flat, cleared acres. During the 1910s and 1920s, the grounds were used as dormitories for loggers. Although those structures no longer exist, some of the original foundation work is visible (photos below).

Best of all, there are an additional 3.2 acres of virgin pine forest, including a campsite once inhabited by the native Mattole Indians!

You won't find anything like it—on Swann's Flat or anywhere else.

This beautiful and historically significant piece of land has never been offered for sale. Currently it is held in trust, with any sale or development subject to approval by the Swann's Flat Board of Supervisors.

The price and full terms will be made available to you upon receipt of the following:

1. Certified copies of your federal and state income tax returns for the three most recent tax years.

2. Certified copies of bank statements showing a minimum of $5 million in cash reserves.

3. Official copies of credit reports from two of the three major credit reporting bureaus (Equifax, Experian, TransUnion).

4. A copy of your professional resume showing current employment and complete employment history.

5. Two letters of reference from industry colleagues.

6. A letter, signed by your CPA and attorney, disclosing any judgments or bankruptcies, past or pending.

7. A portfolio of all real properties currently held.

I've also taken the liberty of attaching some value growth projections. These figures are based on the ten-year total volume and sale history for similar-sized properties on the peninsula and surrounding region. But the unique character of this parcel makes it hard to give a true comp. Still, you should get a sense of what your money can do here.

That's the formal stuff! Don't be a stranger.

Beau

(for EB)

THE TRAIL LEFT by ML was jumbled and difficult to trace.

The trail left by its namesake was anything but.

Emil Richard Bergstrom, born October 13, 1962, Xenia, Ohio. The databases were silent on his childhood, but I surmised it had been less than idyllic: Shortly after his seventeenth birthday, he'd gone into the army.

It must have felt like a safe bet. Vietnam was over; enlistments were down, bonuses up.

Not a good fit. Five months through his term of service, he was discharged.

I couldn't view the complete record to know why he'd been let go. Entry-level separation was at the discretion of the military. The cause could be anything from lack of effort to disciplinary infractions.

By the mid-eighties, he'd made his way to California. And found romance. On December 3, 1984, Emil Bergstrom and Kathleen Adele Jessup wed before the Los Angeles County Clerk.

Alas, fate hadn't smiled upon the union. Though Emil had done better at matrimony than soldiering, toughing it out with Kathleen for three and a half years.

More accurately, she'd toughed it out with him. In 1987 Emil pled no contest to one count of misdemeanor domestic battery. Ninety-day suspended sentence.

Their son, Richard Beaumont Bergstrom, was born the following March. Kathleen had already filed for divorce. Los Angeles Superior Court rendered final judgment two months later, awarding her full custody.

The late eighties and early nineties came across as a tumultuous time for Emil. In addition to the implosion of his personal life, he was paddling against a deluge of lawsuits: His name cropped up on the docket in Los Angeles, Riverside, Orange County, San Diego, and Kern.

He'd sold a lot but never transferred title (allegedly).

He'd misappropriated funds (allegedly).

These early schemes were comparatively crude, less con artistry than blatant fraud. Not all involved land. Bergstrom had dabbled in cars, electronics, scrap metal. Nor had he yet perfected how to erase his tracks. To the contrary: He displayed a flair for public relations, issuing press releases at a blistering pace. Luckily for him, small local papers had column inches to fill.

Valley Times (North Hollywood CA), 19 January 1988—SALES REACH $8 MILLION DOLLAR MARK. Western Development Company achieved a total of $8 million in sales during 1988 according to Emil R. Bergstrom, president of the firm. The company has gained prominence in the past in the acquisition, development and sale of land throughout San Fernando Valley and the Newhall-Saugus area. The firm is located in Sherman Oaks.

Encino Sentinel (Encino CA), 25 April 1990—INDUSTRIAL, DEVELOPMENT FIRMS IN MERGER. California Semiconductor Corp. has merged with Pacific Land Investment Co. and in conjunction with a one-for-10 reverse split, has changed its name to Pacific Research and Development Co. Emil Bergstrom, formerly president of Pacific Land Investment and president of the new corporation said that Pacific Research has signed an agreement to provide a computer programmed economic analysis for Apex-Carlsbad Corp. of Escondido.

Valley Journal (Sherman Oaks CA), 9 July 1991—DEVELOPMENT FIRM FORMS SUBSIDIARY. Symbiotic Systems Corporation has been organized as a subsidiary of the Western Development Corporation, according to Emil Bergstrom, president of the parent firm. The new corporation will be a service organization to handle administration, advertising and direct mail and other assistance to Western Development Corporation and two other subsidiary firms, Numeric Coordination Services in Van Nuys and Property Analysis Corporation in Irvine. The formation of Symbiotic Systems is the latest step in the current expansion program of Western Development Corporation. The land acquisition and sales firm has operations in Southern California and intends to open an office in Northern California later this year, Bergstrom adds.

The similarities between these rackets and Swann's Flat lay in the revolving door of partnerships, the ever-changing names and addresses.

The typical con man's approach to skirting consequences.

Aside from the DV rap, Emil Bergstrom had never been charged with a crime or seen the interior of a jail. He often managed to get civil suits against him dismissed, and any judgments he faced were negligible. At worst he simply closed up shop and reopened elsewhere, sometimes down the hall in the same building. I doubted he'd ever paid out a cent.

In 1993, reality finally caught up to him. He defaulted on a multimillion-dollar loan. The resulting judgment forced Bergstrom to file for bankruptcy.

The plaintiff?

William Arenhold.

The lawsuit constituted my first evidence of the two men interacting. That they then went on to form a fruitful, decades-long collaboration seemed bizarre on the face of it—former adversaries teaming up, like some ill-conceived superhero franchise crossover.

But I could think of an explanation.

Bergstrom's painted himself into a corner. Low on cash. Investors wary. Creditors with pitchforks and torches, bearing down on the gates.

So he and Arenhold strike a deal. Arenhold "loans" him a huge sum of money, backdated. Emil "defaults" and files Chapter 7. Arenhold then lays claim to the liquidated assets—enabling Emil to plead insolvency to everyone else in line to collect.

I pictured him fretting beneath his Stetson, intoning in that folksy twang of his.

Apologies, muchachos. Well's gone dry.

In the meantime, Arenhold funnels the money back to Bergstrom. Minus a service fee.

What read like financial ruin was the opposite: a sweetheart lawsuit, ensuring freedom.

With that done, Bergstrom effectively dropped from the public record. He'd learned his lesson about seeking the limelight. Or perhaps that had been the plan all along.

The land acquisition and sales firm has operations in Southern California and intends to open an office in Northern California later this year.

He'd never opened any such office that I could find.

As with the father, so with the son: I found sketchy information about Beau's early life—his birthday, a defunct Myspace page—but his recent history was blank.

Neither man appeared to own anything of significant value.

Hey Beau,

Thanks so much for your email. It was great getting to know you, too. I'm still sore from our hike.

That property is crazy! You did a great job, it's exactly what I'm looking for.

I understand you need to dot the i's and cross the t's. I'm working on getting together everything you asked for, and I hope you can understand that it might take me a while. I have a bunch of work travel coming up and it's going to occupy a lot of my attention. If you haven't heard from me in a couple weeks, please follow up.

Looking forward to reconnecting soon.

Clay

CHAPTER 18

A disgruntled person is a private investigator's best friend.

A disgruntled *spouse* is a private investigator's BFF.

Kathleen Bergstrom had reverted to her maiden name of Jessup. During the eighties and nineties, while Emil was honing his craft, she'd made a go of it in Hollywood. IMDB listed nineteen credits. A few basic cable leading roles. The majority low-grade fare such as **Screaming Blonde #2** in *Attack of the Face-Eating Pandas* and **Confused Beach Girl** in *Kamikaze Shark 3: Blood Fin Soup*.

Her last gig was 2007's *Right of First Revenge*. **Old Woman.**

By my math she was then forty-three years old.

Time to hang it up.

I called her, introduced myself, told her what I was after.

She laughed and sighed, in that order. "Come on by, we'll talk."

Like her ex-husband, Kathleen had migrated north. Presently she was living her best life at the Rossmoor Retirement Community, a two-thousand-acre independent living development on the other side of the Caldecott Tunnel, where the offbeat urban landscape of Berkeley and Oakland dissolved into open space, tract homes, and big-box stores.

The booth guard examined my driver's license and raised the

barrier arm, and I drove to the Creekside Grill. Kathleen was seated on the patio, lipstick on the rim of her Bloody Mary. Despite the ferocious heat—ninety degrees at ten a.m.—she was impeccably put together: coral twinset, honey hair feathered à la Farrah Fawcett. Discreet makeup emphasized superb bone structure.

She squeezed my fingers and smiled. "What are you drinking?"

"Water's good."

She waved to a white-haired waiter. "Water for my friend, please, Jack."

He brought the carafe. "Will you want another, ma'am?"

"I'm sure I'll need it," she said. "Check back in a few."

He left with a bow.

Golf carts buzzed, sprinklers chuffed, the *pock-pock* of pickleball rang out.

"Emil Bergstrom," she said. "Blast from the not-so-good past."

"Sorry to bring it up."

"Oh, I'm a big girl."

"How'd you meet?"

"He picked me up at a party," she said. "You'll have to take my word that he was good-looking back then. And I was young and naïve. I'm not ashamed to say so. I'd only been in LA a couple of months. He drove a Porsche, too. That impressed me."

"What was he up to?"

"He called himself a businessman. He always had twenty-five deals going at once."

"Do you remember names or details?"

"I didn't understand it and I didn't want to. It was exciting enough for me to go racing from one party to the next. He knew all these wannabe producer types. Guys who had money to spend, or they needed to look like they did. There was a lot of booze and drugs floating around. And Emil can talk the stripes off a zebra.

He'd cook up some cockamamie scheme. Thirty seconds later they're climbing over each other with their checkbooks out."

"When did things start to go bad?"

"For us or for him?"

"Either. Both."

"He couldn't keep it in his pants. We fight, I cry, he swears up and down it'll never happen again. You won't find a single gal in Hollywood who can't tell the same story."

"I read that he was arrested for domestic violence."

She started. "That was an isolated incident. I tried to leave the room and he grabbed my arm. Nothing worse than that."

"You reported it."

"Well, I was pregnant at the time. Things were very tense."

"Were you worried about the baby?"

"No. It was— I was . . . It was an isolated incident."

"We don't have to talk about it," I said.

She stirred her drink with the celery stalk. "It feels like another woman's life."

I nodded.

"It's not in Emil's nature to be physical," she said. "He doesn't have to be. If he wants something, he gets *you* to do it."

"Did you maintain a relationship after the divorce?"

"We saw each other every so often. I wanted him to know his son. Not that Emil cared. He'd send Beau a birthday card with five dollars. Drop in without warning and take him for ice cream. That sort of thing."

"Child support?"

"Off and on. I never felt he was deliberately making my life hard. More that he forgot about us once we were out of sight."

"Are you familiar with a man by the name of Rolando Pineda? He's a lawyer."

"Doesn't ring a bell."

"What about William Arenhold?"

"Him, yes."

"Did you ever meet him?"

"Once. We went to San Francisco for a weekend. It was a nice time, we drove up PCH, had dinner by the wharf. When we got to our hotel, there was this man waiting in the lobby. Emil introduced him as Billy. I remember he was a real charmer. He kissed my hand, and Emil sent me up to the room so they could stay at the bar and talk. I was so mad. Here we are, we've come all this way, it's supposed to be a romantic getaway, and this is what you're doing?"

She drained her drink, flagged Jack for another.

I said, "Any idea what Emil and Arenhold talked about?"

"None. But they were down there for hours. Emil woke me up when he came in, and we had a fight about it. In the morning he apologized. He bought me flowers and we went to tour Alcatraz."

"Approximately when was this?"

"Beau was born in '88. So before then."

And at least five years before the "lawsuit" that had driven Emil out of LA.

I asked Kathleen about that.

"He said he had to leave town. He made it sound like it was temporary. Little did I know."

"Did you ever get up to Swann's Flat?" I asked.

"God, no. Good riddance, as far as I'm concerned."

"What about Beau? How'd he end up there?"

"That came later. I remarried in 2002. Beau wasn't happy about it, and it got worse once I had Ashley. He was so jealous of that child. I thought it was nuts. What's there to be jealous of? She's a baby, you're a teenager. It got to be unbearable. He and Colin were at each other's throats, day and night. I was worried they'd kill each other. After high school he announced he was going to live with his father. I begged him not to. He was so smart, he had good grades. He could have gone to college. But Colin convinced me not to fight it. He said it was healthy to give Beau some space. I should've trusted my instincts."

I remembered Beau's story—horseshit, I now realized—about shooting a mountain lion.

How old were you?

Ten or eleven . . . I basically lived out here as a kid.

"Are you in touch with him?" I asked.

"Not really. Colin died three years ago, and I moved here to be near my daughter. She goes to Mills. Some part of me thought, *Oh, you'll be closer to Beau, too.* It hasn't worked out, though. He calls on my birthday. But we don't see each other."

Jack brought her drink, hesitating when he saw her remote expression.

She smiled and said, "Thanks, as always."

"Ma'am."

He left the glass and took the empty.

Kathleen picked up the celery, stirred. "I've tried to make my peace with it. But it's hard."

I nodded.

"He was a beautiful boy. For the longest time, we were on our own together, me and him, two of us against the world. We didn't have any money but we had fun. We liked to go camping on the beach. We did that all the time."

"A child of the land."

"Come again?"

"That's how Emil described you. 'She was a child of the land, and a child of the land she begat.'"

"Somebody shoulda glued his lips shut years ago."

I laughed.

"He's not wrong, though," she said. "That's one thing about Emil. There's enough truth in what he says that it makes you question yourself." She sipped. "At any rate. I'd like to think Beau knows that he can come to me if he needs. I'll always be his mother."

A tear escaped. She grabbed at her napkin to dab it away.

"When I do speak to him," she said, "it's Emil I hear."

BACK AT MY office, Clay Gardner had an email waiting in his inbox. The sender had a Hotmail address. Mistaking it for spam, I almost deleted it before noticing the first line.

Dear Mr Gardner

My name is Al Bock. I would like to talk to you. Call me at your earliest convenience. I dont have a computer so its better if you call.

His number followed.

PS sorry again about your car

CHAPTER 19

"Did you get the check?" he asked.

"I did, thanks."

"Don't know if that'll cover it. You can also send me the bill once it's fixed."

"I appreciate it. How'd you email me, if you don't have a computer?"

"Library in Millburg has 'em."

"You drove all the way there to get in touch with me."

"I was going anyway. But you deserve the courtesy, after the scare I gave you."

"What's life without a little excitement?"

"Nice and quiet, is what. Let me save you some time, son: I'm not selling. To you or anyone else."

"The property's listed."

"As a public service," he said. "I want folks to understand what they're getting into."

"What are they getting into?"

"A mess. Take it from me: You don't want none of it."

I said, "Mr. Bock, since you're being frank with me, I'm going to do the same. I'm not interested in buying your house. I'm trying to understand how things work in Swann's Flat. I think you're the person I've been waiting for. And if I'm reading you right, I'm the person you've been waiting for."

He said, "About damn time."

LIKE A LOT of people with festering grievances, Al Bock was eager to talk.

"In 1997, I was stationed at the Marine Corps Air Ground Combat Center in Twentynine Palms, California. I saw a notice up on the board. Land for sale. There was pictures of the beach. It looked like a goddamn painting. I called the number and spoke to this fellow who gave me a song and dance. 'Act fast, they're going like hotcakes.' Fourteen thousand and four hundred dollars for a quarter-acre lot."

"Do you remember the salesman's name?"

"I most certainly do. Bill Arenhold."

"Must've been a very persuasive conversation."

"I was ready to be persuaded. That was where my head was at. My marriage just ended. I was staring into the future and seeing question marks. Arenhold—he sent me a buncha charts, showing how much money I stood to make. I know I sound like a damn fool."

"No."

"I *was* a damn fool. Didn't know my ass from my elbow. They teach you a lot of things in the military, but common sense about money ain't one of them."

In 2002, after twenty-six years of service, Bock retired.

"I was supposed to leave before that, but after nine eleven I stayed on a while."

The cost of living in the real world came as a rude awakening. He had his pension, but the divorce and the down payment had eaten up most of his savings. He spent some time in the private sector, scrimping, rebuilding his nest egg.

"Doing what?" I asked.

"Training law enforcement. I taught marksmanship. I did that most of my career."

"You weren't trying to hit me, were you."

"If I was, we wouldn't be having this conversation."

To raise cash, Bock put the Swann's Flat property on the market, expecting a quick sale.

No one wanted it.

"And I mean no one," he said. "It sat there. I called Arenhold. 'You promised it'll be worth ten times what I paid.' He starts yammering on, the economy, blah blah blah. He says, 'Lemme see what I can do.' Soon I get a call from this other guy, says he's a corporate acquisitions specialist. Whatever the hell that is. He offers me seven hundred bucks, take it or leave it."

"You didn't take it."

"Hell no. I told him where to stick it, then called Arenhold and told him I was gonna sue his pecker off. He hung up on me. Stopped taking my calls. I think he figured I'd give up."

"Most people do," I said. "That's their business model."

"They never met me."

Life had handed Al Bock a shit sandwich. He decided to turn it into a tasty lunch.

"My plan was to build and flip. To keep the cost down I did it myself."

"You were the GC."

"No, sir. I mean *myself*."

"You built that house?"

"Yes, sir."

"Alone."

"I had a guy helping me for about a minute. But yeah, me and Godzilla. My puppy."

"I think I met him when I was there."

"No, sir. You met King Kong. Godzilla passed, rest his soul."

"Did you have construction experience?"

"None. I was reading library books, making it up as I went along. I bought a little run-down chain saw mill and used what was available for timber. Anything else I had to bring in, by boat or truck."

"Improvise, adapt, overcome."

Bock chuckled. "Yes, sir. Fubared everything there is to fubar."

"How long did it take you?"

"Nine years. I was living in a tent for the first two, till I got the roof on. Half the time it was too wet to work, and the other half it was so hot I didn't want to."

Along the way, he'd gotten to know Emil Bergstrom.

"I'd had some dealings with him when I applied for permits. He was always polite, and when I first showed up, he came by to introduce himself. He had the boy with him. He wasn't much more than a kid then, Beau. Emil goes, 'Nice to meet you. You need anything, give a holler.' I thought, *There's a neighborly fellah.* Week later I get this notice stuck to my truck from the Board of Supervisors. Assessment. Seven hundred bucks."

"Same amount the acquisitions guy wanted you to sell for."

"Got a sense of humor, Emil does."

Not knowing any better, Bock paid the assessment; the next couple, too. Then he tried to get his water and power hooked up.

"I got a notice. Eight grand."

"Big jump."

"He was testing me. See how deep my pockets were. I canceled the request, bought a couple of used four-hundred-gallon tanks, and put in a rainwater catchment system."

"Smart."

"I thought so. Then I get another notice, saying I still had to pay the fee. I went over to see Bergstrom. He and Beau live in this big house down by the water."

"The third mansion."

"What's that?"

"I was at the other two residences on Beachcomber, the Clancys' and the doctor's. I was wondering who lived in the third house."

"You get around, don't you . . . ? Yeah. That's them. I'm talking to Emil, explaining the problem, and Beau walks in and sits down on the sofa. I didn't think he had any place listening in, and I said so. Emil said, 'My son's my business partner, I don't have any secrets from him.' The whole time Beau was there he didn't say nothing. He watches Emil, watches me."

"Learning the ropes."

"You said it. I told Emil, 'Look, I did the work, it doesn't affect anyone.' No problem. He'll issue me a variance, and they can approve it retroactively. The application fee costs five hundred dollars." Bock paused. "You see what he's doing? He didn't want to run me off before they squeezed out every last cent they could."

With the next assessment, he'd had it.

"I refused to pay. They threatened to take me to court. I told them, 'Go right ahead.' "

Then the real trouble started.

"I was waiting forever for the phone company to put the landline in. The first time they sent a truck, it got stuck, and they didn't want to come back. I wrote 'em a hundred letters before they agreed to do it. I haven't had the line for three days before it goes dead. I go outside, start following it. Few blocks away, a tree's come down and taken it out."

"Cut down or fell down."

"Cut. They weren't trying to hide it. They wanted me to know who it was."

"Did you call the cops?"

"No, sir. What are they gonna do? No offense, but I worked with my fair share of cops. My experience, they'll do as much as they have to and no more. I can take care of myself."

Al Bock's version of self-care was to load up his rifle and drive to Bergstrom's house.

"I told him I was using his phone till he got the phone company out to fix mine. He just smiled. 'Okay, Mr. Bock, calm down.' What do you know? Two days later there's a truck."

A war had begun.

"They'd shoot off guns in the middle of the night to scare the pup. Block the road, so I couldn't get in or out. Every time I left for a supply run, I took a chain saw with me, and I'd let Godzilla loose in the yard, to keep them from trespassing. One time he starts puking. I rushed him up to the animal hospital in Eureka. Vet tells me he got sick from eating onions. I don't grow onions. I don't keep 'em around. Where's he getting onions?"

"You think they fed it to him."

"I don't think it, I know it. Can I prove it? No. I was gone all day, getting him looked at. I get home that evening, every one of my windows is broke."

"Oh my God."

"Yes, sir. I had raccoons running around my kitchen."

"What did you do?"

"Shot his windows out. And he's got a lot more of 'em than I do."

I laughed. "Did he get the message?"

"Yes, sir, he did. He even wrote me a check for three grand."

"I have to tell you, Sergeant, you're the first person I've spoken to who ever pried a cent out of Emil Bergstrom."

"I'll add it to my list of accomplishments."

The harder the Bergstroms tried to dislodge Bock, the more determined he became to stay. Five years in, he realized he had accidentally fallen in love with Swann's Flat. Abandoning his plan to flip the house, he replaced it with a new goal: build his dream home.

"You didn't want to just cut bait?" I asked.

"Why should I? It's my land. I bought it, fair and square. I worked it and made it what it is. I'm a United States Marine. I ain't gonna let some buncha clowns push me around."

"I get that. My question is if it's worth the trouble."

"Oh, we're past all that by now. I'm not gonna say we like each other, but we have an understanding. They leave me alone, and I don't depend on them for nothing. I got my water, I got my solar, I grow my own food, I keep to myself."

"You're still paying fees."

"No, sir. I put an end to that."

"How?"

"I told 'em I wasn't paying no more."

"He agreed? Just like that?"

"Well, maybe I made my point a little more directly."

"Do I want to ask how?"

"Let me put it this way. Inside every bully is a chickenshit pissing his pants."

"Did you ever consider taking legal action?"

"I don't have the money for that."

"You wouldn't have to, if you joined up with other people."

"Like who?"

"Other folks who got burned. Other residents. You can't be the only one who's been harassed."

"Ain't no other residents."

"The doctor. The Clancys."

"I don't think you'll find them to be too helpful."

"Why not?"

"They're on the Board of Supervisors, too."

"All of them?"

"Maggie is, and Jason."

"They work for Bergstrom?"

"Other way around," he said.

"He works for them?"

"Well, for Jason, anyway."

"Why would Bergstrom take orders from Jason Clancy?"

"Because he's married to Leonie Swann."

The name threw me for a loop; I had filed her away as Leonie Clancy.

Bock confirmed that they were one and the same. "She used to be married to Kurt, so that's still how I think of her."

The roadside memorial. "Kurt Swann."

"Yes, sir."

"What about Shasta?"

"You really do get around."

"She's Kurt and Leonie's daughter?"

"Yes, sir."

"Kurt's dead, though."

"Yes, sir."

"How?"

"Accident. His truck went off the road. Now she owns the town."

"What's that mean?"

"Bylaws state that the majority landowner holds veto power," Bock said. "You follow? Nobody lives here less they want 'em to."

"Except you."

"Yes, sir. Although maybe they want me, now."

"Why would they?"

"To show that anyone's free to come and go."

"You're their defense in a lawsuit."

"Listen, son, I'm not saying I don't want to help you out. But I'm tired. I'll be seventy-two in November. My dad died when he was seventy. I'm on borrowed time as it is. I'd like to enjoy what I have left. Now, if you'll excuse me, I got some weeding to do."

I thanked him and put down the phone.

I'd gone into Swann's Flat. And hit a Swann.

CHAPTER 20

The database results on Leonie Swann were strange, and strangely thin.

She didn't just look young to be Shasta's mother. She *was* young—thirty-seven—with no criminal record, no professional licenses, and no addresses prior to 2009, when the mansion at 21 Beachcomber showed up. She paid the utilities but didn't appear on the tax roll.

In a way that made sense. Al Bock's intel suggested a kind of ownership/management structure, with the Swanns retaining title while Emil and Beau ran the show. And if the Bergstroms could teach Leonie anything, it was how to hide assets. She could have placed the house in trust, buried it behind LLCs, transferred it to a third party.

Any such collaboration could not have begun with her. The earliest lawsuits dated to the mid-nineties, when she was in grade school.

Kurt, on the other hand, had been almost twenty years Leonie's senior. The right age for a budding entrepreneur.

I found his obituary in the *North Counties Register.*

SWANN, Kurt. 1/11/1969–12/06/2009. Kurt was born and raised in Swann's Flat, a town founded by his grandfather, Everett. An avid hunter and fisherman, he passed at the too-young age of 40 among the hills that he grew up in. Kurt was generous, supporting the greater Humboldt community and working tirelessly to preserve the character of Swann's Flat for the next generation. He loved Jack Daniel's, playing his Gibson guitar, and listening to classic rock. He is preceded in death by his parents, Charlie and Sarah. He is survived by his wife, Leonie, and daughter Shasta.

"I don't know where I'm going from here, but I promise it won't be boring."

I googled the quote. Attributed to David Bowie.

Erroneous. The real quote ended *I promise it won't bore you.*

I'd asked Jason Clancy: *Bowie as in the frontiersman or as in the singer?*

Singer. His full name's Bowie Stardust.

You're a fan.

I didn't pick it.

Leonie had. Or Shasta, in memory of her father.

A fatal accident likely meant an autopsy.

I called the Humboldt County Coroner–Public Administrator and spoke to a deputy named Zucchero. He directed me to their public records portal. Four-to-six-week turnaround.

I told him I was a former Alameda County coroner. Any way he could speed things up?

"Former," he said.

"Yes."

"What do you do now?"

"PI."

"How's that working out for you?"

"Pros and cons."

"Let me ask you something . . ."

For the next half hour I answered questions about licensing, overhead, health insurance.

"I'll get back to you soon," he said.

I went to the databases on Jason Clancy.

Age thirty-four. His credit was fair. One DUI, in 2008. He didn't have a pilot's license, but he did own a boat, registered to the address on Beachcomber. Previous addresses were in Sacramento; he turned up in Swann's Flat around 2017.

I was wondering if Leonie had put the house in his name. But he didn't appear on the tax roll, either, and when I ran a title search for 21 Beachcomber Boulevard, the actual name on the deed leaped off the screen.

Shasta Swann Irrevocable Trust

An itch in my brain.

I searched again, this time for all titles held by the Shasta Swann Irrevocable Trust.

The results filled fifty pages.

She, a teenage girl, owned the bait shop.

The boat lot.

The boat launch. The marina itself.

Jenelle Counts's name appeared on the hotel's liquor and business licenses. The structure and the land beneath, however, belonged to the Shasta Swann Irrevocable Trust.

In addition to owning her mother and stepfather's residence, Shasta owned the doctor's home at 3 Beachcomber Boulevard as well as the Bergstroms' at number 55.

She owned Beachcomber Boulevard, all four miles of it, including the lot at number 185, the prospectus for which I had open on my computer screen in another window.

This beautiful and historically significant piece of land has never been offered for sale.

Currently it is held in trust, with any sale or development subject to approval by the Swann's Flat Board of Supervisors.

If Clay Gardner bought it, he'd be buying it from Shasta.

The Shasta Swann Irrevocable Trust owned Pelman Auto Service at 27 Gray Fox Run along with Dave Pelman's residence at number 29. It owned the lots with the mailboxes and the empty lots next door. It owned the unoccupied homes and the homes on Airbnb, and I was willing to bet that if I dug deep enough into all those corporations and shells offering properties for sale, that if I traveled to all the courthouses in all the counties in all the states and pulled every file and read through every page, somewhere in the tangle of red tape, I would find Shasta, her trust, lurking behind all of them.

His truck went off the road.

Now she owns the town.

I'd thought Bock was referring to Leonie.

Wrong.

I hadn't hit *a* Swann.

I'd hit *the* Swann.

THE DATABASES SUPPRESS information on minors.

Modern teenagers fill that gap themselves, on social media.

But Shasta's Facebook, Instagram, and TikTok accounts were set to private.

A triathlon website had her winning the girls' under-18 division at the 2023 Race for the Redwoods. She celebrated on the podium, cheeks flushed, hair plastered to her forehead.

That was it.

I swiveled my chair toward the wall, where I'd taped a printout of Nick Moore's missing persons flyer.

Goofy grin. The puka shell necklace and the pendant.

Shasta's social media profile pictures cut off below the chin. No necklace visible.

In the podium photo, her unisuit was unzipped three or four inches. No necklace visible.

I logged into Clay Gardner's Instagram. The sparse feed implied affluence. San Francisco at night, a beach in Vietnam, a Warriors game, a sushi platter. Guys like him didn't post very often. Too busy identifying opportunities and adding value and living in the moment. His five hundred followers had cost me $6.99.

I sent Shasta Swann a friend request.

I did the same from Clay Gardner's Facebook page.

He didn't use TikTok, and she didn't use LinkedIn. A demographic mismatch.

Contacting her could easily backfire.

Who was I, other than some middle-aged rando?

Who'd nearly killed her.

And was now creeping on her.

Gross.

On the other hand, she might accept my requests reflexively.

Who didn't want more followers, especially for free?

THE NATIONAL MISSING and Unidentified Persons System had no record of *Nick Moore*.

Nicholas Moore scored a hit in Santa Cruz County, along the central coast, some 350 miles south of Humboldt. The profile picture showed the same young man whose face was on my wall. Scraggly-haired, no necklace visible.

Why was he missing in one place but on a bulletin board in another?

The NamUs file had been logged in August 2024, two months after date of last contact. Aside from mentioning Santa Cruz, it added nothing to the flyer and was in one respect less accurate, listing the anchor tattoo on his shoulder but not the word across his knuckles.

I did a quick-and-dirty search. The biggest hurdle was his name. *Moore* is the eighteenth most common surname in the

United States. For US boys born in 2004, *Nicholas* was the thirteenth most popular first name.

"Nick Moore" was a long snapper for the Baltimore Ravens.

He was also a minor-league baseball player, a collegiate wrestler, and a lacrosse coach.

He was an actor, a dead poet, a law school professor, a management consultant from Miami, a nurse practitioner in Albuquerque, and an addiction counselor in Waterloo, Iowa. In Santa Cruz alone there were three of him.

Across the room, he grinned at me.

Anyone with information should please contact Tara Moore.

As a rule I steer clear of missing persons cases. There's often little I can do beyond what the cops have already tried, and I won't string along a grieving family.

Some PIs make a decent living doing just that. Their choice.

Try not to get her hopes up.

I dialed the number on the flyer.

"Hello."

"Hi. I'm looking for Tara Moore."

"Speaking."

"Hi, Ms. Moore. My name is Clay Edison. Pardon me for calling out of the blue. I'm a private investigator, and—"

She hung up.

Obviously, mine wasn't the first offer of "help."

I emailed her.

Hi Ms. Moore.

My name is Clay Edison. I'm the private investigator who called you. I was recently in Millburg and I saw the flyer about Nick's disappearance. I was hoping to ask you a few questions.

I suspect other PIs may have contacted you in the past and that you might be skeptical. I'm not trying to get you to hire me.

I just want to talk. If you're not interested, I apologize for the disturbance. I won't bother you again.

You can feel free to contact me via email or at the number below.

All best.

CHAPTER 21

The half hour spent chatting with Deputy Zucchero paid dividends the following day, when a PDF of Kurt Swann's case file showed up in my inbox.

Cause of death was cerebral edema/subdural hemorrhage, secondary to blunt force trauma.

Manner of death was accidental.

I read the narrative, written by lead investigator Owen Ryall.

At 2251 on 12/05/2009, I was notified by the Humboldt County Sheriff's Dispatcher to respond to Swann's Flat Road . . .

Having been in Ryall's shoes, I could imagine his exasperation upon arriving at the scene only to be informed that there was no body yet. It wasn't even clear whether this was a coroner's case.

Kurt Swann was lying somewhere at the bottom of a rocky escarpment, dead or alive, but heavy rain and strong winds had prevented search-and-rescue from making a direct descent. The alternative—hiking up from below in the pitch black, over miles of steep, sludgy, unfamiliar terrain—was worse. They had decided to wait it out.

Al Bock had misremembered one detail. It wasn't Kurt's truck that had gone over the cliff. It was Kurt himself. The truck was still by the side of the road.

By 0315 on December 6, conditions had improved enough to make a second retrieval attempt. SAR threw down ropes. At 0548 they spotted the body of a male meeting Swann's description.

He had fallen approximately three hundred feet along a sixty-five-degree incline studded with boulders and logs, the force of which had thrown him another fifty feet laterally. His clothing was torn, his skin lacerated, his skull bashed in. A branch had impaled him in the groin. He'd lost both shoes and one sock. His hunting vest had stayed on; in an interior zipper pocket was a wallet. Positive identification was made from a California driver's license.

At 0611, Kurt Swann was pronounced dead.

I scrolled through photos.

Broken limbs in a cradle of broken, bloody vegetation.

Right eye popped out onto his cheek.

One small mercy: Rain had deterred animals from picking at him.

Additional photos, taken topside, showed the wicked hairpin turn. A dark-colored Dodge Ram sat close to the edge, jacked up, rear left tire missing. The cliffside had partially given way, as if he'd been in the process of changing the tire and lost his footing.

While Ryall's secondary, Chris King, coordinated with detectives, Ryall proceeded to the address on the driver's license, 21 Beachcomber Boulevard, Swann's Flat. The road was slippery and treacherous, and he didn't arrive until 0900.

He was met at the door by the decedent's next of kin, Leonie Swann, and their two-year-old daughter, unnamed. Ryall asked to speak with Mrs. Swann in private and suggested she call a relative or friend to help with the child. She declined. Ryall then informed her of her husband's passing.

She already knew.

On the previous evening, she had received a visit from an individual named David Pelman, who told her that Kurt had slipped while changing a blown tire and fallen to his death.

Good old Dave, purveyor of four-hundred-dollar coolant.

Ryall again suggested that Leonie call someone for support. This time she agreed. She phoned a neighbor, who arrived within a few minutes. Ryall did not note the neighbor's name but proceeded to David Pelman's residence at 29 Gray Fox Run.

According to Pelman, he and Kurt Swann had left Swann's Flat together before dawn on December 5 to hunt elk. They drove in Swann's truck to their favorite area, Lishin Valley, about three miles northeast of Millburg. All day long they slogged through the cold and damp without so much as sniffing a bull. Pelman was philosophical.

It's called hunting he said *not shooting.*

By midafternoon it was coming down pretty hard. They decided to pack it in.

Weeks of intermittent rain had reduced the road surface to slop. Approaching the hairpin,

> I heard this big bang and we go sliding. The bed was sticking out over the edge and the tire had a rip you could put your fist through. We jacked her up. Some of them lug nuts was rusted on pretty damn tight. Kurt hands me the old tire so's he can put on the spare. I start walking around and I heard him yell. I didn't see nothing cause my back was turned. I just look over my shoulder and he wasn't there no more. I went and leaned my neck out. I couldn't see nothing. He wasn't answering me neither.

Ryall asked Pelman if either man had been intoxicated. Pelman replied that they each had three or four beers over the course of the day. He further stated that Kurt regularly drank beer and that he, Pelman, did not perceive Swann as impaired.

Pelman considered trying to climb down but decided it was too dangerous. Nor could he find the spare, which must have gone over with Kurt.

Left without a choice, Dave Pelman trudged to town on foot, in the rain.

At 2214 he phoned 911 from his residence. Ryall asked why Pelman hadn't stopped at any of the other houses along the way. Pelman replied that nobody else was home.

The 911 call lasted twenty-two minutes. Afterward Pelman changed into dry clothes and proceeded in his own vehicle to the Swann residence to inform Leonie that Kurt was dead.

Ryall asked what time that conversation had taken place.

Pelman guessed it was about eleven, eleven fifteen.

Ryall noted that confirmation of death would not take place for another six-plus hours.

Autopsy revealed extensive injuries. Kurt Swann had suffered fractures to both femurs, both arms, most of his ribs, and six vertebrae. The blow to the skull was determined to be fatal, consistent with high-velocity impact from a blunt object.

Toxicology indicated a blood alcohol level of .022, below the threshold for legal intoxication.

I called the Humboldt County Coroner–Public Administrator and asked to speak with Deputy Owen Ryall. He was Lieutenant Ryall now.

"Former?" he said.

"That's right. Alameda County."

Ryall said, "Let me get back to you."

I stepped out to pick up Amy's dry cleaning and a bowl of ramen. At my desk I pried off the lid, releasing fragrant steam.

My phone rang. I replaced the lid.

"I called your people," Ryall said.

"Who'd you speak to?"

"Brad Moffett."

"What'd he say?"

"You're a pain in the ass."

"Checks out."

"Also that you're the best investigator he ever worked with," Ryall said. "What's your interest in Kurt Swann?"

"I'm trying to get a feel for the family and the place."

"Not sure I'll be much help. That night was the first and last time I was there. We got lost trying to find it."

"A couple things stand out to me," I said. "One is that Pelman goes home to call instead of trying to find a closer phone. Then he tells Leonie that Kurt's dead before there's a body."

"Well, the phone, he had an explanation for that."

"Nobody was home."

"Yeah."

"If he was desperate to get help, there's other things he could've done."

"You mean like break a window?"

"It's a life-or-death situation."

"That fall? Odds are it was instant death," Ryall said. "Probably the same reason he told her Kurt was dead: It's a reasonable assumption."

"How did Leonie seem when you talked to her?"

"What I recall is tired. Like she'd been up all night."

"It also struck me that she didn't want to call anyone at first."

"Could be she was overwhelmed or wanted to focus on the girl. We're talking a toddler."

"You didn't sense she was hiding something from you."

"Nope. People act weird, you know that."

"Do you recall who it was she asked to come over?"

"I don't, sorry." Ryall paused. "You think something's up here."

"I'm asking if there was any doubt in your mind about whether it was an accident."

"Your guy was right. You're a royal pain in the ass."

"I'll take it as a compliment."

Ryall sighed. "You know as well as I do, there's always stuff you can't corroborate a hundred percent. Pathologist said he hit a rock. Okay, but there's ten billion rocks in the vicinity. You can't tell if he slipped and hit his head on the way down, or if someone hit him and that's why he fell. Or if he was pushed. Tire tracks melted in the rain, footprints got washed away, same for blood. Is it impossible Pelman did it? Or someone else? No. But what am I supposed to do? End of the day, we had one eyewitness. He was cooperative and the physical evidence fit."

"Okay. Thanks for your time."

"No prob. Hey, real quick: What made you leave the force?"

"I needed a change."

"Yeah, huh. What do you do about health care?"

CHAPTER 22

Howdy, Clay!

Wanted to check in. Any progress on getting the stuff together?
Let me know if you need anything from me.

Take care,
Beau

I let a day elapse before answering him.

Hi Beau—

Greetings from Aspen. I've been here to ski but not during the
summer. So beautiful.

I'm at a conference till Saturday. Quick stop in New York and
then I'm off to Hong Kong.

I have calls in to my CPA and atty. Letters of rec in process.
Credit reports too. The rest is coming along. Haven't touched
my resume in years, I need to make it current. I'll try to get to it
on the plane.

Stay tuned.
CG

———

WITH THE CLOCK ticking on that relationship, I called Chris Villareal.

We arranged to meet at the office of the estate lawyer helping him. Her name was Priscilla Acevedo. She listened well and asked tough questions. It was a role reversal from when Chris had been fired up and indignant, and I'd had to play wet blanket. Now I was the one advocating action, my frustration mounting as Acevedo calmly poked holes in my arguments.

Every buyer I'd spoken to, including Chris's grandmother, had received disclosures.

Anyone had the right to make a crappy investment. People bought trendy stocks, crypto, NFTs. They played the lottery and the slots.

Whatever we stood to gain would be dwarfed by the cost and the hassle.

William Arenhold was dead. Rolando Pineda's role was ancillary and limited to a few sales. The Bergstroms were worth nothing on paper, as were Leonie and Jason Clancy. Given Shasta's youth, her direct involvement was improbable. Trust documents were not public; we'd need a subpoena to get them, and to get that we'd first need to file suit.

Bottom line, the connections were too flimsy, the stakes too small.

I said, "That's what the scam relies on."

Acevedo shrugged. "I admit, this isn't my area of practice. I'll consult with colleagues and get back to you."

Chris and I rode the elevator to the parking garage.

"We tried," he said. He shook his head. "It sucks. They're going to keep on getting away with it. But I feel like I need to be done with this and move on."

"I understand."

"I'm sorry to quit on you."

"Don't be. You stuck with it longer than most people would."

The doors opened. We stepped out, and he shook my hand.

"Thanks for your work, Clay. Invoice me and I'll pay you ASAP."

I wished him luck.

AMY AND I sat on our back deck, sipping wine and surveying our tiny chunk of the East Bay.

Driveway swirled with chalk petroglyphs. Brown crop circle left by an inflatable pool.

Water guns. Buckets. Tooth-marked foam balls.

Summer was in decline.

"Do our children eat foam?" Amy asked.

"I can't rule it out." I blew a raspberry. "What a stupid day."

"I'm sorry, honey. I know you were excited about this case."

"It's fine. I have to get used to the idea that I can't see everything through to the end."

"That was true when you were a coroner."

"Yeah, but at least that work came to me. I didn't have to chase it down and convince people to keep going."

"Your clients smell better now."

"Poor baby," I said. "How did you live with me for so long?"

"When you love someone you can get used to anything."

"I didn't have to get used to anything about you. You're perfect."

"Aw, thanks."

"*Perfect.*"

"Someone wants sex."

"Did I say that? I didn't say that."

"Years of clinical training have given me a penetrating emotional radar."

"Huh-huh-huh, she said 'penetrating.'"

"And years of marriage to you."

I smiled. "How was your day as a trained clinician?"

"A little worse than average."

"Did something happen?"

"I have a patient in therapy not of their own volition. They're on a court order. And that makes for an incredibly challenging dynamic."

"The lightbulb doesn't want to change."

"The lightbulb doesn't even know it's a lightbulb," she said. "It thinks it's the sun."

"Maybe you're ready for a new career, too."

"Maybe I am."

"What's it gonna be?"

"I don't know," she said, "but it definitely requires us to move to Paris."

"Diplomatic corps."

"Too much pressure."

"Baguette baker."

"Too early."

"Fashion designer."

"I already work with the mentally ill," she said. "I think I'll be a roving street photographer."

"Bullseye. What do I do in Paris?"

"Teach basketball fundamentals to disadvantaged European youths."

I started to hum.

"What are you singing?" she said.

"The theme song to *House Hunters International*."

"It's so cute that you think that's how it goes."

"This bright young American family," I said, "has a budget of eleven dollars."

"Not sure we can be in the city center for that."

"I'm fine being a little outside."

Amy laughed and rested her head on my shoulder, and we watched dusk purple the lawn.

I said, "We do have money now."

She sat up. "You know we can't touch that. It's for her education."

"I'm just pointing out that if we don't have to set as much aside for the future, we've got some wiggle room in the present."

"Not enough to quit our jobs and move to Paris."

"No. But if you were really unhappy and wanted to leave, we'd find a way."

"Thank you."

"You did it for me," I said. "Thank you."

"Do you ever regret it?"

"Leaving the bureau?"

She nodded.

Captain Bakke's top-floor office.

Her flat voice mouthing words of concern.

We need to be realistic, Clay.

The theme of the conversation: realism, and my need for it.

It's not that I don't value you as an individual.

But we need, you and I, to be honest about your service record, and think realistically about your future.

"Not for one second," I said. "Refill?"

"You're trying to get me drunk."

"Is it working?"

"I won't rule it out."

She handed me her glass. I went to the kitchen, took the Chardonnay from the fridge.

"Clay," Amy called.

I figured she'd heard one of the kids crying. But the house was quiet, and she was crossing the living room with my buzzing phone.

The number had a 559 area code. I recognized it. I'd dialed it a week ago.

"Clay Edison."

"This is Tara Moore," she said. "I want to talk to you about my boy."

CHAPTER 23

Five-five-nine was Fresno, three hours southeast of San Leandro. Tara Moore's ground-floor apartment fronted to a noisy drag blighted by strip malls, gas stations, and bottom-feeder motels.

She'd left the door open but the security screen locked. I rang, heard plodding footsteps, saw her shape darken the grate. She cupped her eyes to it before turning the dead bolt.

Old forty or a young fifty, dishwater blond and haggard. A long-sleeved T-shirt declared that LIFE IS GOOD. Its wearer appeared unconvinced.

"Come in."

The apartment reeked of stale tobacco. Tidy, though everything had been used well past replacement point, luster scrubbed down to raw flesh. In Berkeley, people called that living green. In Fresno, it was called being poor.

Younger versions of Nick Moore smiled behind scratched plastic. As a boy, he'd had teeth too big for his mouth—fodder for bullies. By his early teens, the rest of him had caught up, lending him a sinewy masculinity. No resemblance I could see to his mother. I didn't see any photos of men, either. Just Nick and more Nick and, in one shot, Tara wearing a hospital gown, a florid infant in her arms. She'd been even thinner then, distressingly so.

The drive had left me stiff and thirsty. She didn't offer water, just plopped down on a fraying armchair and pointed me to a fraying sofa.

She said, "What do you know about Nicholas?"

Try not to get her hopes up.

"Last month I was up in Humboldt," I began.

"Why?"

"In connection with another case."

"What case."

"I'm sorry, but I can't discuss that."

She folded her stick arms. "What'd you come for if you're not gonna talk."

"I'm happy to talk, Ms. Moore. But I have to respect my client's privacy. I'd do the same for you."

"I'm not your client."

"I know."

"I'm not going to pay you."

"I'm not asking you to."

"Free trial, huh? Then how much? Five hundred an hour? You people are all the same."

She heaved up from the chair and disappeared into the kitchen.

I gave her a few minutes, then followed.

A rear door stood ajar. I stepped through it and out into a poky communal courtyard strewn with castoffs: hamstrung bikes, unplanted pots, a charcoal grill bearing carbonized remains like a bier. Traffic rasped along the drag. Beneath the shadow of the neighboring Exxon sign, Tara sat in a lawn chair, smoking. A ceramic mug nestled in her lap.

"Ms. Moore, we don't know each other. I don't know what promises other people have made. I plan to look into Nick's disappearance, with or without you. My chances aren't great. But they're better if I have your help."

She ashed into the mug. "You were a cop."

"I used to be."

"You helped that boy."

"Which boy."

"The one who was in jail."

She meant Julian Triplett. A Berkeley news site had run a series about the case, detailing my role in vacating his murder conviction. The articles came up when you googled me. The remaining hits were about basketball. As of last season, I no longer held the Cal record for assists.

"Why?" she said.

"He didn't deserve what happened to him."

"How come you quit being a cop?"

"I didn't deserve what happened to me."

Her laughter dissolved into a coughing fit.

"Not me," she said. "I deserve every fucking thing."

She dragged. "This paying client of yours. They got something to do with Nicholas?"

"Not that I'm aware of."

"So what's your angle."

"No angle."

"Pff."

I said, "Can we try again?"

"Hell, it's a free country."

I pulled over a second chair and switched on my recorder. "Start with the last time you had contact with your son."

"It was a year in June."

"Is it Nick or Nicholas, by the way?"

"I put Nick on the poster 'cause everyone else called him that. To me he was Nicholas."

"Did you see him in person, did he call, text?"

"Text." She scrolled on her phone and showed me the screen.

On Monday morning, June 10, 2024, Nicholas Moore asked if Tara had sent the cards yet.

No she wrote.

You said today

I'm at work

Go after

Busy

When he asked.

When I can

K

Your welcome she wrote, adding an eye roll emoji.

"What cards is he referring to?" I asked.

"Pokémon. He used to collect 'em when he was little."

"What did he want them for?"

"Sell 'em, prolly. I don't know what he could get for it, it's a kids' game."

"Did he need money?"

"Everybody needs money."

"I'm asking if he had a particular need. Was there something he wanted to buy? Was he in debt?"

"I don't know. I don't think so."

"Did he gamble? Drink or use drugs?"

She stiffened. "No."

"No to which?"

"None of 'em."

"Not even alcohol or pot?"

"God, you're nosy," she said. "No, period. Okay? He hated that stuff. Never touched it."

"I'm sure you're sick of answering these questions. I'm sorry to make you do it again. That's part of the job."

Her cigarette had burned down to the filter. She fished out a new one and lit it off the first, grinding the butt out into the mug. "Go ahead."

"At the time of these texts, where was Nicholas living?"

"Santa Cruz."

"Was he employed?"

"He worked for a guy who made surfboards."

"Name?"

"Randy. Smythe. With a *y*. And a *e*. He's got a shop in his garage. He let Nicholas sleep there, but he didn't pay him. He called it an internship. Ask me, that's bullshit someone lays on you to get you to work for free."

And maybe the reason her son needed cash.

I returned to the text thread. On Tuesday afternoon, Tara wrote that she'd sent the cards. She included a photo of the receipt showing the tracking number. Shipping had cost $23.65.

CashApp me she wrote.

Friday rolled around and he had yet to reply. Tara tried again. *Did u get it*

Subsequent texts reflected her growing irritation. She took time out of her day to do him a favor. The least he could do was say thank you.

Another week went by with no response. On June 18, Tara fired off a series of lengthy, angry texts, excoriating him for his selfishness.

"I was mad," she said. "I thought he didn't want to pay me. Then I saw his TikTok."

She took the phone and opened up Nicholas's profile.

I'd missed it because his name didn't feature: His handle was wat3rwh33l, the picture an image of *The Great Wave off Kanagawa*. He had 39 followers and followed 210 other accounts. The earliest posts revolved around skateboarding. On average they garnered a dozen likes. Never an especially active user, in spring 2023 he seemed to lose interest. He didn't post again for over a year, resurfacing on June 19, 2024, with a video lasting twenty-six seconds.

It began with Nicholas standing in a dirt turnout along a two-lane highway dividing silver ocean from green-and-tan hills. Wind crackled. It could have been anywhere along the West Coast. He'd propped his phone on the ground and was shirtless in cutoff jeans and hiking boots. The puka shell necklace smiled against his chest, the pendant winked.

The caption read *In the name of the father.*

Raising his face and hands to the sky, he turned in a slow circle, his expression euphoric, sun shining on his shaven scalp. I glimpsed the anchor tattoo on his shoulder.

He completed a rotation and strode forward. The pendant swung away from his body as he leaned in to grab the camera. He straightened up, holding the camera at arm's length and grinning broadly. I realized I was looking at the source for the flyer photo.

He displayed his left fist. The letters F A S T were tattooed across his knuckles in serifed font, oriented backward and upside down.

He extended his middle finger. Held the gesture for a three-count before poking at the screen.

The clip ended.

Tara Moore said, "That's the last I seen of him. No texts, no calls, no nothing."

"Do you understand what this is about?"

"He was mad at me."

"What for?"

"'Cause he didn't want to pay me what he owed."

"The cost of shipping the cards."

She nodded.

"What about the rest of it?" I said. "The movements. Is he acting something out?"

"I thought it's just him being a dumbass."

" 'In the name of the father.' Does that mean anything to you?"

"Not really."

"Was Nicholas religious?"

"We did Christmas but that's about it."

"Can I ask what the situation is with his dad?"

"He's dead. He died when Nicholas was a baby. We were never together."

"What's his name?"

"Warren. Pezanko."

I scrolled through the profile's FOLLOWING and FOLLOWERS. Shasta Swann was not on either list. "What can you tell me about this necklace he's wearing?"

"I never seen it before. He musta got it after he moved out."

"Do you have a sense of where the video was taken?"

"Mendocino. Above Fort Bragg."

"How can you tell?"

"There's a mile marker," she said. "You can see it when he bends over."

I hadn't noticed, too busy focusing on the pendant.

I replayed the clip.

The postmile flashed between Nicholas's legs as he reached for the phone. Glare wiped out the lettering. I fiddled with the slider, bringing it into view one character at a time.

MEN 83.261

"Great catch," I said.

Tara Moore waved that away. "Not me. It was this lady Regina Klein. You know her?"

I shook my head. "She's a PI?"

"I figured you guys all hang out together."

"You were working with her."

"For a little bit. Haven't spoken to her since prolly the beginning of the year."

"What made you stop?"

"I couldn't afford to pay her no more. I spent everything I had on the first two guys. Who were assholes."

Tara scratched her nose with her cigarette hand, spilling ash on her T-shirt. She brushed at it apathetically. "I don't blame her. She's got a business to run. But it's my son, you know?"

I nodded.

"I'm just so tired of chasing my tail," she said. "I put twenty thousand miles on my car in the last year. Everything I make goes to gas and copies."

"What brought you to Millburg?"

"I wasn't looking there in the beginning, I thought he was still in Santa Cruz. Once Regina showed me the mile marker, I started driving out every weekend, going around and putting up his poster. I went into this shop to ask the lady if I could put one in her front window. She told me about this big bulletin board. 'You should go there, everyone knows about it.' "

"I also saw his profile on NamUs."

"I'm on all the sites. There's about a million of them. I can't keep track. It's all just a bunch of useless fools crying to each other about how nobody'll help them."

"Let's back up a sec," I said. "You saw the video. Is that when you started to feel that something was wrong?"

"He missed my birthday."

"When's that?"

"August 18. I don't care how mad we were, he wouldn't do that."

"At that point you haven't had any communication from him in about two months."

"Yeah."

"Was it normal for you to go that long without speaking to each other?"

"Once he left, he didn't want nothing to do with me. And, and"—her voice escalated—"why should I have to beg him? *He's* the one owed *me* money. *He's* the one flipping *me* off. He should be apologizing to me."

"I'm not putting anything on you, Tara."

She sucked on her cigarette. A vein ticked in her neck.

"He missed your birthday," I prompted gently.

"Yeah. I started to get scared. Like, what if he got into an accident? He didn't answer my texts and every time I called it went to voicemail. I didn't know what else to do. I called the surfboard guy."

"Smythe."

"He said *he* hadn't seen him, either."

"Since when?"

"Around the same time."

"June."

She nodded. "He said he went out one morning and Nicholas is gone, his stuff's gone, his car's not in the driveway."

"Did Nicholas tell him where he was headed? Did he leave a note?"

"The guy didn't know a damn thing. He just kept saying, 'Buuuh, duuuh, I dunno, he's not here, he left.' I got in my car and drove straight over there. I didn't even stop to pee. I'm banging on his door, and he comes out with his hair sticking up, like I woke him up at two in the afternoon. I made him show me where Nicholas was sleeping."

She scowled. "Internship my ass. Smythe had him cooped up in the garage like a friggin' prisoner, machines everywhere, fiberglass dust. 'No wonder he left, look at this shithole.' He starts acting all huffy, saying calm down or he'll call the cops. 'Fuck you, I'll call them myself.'

"I went to the station. Waited three hours for someone to talk to me. They told me Nicholas is an adult, he can do what he wants. I said, 'What about this guy, Smythe, maybe he did something to Nicholas.' They had me fill out a report and sent me home. Next day I called. They didn't have a clue what I was talking about. They said I had to come back in and file a new report. I was ready to lose my mind."

"I'm sorry you had to go through this, Tara."

"You got no idea. I'm calling them every day and getting the runaround. Finally this one detective goes, 'Ma'am, I was you, I wouldn't sit on my hands.' I started with the posters. Every wacko in town's calling me up, saying they know Nicholas or they seen him. Then this guy calls and says he's a private investigator. Portis?"

"Don't know him."

"Asshole . . . All he did was ask for money. The next guy was the same."

She ashed into the mug. Her foot twitched anxiously.

"Kills me, you know?" she said. "Not just the money, how much time I wasted."

She yanked out the pack and lit another cigarette. I let her smoke in peace for a bit, then said, "I'm curious what took Nicholas to Santa Cruz to begin with. Was that his thing? Surfing? I know he was a skateboarder."

"Please. He never got wet."

"So why do you think?"

"Beats the hell out of me. Senior year he dropped out. Said school's for sheep. 'Yeah, sheep who like to eat.' I made him get a job, you're not gonna hang around all goddamn day in your underwear playing video games. He started over at the Dick's on Blackstone. Every day he came home whining. 'They don't respect me.' No shit. Why should they? You don't have a high school diploma. He quit and went to Chipotle. What do you know, it's the same thing. Always been this way. His brain shuts off. He doesn't think, he just does things. One day he comes home with this dumbass anchor tattoo, talking about his heart belongs to the sea. I said, 'You dipshit, you can't hardly swim.' He got all offended.

'Shows what you know, real sailors don't know how to swim.' Fine, Popeye. Go wherever the fuck you want. Just don't come crying to me."

She wiped her eyes roughly. "Shit."

I offered her a tissue from a small pack I carry. A habit from my coroner days.

"Thanks," she said.

"Do you need a break?"

She blew her nose. "Do your thing."

I said, "In the last fifteen months, has Nicholas been in touch with anyone else?"

"Everybody says they haven't heard from him."

"His friends?"

"I don't know who he hung out with over there. He didn't tell me."

"What about friends from Fresno?"

"They're a bunch of idiots."

"Be that as it may, they may know something."

"They don't. Call them yourself, you don't believe me."

"I believe you," I said. "Who else is in his life? Siblings?"

"Just him."

Her answers about extended family were similarly curt. No uncles and aunts locally, no grandparents to speak of.

A lonely, claustrophobic self-portrait.

"Could he have reached out to one of these people without telling you?"

"I asked my sister. She said no. She said anything happens, it's on me, for fucking him up while I was pregnant."

"I'm sorry, Tara."

"She's right."

Smoke twined lazily toward a baked beige sky. Hard to believe that one of the most beautiful places on earth, Yosemite National Park, was less than seventy miles away.

I asked if Nicholas had any medical conditions or took medication.

"Adderall for his ADHD."

"Anything else?"

"Like what."

"Diabetes. Migraines. Seizures. Other mental health issues. Anything at all."

"No."

"Any history of self-harm or suicide attempts?"

"No."

"What about the rest of the family? Illness or mental health issues?"

"Warren's a fuckin asshole. Does that count?"

I smiled. "We'll stick to official diagnoses."

"No."

"Does Nicholas have a criminal history?"

"Not really."

I waited.

"When he was fourteen he and some friends got caught climbing the school fence. One kid had a can of spray paint in his backpack. Idiots," she said. "They were going to charge them with breaking and entering till the principal got them to drop it."

"What about as an adult?"

"No."

"Hobbies, other than skateboarding?"

"Video games."

"Did he have friends through either of those activities?"

"I told you, he didn't talk to me about it."

She looked uncomfortable. Bumping up against the limits of her knowledge.

"What kind of vehicle did Nicholas drive?" I asked.

"A Civic."

"Do you have the license plate?"

"I got it written down. Regina had me get all that stuff together. She sent it back when she was done. It's in a box, in his room. You can have all of it."

"Great. Anything else you want me to know? What should I be asking, that I'm not?"

"I'm sure I'll think of something as soon as you leave."

"Call me, or email me. No matter how insignificant it seems. I'd also like to speak with Regina. I'll need your permission."

"You have it."

"It'll be faster if you call her yourself."

"Yeah, okay."

"Thank you. How'd you find her, by the way?"

"Internet." Tara tugged out her menthols. The pack was empty, and she crushed it.

THE APARTMENT HAD a single bedroom. A bare mattress lay on the carpet, striped by the shadows of window bars. Remnants of adolescent passions: vacant reptile tank, posters of Bruce Lee and Walter White. The gaming setup included a flat-screen, newer and larger than the TV in the front room.

I asked Tara where she slept.

"The couch pulls out."

She hadn't taken over her son's space.

Too painful.

Hopeful, too. Keep the bed free, in case he comes back.

She towed a cardboard box from the closet. "When am I gonna hear from you?"

"When I learn something."

I wanted to temper her expectations. I thought she might snap back at me, but she nodded, as if drawing courage from the admission.

She saw me to the front door, watching as I buckled the box into the passenger seat.

CHAPTER 24

Regina Klein had begun her investigation the same place I would have: at the computer.

The box contained copies of Nicholas Moore's vital records, public records searches, a preliminary timeline. His driver's license listed Tara's address. He'd never paid a utility bill, in Santa Cruz or elsewhere, never bought or sold a property. His tenancy with Randy Smythe had been informal to the point of invisibility.

The Civic was a 2009, black, bought used in 2020. Registration had expired as of December. No record of resale or transfer.

The postmile in the TikTok video mapped to Shoreline Highway at the southern end of the Lost Coast, right before the inland detour that gave the region its name.

Thirty miles to Swann's Flat as the crow flies.

Crows could bypass the punishing road.

Still, feasible. Though I couldn't fathom why Nicholas would want to go there.

His bank account had lain dormant since his disappearance, the last debit card charges posting two days after the final text exchange with his mother. He'd spent six hundred dollars at a Santa Cruz camping outfitter. Klein noted the purchases: pack, boots, sleeping bag, and tent.

To know that, she would've had to sweet-talk some gullible employee into retrieving the sale record.

So sorry to bother you, my wallet was stolen, I'm worried someone else may have used my card. Would you mind terribly checking? Here's the number.

Canvass of Randy Smythe's neighborhood turned up only one person who recognized Nicholas: the clerk at a nearby minimarket. He recalled Nick coming in a few times a week for milk, bread, peanut butter, premade sandwiches.

A thumb drive held photos of Smythe's property, backyard, and garage workshop, plus an audio file of Klein's interview with him. Under pressure, Smythe stuck to his guns: He didn't know where Nick had gone. Their relationship was professional, not personal.

At times Smythe came across as cagey, though that could've been due to Klein's aggressive style. Her voice was girlish and high-pitched; his, marble-mouthed and narcotized. It was like listening to Betty Boop grill Matthew McConaughey.

You let him live in your house she said.

In the garage.

I don't have anyone living in my garage she said. *You just let anyone move in? You didn't get references?*

He said he wanted to learn. That's how I learned.

Paying it forward.

Yeah.

Did he have a girlfriend?

I don't know, man.

Boyfriend? Come on, Randy. A year? You never saw him with anyone?

It's none of my business.

You have eyes.

That's all I know. I'm busy.

Klein had called hospitals and shelters. She'd visited local skate-parks and skate shops to show Nicholas's photo around, and had begun working her way through gyms and bars. The lack of an active social circle was striking. A short list of friends and co-workers drew wholly on his previous life in Fresno—the people Tara Moore had referred to as *a bunch of idiots*. The first six names were starred. Presumably that meant Klein had spoken to them, but her reports didn't indicate any pertinent findings.

In any event, she'd had almost no time to follow up. Invoices stamped PAID showed two weeks of work in January and February.

She'd tacked on a third week, gratis.

I left her a voicemail and began calling idiots.

GABE ESPINOZA WAS from Fresno, a fellow skater—not an idiot at all, but bright and helpful. With a note of hurt, he told me that Nick had dropped off the face of the earth. They hadn't spoken in close to two years.

"We've been friends since first grade. Now you won't text me back? What?"

"Why do you think he left?"

"Shitty job. No girls. His mom's psycho. What's keeping him?"

"What makes you say that about his mom?"

"Did you meet her?"

"I did."

"And you thought she's normal?"

"How did she and Nick get along?"

"They didn't. Every time I was over, they were fighting and yelling at each other."

"About?"

"Money. School. Everything. And not the normal way you fight with your mom, okay? She's cussing and calling him names, like he's her boyfriend and she caught him cheating."

"She was controlling."

"*Hella* controlling. He told me once he wanted to go visit his dad's grave. She wouldn't tell him where it is. How messed up is that?"

"Why didn't she want to tell him?"

"'Cause she's psycho. I don't know. Ask her."

I would. "Did he talk to you about his dad?"

"Not much. I think it made him depressed. So, yeah. I can't blame him for getting out of here. I would, too. But you don't have to be a dick about it."

"Why Santa Cruz?"

"I guess he wanted to get as far away as he could. It's like the opposite of here."

"Tara told me he had a thing about the ocean."

"Yeah, *that* was random. He started reading books about sailors. He tried to get me to read them, too. I was like, 'Bro, I literally do not care about this.'" Espinoza laughed. "He's intense, you know? Nothing halfway. He finds some thing and goes ham. Then he gets bored and drops it and jumps to the next thing. We used to make these TikToks? At the skatepark?"

"I saw them."

"It was stupid shit, just us messing around. Out of nowhere Nick tells me he won't do it anymore. 'I hate social, it's poisoning our brains, megacorporations profiting off us, stealing our souls, stealing our DNA.' Some of what he was saying I agree with, but then he started to get into some straight-up conspiracy theory shit. He wanted to delete everything. I was like, 'Hold up, I shot those, they're mine, too.' So he left them. But the rest he took down. Discord, Twitch, IG, Snap."

"Have you seen his last TikTok? Where he's standing by the highway?"

"I think. I don't remember."

"Would you mind taking a look?"

"Hold on . . . okay, yeah. This."

"Any idea what he's doing?"

A beat while he watched it to the end. "He looks like a skin-head."

"Was he into that?"

"What."

"Skinheads."

"*Nick?* No. He just looks weird without hair."

"Any thoughts?"

"Not really."

"Do you recognize the place?"

"Sorry."

"That's okay. Gabe, did Nick have mood swings?"

"I mean, he was never Mr. Happy. Shit was tough for him."

"Did he ever have periods where he would get overly excited or skip sleeping? Talk fast? Ever describe hearing voices?"

"Nothing like that."

"Did he use drugs or alcohol?"

I expected his answer to differ from Tara's, or at least be less absolute.

But he said, "Never."

"You're sure about that."

"Completely. He was straight edge. It was really serious with him, because his mom used to be a meth head. He wouldn't even touch cigarettes."

"Tara told me he was on Adderall."

"I mean. Who isn't?"

"Did he ever take more than he was supposed to?"

"He didn't take it at all."

"He stopped his meds?"

"Yeah."

"Is that when his behavior started to change?"

"No, he stopped a long time ago. I think before high school."

"What did he do with the extras?"

Espinoza hesitated.

"No judgment," I said. "But I'm wondering if that's how he made cash."

"Lots of people do it."

"I know. That's why I'm asking."

"He's not, like, Pablo Escobar."

"Okay. Tell me about Nick's relationships. Was he dating anyone?"

"He never really had a regular girlfriend. He would get obsessed with one person, then switch to someone else."

"That was his pattern."

"Yeah." He paused. "You know what. There was this one girl he was into for a while. Naomi Cardenas. She goes to Santa Cruz."

"To UC?"

"Yeah. Or, I mean, she got in. I don't know if she's still there."

"Were she and Nick together?"

"No way," he said. "That's what I'm telling you: They weren't even friends. I don't think he said one word to her, all of high school. She was in a completely different universe. And I'm pretty sure she had a boyfriend, so it was never going to happen. Stupid, you know. Don't tell Nick I said that."

BY WEEK'S END, I'd left Regina Klein four voicemails and sent three emails.

I called Tara Moore. "Did you get a chance to speak to her yet?"

"I did it the day you were here, right after you left."

"Can you remind her?"

"Yeah."

"Thanks. Couple questions, while I have you. Did Nicholas ever mention someone named Naomi Cardenas?"

"No. Who's that?"

"He went to high school with her. Had a crush on her at one time."

"News to me. Does she know anything?"

"I'll let you know once I've spoken to her. Now," I said, "I have to ask you something tough, and I'm sorry. You told me Nicholas's father was dead. I looked up Warren Pezanko. I'm not seeing a death record that fits. I am seeing someone by that name in the prison system."

"You have no right," she said. "No right."

I kept silent.

"He's *trash,*" she said. "Evil trash. I didn't want Nicholas anywhere near him."

"He's housed at Pelican Bay."

"I don't give a shit where he is."

"My point is that's in Northern California. Up the highway. Is it possible Nicholas went to see him?"

"No. How would he? I told him his father's dead. That's all he ever heard from me."

"Did he ask you about visiting the grave?"

"Why would he? Why are you getting into this?"

Not lying, quite, but covering up.

I said, "What if he wanted to see the grave, so he started calling cemeteries himself? They all tell him, no, sorry, nobody here by that name. Now he's wondering, what's going on here? He starts looking online."

"He couldn't, even he wanted to. I told him a different name."

"What name?"

"Warren Smith."

"Is it possible he found something with Warren's real name on it? A birth certificate?"

"I didn't put that piece of shit on the certificate. I said I didn't know who the daddy was."

"Maybe a letter, or a card, a picture?"

"I didn't hold on to nothing from him."

"All right." I paused. "Is there anything else I should know? Now's the time."

"He's a fucking garbage piece of shit," she muttered.

I was starting to get the feeling she didn't like him. "Okay. You'll call Regina for me?"

A beat.

"Yeah."

NAOMI CARDENAS WAS more representative of her generation than either Nicholas Moore or Shasta Swann, leaving her many social media accounts wide open for the world to see.

Her favorite tags were #womeninSTEM, #womenwhoSWIM, #brainsandbeauty, and #scienceissexy. She sliced through the pool, twirled on the beach, smirked in a lab coat with her swim goggles in one hand and safety goggles in the other. A thirty-second makeup tutorial promised to teach you how to achieve that soft, seamless look. The secret, I inferred, was to be Naomi Cardenas and be born with flawless skin.

If she was half as vivacious as she wanted people to think, it was hard to picture her going for Nick Moore.

My phone rang.

"Clay Edison."

"I know who you are," Regina Klein said. "You're the motherfucker trying to steal my case."

CHAPTER 25

Santa Cruz is a mellower version of Berkeley: surfers and locals, students and tourists, drifting in a tranquil stupor brought on by an overload of natural beauty.

The world might be ending, but not here.

How could it, with that view?

Regina Klein, licensed private investigator, smashed the myth.

"Adultery," she said.

I'd asked about her caseload.

"Insurance fraud," she said. "Bread-and-butter shit. People are the fuckin same everywhere."

We sat outside a coffee roaster and vegan bakery on Beach Street. It was a bright, blustery day, the ocean bejeweled, palm trees doing a slow hula. Breezes carried the cloying scents of cotton candy and kettle corn, punctured by fetid spurts of sea lion. The table was cramped and my knees butted the post.

Not a problem for Regina at four foot eleven. Lemon-yellow Keds grazed the sidewalk; dyed-black bangs framed a doll-like face; oversized horn-rims further magnified her brown, owlish eyes. To judge from appearance alone, she'd be good at disarming people and getting them to lower their guard.

Assuming she could tone down the stridency a hair.

She wasn't making any such effort with me.

That was *her* case. *Her* legwork. If Tara Moore could afford to hire a PI, why hadn't she called Regina to finish what she'd started?

"What the actual fuck, man? Have you ever heard of professional fucking courtesy?"

I offered her a second oatmilk latte.

"Do I look like I need any more fucking caffeine? Get me a peach poppyseed scone."

I bought one and brought it to her.

"One thing about these hipster scum," she said, "they know how to make a pastry."

She stuffed a chunk into her mouth. "So what's your deal, Mr. Pro Bono? You're a trust-fund baby? Why do you want my case?"

"It caught my eye."

"Nice try, friendo. You don't get to horn in on my shit and then act like a fuckin schoolgirl. Pay to play."

I sketched the contours, leaving out Shasta's name or anything material to Chris Villareal. When I mentioned the necklace, Klein waved dismissively toward the boardwalk.

"They sell those everywhere. Tourist crap."

"Long way from Humboldt. How'd it get there?"

"Really, Poirot?" she said. "Okay. Here's a few theories. It's a different necklace. Or it's the same, but your unnamed person of interest was a tourist here, bought tourist crap, and took it home. Or they bought it on the internet. Or Nick pawned it and your person bought it. Or he dropped it on the sidewalk and they found it. He met them and gave it to them and moved on. Now he's in Outer Mongolia eating yak cheese. You want more? I can do this all day, as long as you're buying."

"There's no evidence of him being anywhere else."

"There's no evidence of him being anywhere, period."

"Except the necklace."

She rolled her eyes.

I said, "The TikTok's his first post in a year. He's dumped all his other social media, but he wants the world to see where he is. What's the significance of that spot? Where's he headed?"

"Oh, you're one of *those* guys."

"Which guys."

"Armchair shrink." She affected a plummy, pompous voice. " '*My* guiding principle is that the *why* is more important than the *how*. Thank you for coming to my TED Talk.' "

"I take it you're a how kind of person."

"All there is, sugar tits," she said. "Who did what to who, how hard and how long. The rest is Monday-morning quarterbacking. Your wife cheats on you? I'll sit in my car for nine hours and get you the proof. You want to know what's in her head, buy a saw."

"You're right," I said. "It's thin. That's why I'm here."

"What do you want from me?"

"Whatever's not in the file."

"The file is what's in the file."

"You expect me to believe you haven't thought about it?"

"Sorry, Freud, my compartmentalizing skills are world-class."

"Did you know that Warren Pezanko is alive?"

She shrugged.

"You knew."

"Of course I knew."

"You didn't put that in the file."

"I was off the clock," she said, cramming in the last bite of scone.

"What will it take for you to trust me?"

"You could share your Netflix login."

"I'm serious."

"So am I," she said. She wiped her mouth. "I've missed the last two seasons of *The Great British Baking Show*."

"How about another scone?"

"Cherry walnut."

I brought it to her.

"It's a start," she said, breaking it in half.

"I'm asking about Pezanko because I think it could be relevant."

"How?"

She had put down the scone and was paying attention. A turning point?

"Could explain why he's heading in that direction," I said. "I think it's more than theory. The video's called 'In the name of the father.'"

"It's a TikTok, for fuck's sake, not the Bible. And how's he finding out? Tara never told him the guy's name."

"Maybe it wasn't Nick who found Pezanko. Maybe Pezanko got in touch with him."

"Same problem. How's he gonna know where Nick is?"

"I don't know. I put in a call to the warden at Pelican Bay to see if he'll talk to me."

"And?"

"I haven't heard back yet."

"You're a disappointment and a half."

"All I'm trying to do is avoid reinventing the wheel."

"Easy for you. I gave you a head start. What're you going to give me?"

"Gabe Espinoza."

"The fuck is that?"

"Number thirteen on your list of friends and co-workers."

"Once again: my legwork."

"No argument from me."

She picked at the scone, trying, unsuccessfully, to squash her curiosity. "What'd he say?"

"Nick had a thing for this girl, Naomi Cardenas. She lives here."

"In Santa Cruz?"

I nodded. "I'm headed over to her next."

She was quiet for a long time.

"Okay. That's a good lead." Begrudging admiration.

"I'm sure you would've found her eventually."

"Don't you condescend to me."

"I'm not. I'm rubbing it in your face."

She laughed. "Get bent."

"Despite your uncontrollable hostility, I'll keep you in the loop."

"No fuckin thank you." She wiped the crumbs from her hands, shaking her head vehemently. "He's all yours now."

CHAPTER 26

Before leaving the beachfront I made a quick circuit of the neighborhood souvenir shops. Of the many puka shell necklaces for sale, few featured pendants and none of those were a rooster. The shopkeepers claimed they'd never seen or sold anything like it. One guy suggested I try a "real jewelry store." I asked for recommendations and he told me to google it.

Naomi Cardenas lived on the south side of campus. I loitered by the building entrance, pretending to talk on the phone and catching the lobby door as a resident left.

The roommate who answered my knock had me wait in the hall.

I heard the chain go on.

A moment later Naomi opened the door, peering at me through the crack. "Yes?"

I introduced myself and showed my license. "I wanted to ask you about Nick Moore."

She flinched slightly; glanced back into the apartment. "One second."

Taking off the chain, she stepped out into the hall and shut the door behind. She was less glamorous in person but prettier for it, wearing mesh shorts and a tank top and a messy bun. Dark circles under her eyes. Long night at the lab?

"What's going on?" she asked.

"You know Nick."

"Sort of."

"When were you last in touch with him?"

"Is everything okay?"

"His mom hasn't heard from him. She's worried. It would help to know how long it's been since you spoke to him."

"A year? More."

"What's that mean, you 'sort of' know him?"

"We went to high school together. But I didn't know him then, we only met here."

"How?"

"I was on my way to class and I heard someone calling my name. This guy comes up to me. He's like, 'I went to Hoover. You probably don't remember me.'"

"Did you?"

"Kind of? I think I recognized his face. You know what it's like when you're out in the world and you run into someone from your hometown. You feel this . . . bond. Even if you don't really know them. We were just, like, chatting about places and people. After that we started texting a little."

"Was there anything romantic between you?"

"With Nick? Nooo. Nooo. Totally platonic. Truthfully, I felt bad for him. He seemed kinda lost. I think he was having trouble meeting people. I invited him to this Halloween party we were having. I didn't think he'd actually show up."

"But he did."

"Yeah. And . . . Yeah."

I said, "What happened?"

With another backward glance, Naomi led me down the hall and into the stairwell.

She said, quietly, "He hooked up with my roommate."

"The one who answered the door?"

Naomi nodded.

"What's her name?"

She stubbed the concrete with her flip-flop. "I shouldn't even be telling you this."

"I wouldn't ask if it wasn't important."

". . . Maddie."

"Maddie what?"

"Zwick."

"Do you think she'd be willing to talk to me?"

"That's not a good idea. Her boyfriend's over right now."

"Was he her boyfriend at the time?"

"They were broken up when it happened. Plus she was *really* drunk."

A door slammed on an upper floor. I waited for the echo to fade. "Did Maddie and Nick have a relationship or was it a one-time deal?"

She touched a fingertip to her lips. "Well, it's not like they were dating."

"But?"

"For a while they were hanging out, and he'd stay over sometimes. Then she got back together with Alex. But it became this whole big drama. Nick kept texting her. She blocked him and he started sending her letters. Actual letters, written on paper. Who does that?"

"What did they say?"

"I didn't read them."

"Does she still have them?"

"I'm sure she threw them out. One night he showed up, banging on the door. Alex was there. He and Nick got into a fight."

"How serious?"

"It was mostly yelling and shoving. Alex was like, 'Stay away from her or I'll kill you.'"

"Was that a real threat?"

"Alex? *No.* He's pre-med. Trust me, Nick was out of control."

"When was this?"

"Last year. Spring quarter."

Prior to the disappearance.

"Has Maddie been in touch with Nick since then?"

"I don't think so."

"It would really help if I could talk to her."

"I can ask, but not while Alex is here."

"I'm in town for the rest of the day. If you can get the message to her, I'd be grateful."

She accepted my card. "I hope Nick's okay. I mean, he shouldn't have acted like that. But he's not a bad guy. Just . . . confused."

I nodded.

She said, "He said some cuckoo things that night."

"Such as."

"He loved her, he was going to kill himself if he couldn't be with her. Maddie was totally traumatized. So, I hope he's okay, for his sake. But for hers, too."

RANDY SMYTHE'S COTTAGE was tiny and decrepit, six or seven hundred square feet worth six or seven hundred thousand dollars due to its prime location on the San Lorenzo River.

The whine of machinery drew me along a driveway lined with kinetic sculptures in steel and wood.

The garage was a one-car, its door shut while work took place in a postage-stamp yard. Two men wearing dust masks hunched over a surfboard propped on sawhorses. The younger used an orbital sander to shape the board, while his companion—twice his age and taller, with steel-wool hair and a rawhide complexion—traced curves in the air to guide him. More sculptures rotated.

I waved. "Excuse me."

The younger man glanced up and shut off the sander.

"Randy Smythe?" I said.

The older man said, "Yes?"

"My name is Clay Edison. If I could have a few minutes of your time—"

"We're right in the middle of this."

"It's about Nick Moore."

Smythe tugged down his mask. Taking a water bottle from the grass, he chugged it and waggled it at the young man. "Fill this up for me."

The assistant obediently carried the bottle into the house.

Smythe said, "I've gone over this."

"I realize that, but Nick's still missing."

"I don't know what you want me to say, dude. I don't know where he went, he didn't tell me, I haven't heard from him."

"Let's try to jog your memory."

"There's nothing to jog."

"Did he ever mention a girl named Maddie Zwick?"

"No."

"Did he ever bring people over?"

"No. That's a shop rule. I don't care what you do in your free time, you can't do it here."

"Before he left, did you notice changes in his behavior or mood?"

"Man, I don't know. We were focused on the task. This is an art. It requires concentration. I can't be having distractions."

"How was he as a worker?"

"Fine. He learned quick, he didn't complain. Creative. I liked him."

"He was sleeping in the garage."

"That's how it works."

"It's not an accusation."

"I fed him. I shared my knowledge. When I was in the same situation nobody paid *me*."

"I'd like your permission to have a look in there."

"Dude. I'm tellin you, there's *nothing,* okay? He took everything with him when he left."

A voice behind us said, "There was some letters."

We pivoted toward the house. The shop assistant stood on the back steps. He'd removed his mask and was holding the refilled water bottle.

"What letters?" I asked.

He glanced at Smythe nervously.

"What's your name?" I asked.

"Aiden."

"Aiden, what letters?"

"They were in the locker," he said.

I turned to Smythe.

He sighed. "Fine."

He hauled up the garage door. A scalding, chemical stench billowed out.

I saw surfboards in various stages of completion: heaped on tables, drying on racks. Hand tools, power tools, oxyacetylene torch, fiberglass cloth, tubs of epoxy, a spray paint rainbow.

One errant match would level the neighborhood.

Good reason to work in the yard.

The three of us single-filed toward the back, where floor space had been carved out to accommodate an army cot. Creature comforts included a battery-operated fan and a clamp lamp. Aiden's personal possessions fit into a duffel bag and a footlocker, also military surplus.

"May I?" I asked.

Aiden looked at Smythe. Smythe said, "You invited him, kid."

I opened the footlocker. Sour Patch Kids, marijuana, a bong, lighters.

"Where are the letters?" I asked.

"I threw them out," Aiden said.

Smythe shut his eyes. "Unbelievable."

"I didn't know I was supposed to keep them."

"Why'd you tell us you had them?"

"I didn't say that, I said they were there before."

"Do you remember what they said?" I asked. "Who they were addressed to?"

"I wasn't paying attention. It was somebody's private stuff."

"How many were there?"

"Uh . . ."

"A lot, or just a few."

"Like ten?"

"Are we done, please?" Smythe said.

"Those sculptures," I said to him. "Are they yours?"

"Yeah."

"Do you ever make jewelry?"

"No."

"But you have the tools to do it."

"Nothing fancy."

"What about Nick? Do you recall him making any jewelry?"

Smythe said, "Now that you mention it, yeah. He was cutting a piece of steel and broke a saw blade. I was *not* happy."

I showed him the photo of the pendant. "Was it this?"

"Could be."

If so, the rooster was one of a kind.

My phone buzzed with a text.

It's Naomi. Alex left Maddie says you can come over

CHAPTER 27

T hanks for agreeing to meet with me," I said.

Maddie Zwick nodded.

She sat curled up on the living room futon, long legs folded beneath her, gnawing the cuff of her sweatshirt and gazing at me with watchful blue eyes. A miniature floral tattoo adorned the inside of her wrist. The sweatshirt read BANANA SLUGS SWIMMING & DIVING.

After making introductions, Naomi Cardenas had excused herself to class. We weren't alone—a third roommate was working in her bedroom—but Maddie still seemed uneasy, and I offered to move the conversation someplace public.

"It's okay," she said.

I said, "What's your event?"

"One hundred fly and two hundred IM."

"Cool."

She reevaluated me. "Do you swim?"

"Dog paddle."

She smiled cautiously. "That's not an event."

"Not yet. I did play basketball at Berkeley. Used to arrive for morning practice and the swimmers would be leaving. They'd already had two hours in the pool."

"My alarm's set for four thirty."

"Brutal."

"Yeah, it sucks." Her posture eased. "In high school I lettered in basketball. Volleyball, too."

"Triple threat. Lemme see. You're what. Five-nine?"

"And a half."

"Two guard."

"Yup," she said. "Point?"

"You know it."

She smiled again, more fully.

I said, "Like I said, I really appreciate this, Maddie. I know you had a rough experience with Nick and I'm sure it's not fun to talk about. Naomi told me some, but I'd like to hear it from you. Take as much time as you need."

She spat out her cuff and shoved it up her forearm, irked by her own bad habit. "We had a party and she invited him. She must've forgotten, or she was ignoring him, because I went to my room to get something. He was in there."

"Doing what?"

"Nothing. Standing there, with his hands in his pockets. I was like, 'Uh, excuse me?' He apologized. He said he came in to get some space 'cause he felt out of place. He didn't know anyone except Naomi."

"What was your first impression?"

"Part of me was creeped out, but at the same time it was kind of sweet and awkward. How he admitted it right away, most guys would be like, 'Oh no, I'm good.' We started talking, and you know. One thing led to another."

"Naomi said it wasn't serious between you."

"Not for me."

"For him?"

"I mean. It's my fault."

"Why do you say that?"

"I should've been clearer. I'd just broken up with Alex, I was feeling shitty about myself. Nick . . . He was cute. And—I did like him. Just not the way he liked me."

"How long did it last?"

"About seven months. But that makes it sound like more than what it was. We didn't do, like, couple things. We never went anywhere together. I didn't want to run into Alex, and Nick wasn't allowed to have guests, so he'd come over and we'd sit and watch TV and talk."

"What did you guys talk about?"

"Normal stuff. Life. He wasn't my usual type. I had a typical suburban childhood. My dad sells insurance, my mom's a nurse. Very Orange County mid. Naomi was like, 'It's so adorable, you're going through your dirty hippie boy phase.'"

"Opposites attract?"

"Yeah, maybe. For a little while."

"And then?"

"It felt out of balance," she said. "Almost from the beginning."

"Can you give me an example?"

"Well, like . . . He gave me this necklace?"

"The rooster."

Her eyes widened. "You saw it?"

I showed her the still from the TikTok video.

"Yeah," she said. "I gave it back when we broke up. I never wanted it in the first place."

"That's what you mean by out of balance."

"Exactly. I get that he meant to be sweet. But I'd known him like three weeks. You should not be buying me gifts. He goes, 'I didn't buy it, I made it.' If you think about it, that's even weirder. When did you start working on it? The day after we hooked up?"

The cuff had found its way into her mouth again.

"He's a talented guy," she said. "It was good. But it's a *chicken*. I don't want to wear that. When I tried it on, he looked so happy.

I didn't want to hurt his feelings. I'd wear it when he was around and take it off when he left."

She pulled the cuff from between her teeth. "I'm not the best at setting boundaries."

"Was the necklace supposed to represent something?"

"He said it was good luck for sailors. He told me that on ships they keep the pigs and chickens in crates. If it sinks, they float to shore and don't drown."

"At least he didn't give you a pig."

She laughed. "Oh my God. I can't even."

"The sailor fixation—what was that about?"

"We were comparing tattoos once. Mine," she said, touching her wrist, "is for my grammy Lily. He showed me the anchor and was all like, 'Life is a storm.'"

"What's that mean?"

"I just thought he was being extra. Part of his moody-guy thing."

"Tell me more about that, Maddie."

"He took *everything* so seriously. The world's black and white, everything has to mean something. He was *very* self-conscious that he'd dropped out. I think he felt he wasn't good enough or smart enough so he had to prove himself constantly."

"To you."

"Actually, no. It wasn't about me, it was about him. I'm an English major, right? So he'd always try to talk to me about books. *Catcher in the Rye*? High school stuff. He must've realized what I thought, because he started asking for recommendations. Anything I gave him, he'd read in a couple days and ask for more. It bothered me. You're not seeing me, the person; you're using me to fill in the holes in your life."

She paused. "Does that make sense?"

"Perfect sense. Is that why you decided to end it?"

"Kind of. I let it drag out. But then it got really weird, really quickly, and I knew I had to just cut it off."

"Weird how?"

"I was showing him the reading list from this seminar I took on Chicano literature. Sandra Cisneros, Richard Vasquez, people like that. I asked Nick if he'd ever read Octavio Prado."

"I'm afraid I don't know who that is."

"He wrote this book, *Lake of the Moon,* about growing up in Fresno. That's why I thought of it. I was like, 'Oh, this guy, he's from Fresno, too.' I wasn't implying anything about Nick personally. I just thought he might like it 'cause of the connection."

"Is that how he took it? Personally?"

"That's the weird part. I let him borrow it. The next morning he came back. He'd read it overnight and he was *freaking* out."

"About?"

She exhaled. "So you know he never met his dad?"

"He discussed that with you."

"No discussion, he just told me. It felt too heavy for what we were. I wasn't thinking about it when I gave him the book. There's a part where Prado writes about getting a girl pregnant. Nick . . . He was *convinced* the girl was his mom and Prado's his real father."

"That's what he said?"

Maddie nodded.

"What gave him that idea?" I asked.

"No clue. I mean, I thought he was joking. Obviously. Then he starts showing me his notebook. He's copied out all these passages from the book. Names and dates. And charts he'd created. Pages and pages, he must've been working on it all night. I'm looking at it and he's pacing around my room, talking a mile a minute. 'Don't you get it? Everything lines up. This is why I came here, this is why we met, it's destiny.' It was insane."

"Sounds like it."

"Yeah. Then it started to get scary. He's asking questions about Prado and getting angry when I can't answer. I told him, 'I don't know anything else, that's the only thing we read in class.' Eventually he got fed up and left."

"Had you ever seen him act like that before?"

"No. Never."

"You described him as moody."

"Okay, but this . . . It was a whole 'nother level."

"What's the character's name? The woman he thought was his mom."

". . . Sandra, I think."

"Do you have the book?"

"He never returned it."

"When did you lend it to him? Approximately?"

"I took the seminar winter quarter, so right after that."

"Spring 2024."

"Yeah."

"What happened after he left?"

"I didn't hear from him for a few days. I was worried, but also relieved. It felt like a wake-up call. I texted him that I needed a break."

"How'd he take it?"

"Better than I expected. He apologized. I told him we could be friends. He didn't text for a week or two. Then it was nonstop."

"Do you have the messages?"

"I erased them when I blocked him."

"He began sending real letters."

She nodded.

"Do you remember what they said?"

"I only opened the first one. I started to read it, but it was too upsetting. The rest I put straight in the trash. I'm sorry."

"You have nothing to be sorry for, Maddie."

She bit her lip. "I just wanted it to stop."

"Of course. And this went on till the night of the fight with Alex."

"Yes."

"Are you okay to talk about that?"

She started to go for her cuff but caught herself. "I think so."

"Whenever you're ready."

She drew the hem of the sweatshirt over her knees. "Okay, so. It was late. I'm asleep, Alex's studying in the kitchen. He and I had gotten back together. Naomi heard a knock and saw it was Nick through the peephole. She told him to go away, but he kept banging. Alex opened the door, and the two of them started arguing. It woke me up so I came out of my room. I almost didn't recognize Nick. He'd shaved his head, and he was sort of sticking through the door, trying to force his way inside. It was like that scene from that movie. The guy with the ax?"

"*The Shining?*"

"Yeah. I was afraid someone was going to get hurt. I said I could talk to him, but only if he calmed down. He goes, 'I'd never hurt you, I love you.' Alex heard that and went ballistic. He pushed Nick into the hall, and they started wrestling. Now I'm trying to calm *him* down, too."

She'd crossed her arms protectively over her chest and was staring at the door, as if she could see them rolling around.

"What a thing to go through, Maddie."

She swallowed. "Yeah."

"Do you remember what Nick was saying?"

"Not really. More of that destiny crap. Basically he wanted me to come with him."

"Where?"

"I don't know. He was babbling, not making any sense."

"This might sound strange, but did he mention the writer? Prado?"

"I . . . There was a lot going on. No, I don't think so. I was just trying to say whatever I could to get him to calm down. All of a sudden he stops and looks at me. 'You're not wearing it, why aren't you wearing it?'"

"The necklace."

She nodded. "I couldn't tell him the real answer, which was that I never wore it anymore. I didn't want him to lose his shit. I said I took it off to sleep. His whole vibe changed, like *that*. He sort of . . . deflated? It was awful. I thought he would start crying. He asked me for it back. I gave it to him and made him promise he would leave."

"After that?"

"I never talked to him again."

"He never tried to contact you."

"No. Well—he put up a TikTok, flipping me off."

"You think that was directed at you."

"I mean. Yeah. Who else would it be?"

"Do you recognize the location in the video?"

She shook her head. "Do you?"

"Mendocino County. About a five-hour drive north of here."

"What was he doing all the way up there?"

"Good question. Did he ever talk about heading that way? When he was trying to persuade you to come with him?"

She bit her lip again. Hard enough to leave a rosy crescent. "I'm sorry, I really don't remember." She wiped her nose on her sleeve. "Everything was so chaotic."

"You're doing great," I said. "And you can always call me later if something comes back to you."

She nodded.

"One last question. Do you know the date of the fight with Alex?"

"Not off the top of my head. But . . . Hold on."

She took out her phone, began scrolling. "I couldn't sleep 'cause I was so shaken up. I texted my coach and told her I wasn't feeling well. One second, I have to find it . . . Okay, I wrote to her at four a.m. on June 12. So the night before."

June 11. The day after Nicholas's last message to his mother.

I thanked Maddie and left her looking forlorn.

CHAPTER 28

Octavio Prado was the writerly equivalent of a one-hit wonder. *Lake of the Moon,* first published in the fall of 2005, was long out of print. I browsed reviews left by a tiny, loyal following.

My favorite book of all time

Why is he not more famous?

Unsung master, so much better than today's "literature"

Used hardcovers went for a penny, plus shipping and handling. I ordered one, expedited.

Two thousand five. Prado had had the good or bad fortune of making his debut immediately prior to the advent of Web 2.0—that brief window when the internet held nothing but promise and privacy still existed. His Wikipedia entry was a stub, and he didn't maintain a webpage or use social media. The bulk of the links about him were broken. More recent pages referred to him in the past tense and regurgitated the same set of factoids.

Wunderkind, published at nineteen to raves and nominations. Hollywood knocking.

He didn't win the awards. There was no movie, no cushy post teaching creative writing at a liberal arts college. No heroic sophomore effort.

A supernova, there and gone.

———

MY COPY OF *Lake of the Moon* arrived two days later. The cover depicted a hybrid creature: eagle's head, human body, dressed in baggy shorts and smoking a limp cigarette.

I opened to the back flap.

A young Latino man glared at the camera, doing his utmost to compensate for a baby face. Shaved head, pencil goatee, a soft bulge beneath his chin. But for the bare scalp, no resemblance to Nick Moore.

Octavio Prado was born in Fresno. This is his first book.

It ran to 166 pages, written in a terse, crackling style and covering three weeks in the life of its adolescent protagonist, Félix Santiágo de Jesús y Tlalolín. Aka Grillito, aka Cricket.

In the first scene, he woke up in the bedroom he shared with three brothers. Over breakfast he endured merciless teasing from his three sisters. He rode his skateboard to school. He got a B on a creative writing assignment. He talked shit with his friends in the hallways.

During lunch, a white girl flirted with him unexpectedly. Her name was not Sandra, as Maddie Zwick remembered, but Sarah.

After school he rode his skateboard to his grandfather's house. He and the old man were rebuilding a Rolls-Royce from parts. When they were done, Abuelo gave him ten dollars from a coffee can under the kitchen sink.

At home Cricket couldn't stop thinking about Sarah. He went into the bathroom to masturbate but forgot to lock the door. His sister walked in. She screamed and called him disgusting.

Fleeing the house in shame, he rode to a local skatepark, gliding over the ramps till nightfall.

Someone called his name. Sarah was walking toward him. They sat alone at the edge of a lake-shaped pit, talking and kicking their feet. She said she was driving home from tennis practice and saw him. She said she liked Mexican guys. She didn't know why, she just did. She leaned over and kissed him. They went to a secluded corner of the park, lay down in the weeds, and had sex.

Post-coitus, the action jumped ahead.

Sarah confronted Cricket at school. She told him she was pregnant and demanded five hundred dollars for an abortion, implying that if he refused she would accuse him of rape.

He rode to Abuelo's house. He intended to borrow the money, but Abuelo didn't answer the door. Cricket went around and let himself in with the key under the flowerpot. The old man was asleep on the living room sofa, his snores boring through the drone of the TV. Cricket took the coffee can from under the kitchen sink. He peeled the lid off.

The novel ended with him staring into the can at a mess of small bills, listening to the old man's exhausted wheezes.

On another day, I might have enjoyed it. But this wasn't pleasure reading; I was searching for any link to Nicholas Moore, however specious.

Fresno. Skateboarding. A white girl.

Sarah rhymed with *Tara*.

The year of publication coincided with Nick Moore's birth.

Still, not much.

But that was beside the point. It didn't matter how a rational person would respond, only how Nick would. Everything I'd learned about him—intense mood swings, grandiose thoughts—suggested an undiagnosed mental illness beyond his childhood ADHD.

What *Lake of the Moon* left out was more important than what it contained.

We never learned if Cricket went through with his theft. If Sarah had the abortion. If, for that matter, the pregnancy was real or a shakedown.

Blanks for an overactive mind to fill in.

I looked up the seminar Maddie Zwick had taken.

Lit 193C, Chicano/a Voices, was taught by a UC Santa Cruz associate professor named Eli Ruíz. His CV positioned him as a leading authority on Prado—the sole authority, having planted his flag with a single journal article titled *"Autonomía o autotomía?: Violence, Liberation, and De(con)structed Selves in Lake of the Moon."*

I emailed him and was surprised to get a callback within the hour.

He spoke at a breakneck clip, excited by my interest. As a teenager growing up in Whittier, discovering Prado had been a formative experience: the first time Ruíz recognized himself on the page. The slang was his slang, the characters intimately familiar.

I asked what Prado was doing now.

"No one knows. He left Fresno and withdrew from the public eye. I've reached out to his family, his literary agent. They haven't heard from him in years. I've come to the conclusion that he doesn't want to be found."

"Why?"

"The novel caused an uproar in his community. Prado's family is very traditional, very Catholic. More than that: His mother is fanatically religious. I gather he was made to feel excruciatingly unwelcome at home. He may have been threatened, or felt that way."

"It's fiction."

"A fine line, Mr. Edison. And Prado didn't do himself any favors, there. He's also the youngest of seven, also three brothers and three sisters. His mother's name is Celia; in the book it's Celene. He mentions her church by name. He really did rebuild a Rolls-Royce with his grandfather. And so on. And, by the way, his grandfather died of a heart attack shortly after publication. Celia is quite firm in blaming Octavio."

"What about the Sarah character? Who's she?"

"That's trickier. Prado attended Roosevelt High from 1999 to 2003. The student body is predominantly Latino and Latina. It shouldn't be hard to narrow her down, but everyone I've spoken to denies it. The name Sarah can sometimes signify a generic white female. I'm inclined to think she's a composite."

"Was the pregnancy factual?"

"Not to my knowledge."

"That would be a good reason to want to leave town."

"Yes, although I doubt he needed another."

"Any idea where he went?"

"If only. His agent told me she was forever trying to get ahold of him, but he moved often, without warning. My impression is that he was homeless by choice."

"I'd like to speak to her. Would you mind putting me in touch?"

"Let me ask her permission."

"Thank you."

"One thing you might find of interest: Prado finished a second book but it was never published."

"How come?"

"It's somewhat . . . unruly."

"You've read it."

"The agent donated it to UC Merced. I had a scan made. I can send you the PDF."

"That'd be great. What's it called?"

"*Cathedral.*"

My scalp prickled.

A grove of redwoods, whirling like dancers, writhing like flames.

The Cathedral.

I asked what the book was about.

"Easier to say what it's *not* about," Ruíz said. "You can't characterize it as a novel, as such. More like a mosaic. There's no traditional narrative. One senses Prado striving for a new mode of communication. He doesn't succeed, in my opinion. But some of the writing is highly memorable. Sublime, even."

"What does the title mean?"

"As far as I'm aware, the word doesn't appear in the body of the text. Full disclosure: I've only read chunks, never the whole thing straight through. I love Prado, but that would be a lot to ask of anyone."

"Professor, have you ever met a young man named Nick Moore?"

"He's a student?"

"No. I'll text you a photo."

Seconds later: "Oh. *That* kid."

"How do you know him?"

"I don't," Ruíz said. "I met him once. He showed up to my office hours." A beat. "He wanted to talk about Prado, too. Lots of questions. Not dissimilar from yours, in fact. What else did Prado write, where is he now."

"You told him about *Cathedral*."

"Probably."

"Did you send him the PDF?"

"I can check. What am I looking for?"

I gave him Nick Moore's email address.

"No, I don't see it," Ruíz said. "Who is he, if not a student?"

"A young man. Also missing."

"Oh no. Really?"

"For about fifteen months."

"That's terrible. Uch. His poor family."

"Do you remember when you talked to him?"

"I had recently finished teaching the seminar, so it must have been around then. Or a little after . . . ? I'm sorry. I don't want to tell you the wrong thing."

"No worries. Thinking back on the conversation, does anything jump out about him or his behavior? Was he upset, excited?"

"I couldn't say. As I recall I was on my way to class, running out the door, and we only spoke for a few minutes. What's his connection to Prado?"

"He's from Fresno. He was born the same year *Lake of the Moon* was published, and he seems to have come to the conclusion that Prado was his biological father."

Ruíz spluttered a laugh. "What?"

"Could that be possible?"

"No. No. Out of the question." Then, doubtfully: "*You* don't think it's possible?"

"He and Prado have a few superficial things in common."

"Such as."

I described the similarities. When I got to Sarah and Tara, he scoffed. "Come on."

"I agree with you. But I try to keep an open mind. I'd rather ask the question and sound stupid than be smug and miss something."

"You should steer clear of academia, then."

"Noted. I will say, Professor, you're a pretty good PI."

"I'm up for tenure soon. Depending on how it goes, you might be hearing from me re: a career change."

"I'll be ready," I said. "Nick didn't ask you directly about any of this, though."

"No."

"What about the manuscript at Merced? Did you mention it to him?"

"I might have. As I said, it was a brief conversation. I'd forgotten about it until you sent me his picture. But—look. He's far from the first person to overidentify with a writer or character. When it comes to Prado, I'm just as guilty. Any great literature, Mr. Edison, is a mirror."

CHAPTER 29

I f books were mirrors, *Cathedral* belonged in a fun house.

One thousand, nine hundred twenty-three mind-numbing, handwritten pages, clogged with strikeouts, erasures, words running left to right but also backward. Or vertically. Or diagonally. Many sheets were blank or featured a single word. Others had been victimized by marker bleed.

Prado catalogued the shelves in an AM/PM mini-mart.

He drew motorcycles. Drew a poor rendition of Keanu Reeves in *The Matrix*.

A wrinkled blotch marked where he'd spilled some sort of amber liquid.

Occasionally I stumbled across passages that demonstrated his skill and concision: sharp snippets of dialogue, crystalline descriptions of people or places. But these lucid moments were few and far between, and I couldn't pinpoint any chronology or geography, making it impossible to extract actionable leads.

On page 450 I broke for coffee and ibuprofen.

On page 889 I stopped dead.

A rectangular block of text crowded the screen. At its center was a pencil sketch about the size of a baseball card.

Prado's drafting skills were rudimentary. But I got the gist.

Saw-toothed water.

Lumpy hills.

Two convergent lines forming a road.

On it, a stick figure.

One arm up.

One giant middle finger extended to the sky.

Sea, mountains, highway; fuck you.

I opened Nicholas Moore's final TikTok, let it play.

Sea, mountains, highway.

Fuck you.

The drawing was far too crude to call it a match.

Was I committing the same error as Eli Ruíz or Nick Moore or countless others?

Craving meaning, finding it in the mirror?

I combed through the surrounding text, a stew of Spanish and English.

A phrase was tucked into the bottom right corner.

En el nombre del Padre, y del Hijo, y del Espíritu Santo A Men 83261

In the name of the father.

I zoomed in. The writing was faint. But then I saw it. A speck between two digits made it *83.261*.

And that reminded me of something.

I replayed Nick's final TikTok, pausing on the frame where he stooped toward the camera.

As I adjusted the slider, the postmile sign came into focus, one character at a time.

MEN

83.261

———

FOUR DAYS AND one bottle of ibuprofen later, I had yet to find another real-world reference.

That didn't mean there weren't any. The scan quality worsened steadily; I imagined the unfortunate work-study student assigned the task, drowning in boredom. Prado's handwriting deteriorated, too. By the end it was a hectic scrawl that tore holes in the paper.

Something might be in there, but I wasn't going to find it in a PDF.

I booked an appointment at UC Merced for the following afternoon.

IN THE MORNING I dropped Myles off at daycare and drove Charlotte to Chabot Park for camp. As I was walking back to my car, a counselor chased after me, calling urgently.

"Excuse me." She was about fifteen, with box braids. "You're Charlotte's dad."

"Yes?"

"I wanted to talk to you about something that happened yesterday."

I braced myself. "Okay."

"The kids were taking turns on the swings, and there was a child who was getting upset because he had to wait so long. Charlotte was next, but she let him go ahead. It was so kind of her."

"I thought you were going to tell me she did something wrong."

"*Charlotte?* Oh no. She's the sweetest thing ever."

"You know what? You're right. She is. Thanks . . ."

"Nia." She grinned. "Anyhow. I thought you'd want to know."

"I do. Thanks for sharing it with me."

"You're welcome! Have a great day!" She ran off, braids flying.

I took out my phone to text Amy and tell her. It rang before I could call. Blocked number.

I said, "Hello?"

"This is Maeve Ferris. Octavio's agent." A mid-Atlantic accent broadened the *a*'s in Prado's name. "I believe you wanted to talk to me."

"Yes. Hi. Give me one second."

"Bad time?"

"No, I just need to grab my notebook."

I got it from the car and jogged along Estudillo Avenue, away from the noisy drop-off area and toward the picnic tables.

"Thanks for getting back to me, Ms. Ferris. I'm not sure what Professor Ruíz told you."

"You're searching for a boy who thinks Octavio is his father."

"Correct."

"Allow me to assure you: He's not."

"And you know that because?"

"Because Octavio was a virgin. And I know *that* because he told me."

"Could he have lied?"

"Not a chance," Ferris said. "He was utterly sincere. Tell me: Have you ever met a man who lied about that? Only the very best ladies do. Plus there are the issues of content and context. Anyone reading that sex scene could tell it wasn't written from experience."

"What I read was very short."

"You should've seen the original, before I made him take a machete to it."

"That bad, huh."

"The word *loins* made multiple appearances," she said. "One of my conditions for representing him was that he walk me through the manuscript, to review it for potential libel. You probably don't remember, but a number of books around then straddled the line between novel and autobiography, and several of those authors ended up getting sued. Given Octavio's subject matter, I thought it prudent to have him on record. The sex, the pregnancy—it was all made up."

"Was Sarah a real person? I ask because the mother of the boy I'm looking for is about the right age, and her name is Tara."

"Perhaps Octavio knew her or was inspired by her, but he certainly didn't impregnate her. Short of a Christmas miracle, I don't see how this boy could be his son. Who is he, anyway?"

"His name's Nicholas Moore. He was born around when *Lake of the Moon* came out. Has he ever contacted you?"

"No," she said. "Born when, exactly?"

"May 3, 2005."

"Well, that's another way to know. Octavio and I spent at least a year editing together, and then we had to wait for his place in the publication cycle. The first draft would have been finished no later than about 2003."

"Ah."

"Sorry to disappoint, Mr. Edison."

"That's all right. I told Professor Ruíz I didn't think it was plausible. But it is possible Nick convinced himself it was the truth."

"*That* wouldn't surprise me. Fiction can be a springboard for all sorts of fantasies. Now, if there's nothing else—"

"A couple questions about Prado, if that's okay."

A beat. "Be my guest."

"How'd you come to work with him in the first place?"

"I'd love to claim I divined him with my exquisite literary antennae, but it was pure chance. He sent in the manuscript unsolicited. My assistant pulled it out of the slush pile. Lauren. Smart girl. She went back to law school . . . Regardless. She liked it, passed it to me. *Et voilà*. Back then we could afford to take risks. Not anymore. One reason I got out."

"Professor Ruíz said the book upset Prado's family."

"Yes, it was rather tragic. They booted him out of the house.

Next thing I know he's calling me from a bus station pay phone in San Francisco."

"Is that where he settled?"

"Not for long. He kept picking up and moving. He was terribly frightened."

"Of?"

"His brothers had given him a righteous beating. I think they intimated that they'd do it again, or worse, if he dared to write another book. Remember, he was nineteen. To become simultaneously a darling and a pariah was a shock to his system."

"He struggled with the spotlight."

"Oh, did he. He was shy to begin with. Getting pummeled wasn't nearly as threatening as being trotted out in public. It triggered a streak of paranoia in him. I invited him to come stay with me but he was afraid of flying. So he just went along like that, hopping from one fleabag to the next. I wouldn't hear from him for weeks at a stretch. Whenever a check came in, I'd hold the money. Sooner or later he'd call needing cash, and I'd send Lauren over to Western Union."

"Do you know where he was? Specific locations?"

"I do not. California's one big plate of avocados to me."

"Any chance you still have the transfer receipts lying around?"

"Goodness, no. What kind of hoarder do you take me for?"

I smiled. "How much did he make?"

"For *Lake of the Moon*? I think the advance was about thirty-five thousand."

"That doesn't go very far around here."

"Well, it was twenty years ago. And there was option money, too, and a handful of foreign sales. Fifty or sixty K, in all. But yes, I knew he was going to run out. I kept pressing him to sign another deal, strike while the iron's hot. He wouldn't hear of it. He was busy, he had to concentrate, something big in the works. I said, 'Wonderful. May I see a few pages to get the flavor?' No, it's not ready, he's writing as fast as he can. All the clichéd excuses you get from writers who are choking. Then he stopped communicating altogether. Months went by, a year, two. I'd just about written him off. You can imagine my astonishment when this twenty-pound package crash-lands on my doorstep."

"*Cathedral*."

"Ah, yes. *Cathedral*." She sighed. "I want to be kind. It's a work in progress. And I believe Octavio would've gotten there. In time. But clearly it's not publishable as is. He must have known it, because he sent a follow-up letter, instructing me to burn the manuscript."

"You didn't."

"Naturally. I've worked with too many writers to heed those sorts of hysterics."

"Where does the title come from?"

"I've always thought it referred to one of those medieval churches that take five hundred years to complete. You begin building knowing someone else will finish it."

"You helped him with his first book," I said. "Could he have wanted you to take over on this one?"

"If so, he was delusional. *Lake of the Moon* had its issues, but at the core it was a *story*, amenable to refinement. *Cathedral* is . . . was well beyond my skills. Those of any agent. Or editor, for that matter. In any event, all that's irrelevant. Octavio never contacted me, and I had no way of reaching him. There was nothing for me to do but sit and wait for him to call."

"When did you realize he wasn't going to?"

"It wasn't an epiphany. He simply faded from my consciousness."

"You made the decision to donate the manuscript."

"I hung on to it as long as I could. After I retired I was cleaning out my office and found it in my file cabinet. Taking up the better part of a drawer. Sap that I am, I couldn't bring myself to toss it.

Couldn't very well give it to his parents, either. I had my assistant look up libraries specializing in California literature. I can't remember who took it."

"Merced."

"Sounds exotic."

"Only if you like cows. I'm headed there today."

"I thought that professor sent you his copy."

"He did, but I'd like to see it in the flesh. I'm not sure how well you remember it—"

"Not in the slightest."

"At one point, there's a stick figure giving the finger, and the line *En el nombre del Padre, y del Hijo, y del Espíritu Santo. A Men 83.261.*"

"That sounds like a Mass."

"It is. But the word *amen* is broken up. You can read it as two words: *A*, 'to,' and *Men 83.261*. The number corresponds to a mile marker in Northern California. Mendocino County, 83.261. In other words, 'I'm going to this place,' and then the precise location."

She said, "Goodness, that's clever. If I was still in the business, I'd talk to you about a book. The real-life adventures of a preternaturally clever private detective."

"Thanks, but the job's mostly plodding along."

"So is writing."

"Did Prado ever mention Northern California? When he called to have money wired—"

"Sorry, no. As I said."

"Please indulge me for a second and I'll name some towns. Stop me if any of them ring a bell. Fort Bragg. Millburg. Swann's Flat."

"Avocados," she said.

"Okay. Thanks anyway."

"You're welcome. It's nice to think about Octavio. Amend

that: *bittersweet*. He was a sweet boy. A sweet, sad boy. I wish I'd done more to help him."

"What else could you have done?"

"Flown out, bought him dinner, bucked him up." A beat. "We never met in person, you know."

"Really?"

"Really. Everything was phone calls. That's how we operated, in those days. Now I have to go. Husband, cigarettes, martini, then walk the dog."

"Thanks for your time, Ms. Ferris. I'll send your regards to the manuscript."

"Please do," she said. "It broke my heart to let it go. As if I was signing Octavio's death certificate."

CHAPTER 30

The newest addition to the University of California, UC Merced, was built in 2005 to serve the undereducated, low-income agricultural communities of San Joaquin Valley. From the East Bay it was a two-hour drive inland, all fields and cattle farms till the campus sprouted from the earth like some modernist bumper crop. I'd never been there before and was struck by the contrast between its boxy, no-nonsense layout and the august, tree-lined pathways of my alma mater.

Kolligian Library was one of the larger boxes. I rode the elevator up to Special Collections.

The desk librarian was a dyspeptic middle-aged guy with a waxed mustache. In exchange for my reservation number, he handed over a pair of white cotton gloves, a golf pencil, and a baggie of weighted shoelaces.

"I'll retrieve the item from storage and deliver it to you in the reading room. Are you planning on taking pictures?"

Without waiting for an answer, he shoved a tray of forms at me. "You'll need to fill this out. Every image requires a separate form. No flash photography."

I held up the shoelaces. "What are these for?"

"Keeping pages flat." As if I should've known. "*Never* press down on the binding."

"It's a manuscript. I don't think it's bound."

"Do we have a problem, sir?"

"No problem."

"End of the hall. I'll meet you there."

"Thanks. One other thing: Can I view the request history for the item?"

He reacted as though I'd asked for nudes of his grandmother. "That information is confidential."

"Okay."

"How would you like it if I told people what you were reading?"

"I admire your commitment to privacy."

He sniffed. "End of the hall."

Along the way I passed a walnut display rack stocked with the current issue of *California,* the UC alumni magazine. My own copy had come in the mail a few weeks ago. The cover story, "Cuisine of Culture," was about lab-grown meat.

I hadn't read it or any of the articles, skipping straight to the class notes to check on my peers. Who'd made partner; had a baby; won a prize; written a book. Then there were the obits, citing car accidents and cancers. No cause given translated to suicide.

The reading room was glass-walled and light-drenched. A white-haired woman pored over a folio. I chose the seat farthest from her, by a window overlooking a wide, grassy expanse. Sprinklers hiccuped in the wavy heat.

The woman cleared her throat and turned a page.

The desk librarian arrived, pushing a cart loaded with archival boxes.

He hiss-whispered, "Gloves. Please."

I obliged, and he gently set out the boxes—five of them, made of sturdy gray cardboard with protective metal edges. They touched down on the table with a soft, confident *thunk*. Call labels displayed a barcode, catalog number, and author information.

I nodded thanks and the librarian departed, looking back once to ensure obedience to protocol.

I pried up the cover of box one. It resisted, then rose with a farting sound, emitting the scent of old paper and attracting the white-haired lady's disapproval.

I set the cover aside and leaned in.

I expected Prado's frenzied handwriting, chaos in black and white.

Instead I saw a glossy full-color photo of a tentacle grasping a sealed jar.

CALIFORNIA

THE MAGAZINE OF THE UNIVERSITY OF CALIFORNIA
ALUMNI ASSOCIATION

It was the May–June 2024 issue. The cover story, "Sucker for Learning," was about octopus intelligence.

I removed the magazine.

Beneath it was another, identical issue.

Below that, a third.

I reached into the box and removed the entire stack.

Octopi.

Same for boxes two, three, four, and five.

I refilled the boxes and balanced them in my arms. The white-haired woman glanced up as I butted through the door and into the hall.

Seeing me coming, the desk librarian began to hop up and down in alarm.

"Excuse me, sir. You can't do that. *Sir.* Please wait while I get the cart."

I dropped the boxes on the counter. "We have a problem."

"*Excuse me.* Special Collection items are *not* to leave the reading room."

"They already have. Take a look."

He frowned. Opened a box. Frowned harder.

"What is this?" he said.

"It's supposed to be a two-thousand-page handwritten manuscript," I said.

He started removing magazines one by one, piling them sloppily on the counter.

"What is this," he mumbled.

"I know what it looks like to me."

He didn't answer. He seized the next box, shook off the cover, and dumped the contents out. Magazines slid to the floor.

"The fuck," he said.

I held up my PI license. His pupils dilated.

I said, "How about we rethink your commitment to privacy?"

THE HEAD OF library security, Roy Trujillo, was a retired twenty-seven-year veteran of Merced PD, easygoing and happy to shoot the breeze with a fellow ex-cop.

He didn't mind civilian life. His might not be the most exciting job, but it came with a respectable benefits package. He'd tweaked his schedule to spend Fridays with his granddaughter. Add in his pension and he was doing pretty well.

"I toyed with applying to the Forest Service," he said.

"What stopped you?"

"My wife has this thing about bears. *Hates* 'em. I told her: They're more scared of me than I am of them. She said, 'Then *you* need to be more scared.'"

We were sitting in Trujillo's windowless basement office, reviewing CCTV footage from May 11, 2024: the day a man calling himself Nicholas Prado had visited Special Collections to view the manuscript of *Cathedral*.

"You think somebody'd notice he used the same name," Trujillo said.

There were no cameras in the Special Collections reading room. The closest was by the front desk, offering a slice of the hallway, including the magazine rack.

Trujillo had set the playback speed to 3x. Bodies zipped in and out at a rate of one or two per hour.

"Hold up," I said.

He rewound a smidge and set the playback to normal.

A man walked down the hall in the direction of the reading room. He wore shorts, a backpack, and a hoodie, and was carrying a pair of white gloves and a baggie of shoelaces. His back was to the camera. The timestamp read 14:12:50.

Five minutes later, the desk librarian appeared, pushing a cart loaded with archival boxes.

He returned two minutes after that, having deposited his cargo.

At 14:37:48, Hoodie re-emerged. He'd left his backpack behind and was wearing the library-issued gloves. I couldn't make out his face before he turned to the display rack and began grabbing magazines by the handful.

"Son of a bitch," Trujillo said.

"Can't return empty boxes."

The gloves were making it hard for Hoodie to hold on to the slippery magazines. He kept dropping them on the carpet and snatching them up, stuffing them under his arms.

He left, was gone for a few minutes, came back for more.

And again.

"Big-ass book," Trujillo said.

The next time Hoodie appeared he had the backpack on.

He walked toward the camera.

The light caught his face. Trujillo hit PAUSE.

I said, "It's him. Can you follow him out?"

Trujillo switched cameras, tracking Nick as he took the elevator to the first floor. The backpack sagged with the weight of the manuscript.

In the lobby he stopped, staring at the main entrance.

"What's he waiting for?" Trujillo asked.

"Maybe worried about setting off the theft detector."

"He doesn't have to be. The tag's embedded in the boxes."

I raised an eyebrow.

Trujillo put up his palms. "Not my system. I inherited it."

On-screen, Nick was still frozen. Students skirted him as if he were furniture.

He started forward, his gait stilted and unnatural. Cleared the detector pillars and pushed through the doors.

Trujillo switched to an exterior camera.

Nick crossed a concrete plaza toward the parking lot.

"What's he drive?"

"Black 2009 Civic."

Trujillo switched to the lot exit camera.

He said, "There he goes."

The Civic followed Scholars Lane to the edge of campus, turning onto Lake Road toward town. Then off-screen and out of sight.

Trujillo tapped PAUSE and faced me. "Can you get my book back?"

I thought it ironic that Prado's work, ignored during his life, had value now that it had been stolen. By the one person who cared about it most.

I said, "I'll try."

I ATE LUNCH on the drive back to my office, where I checked the jet-setting Clay Gardner's accounts for the first time in weeks.

Howdy partner.

Hope you're doing well and enjoying your travels. How's Hong Kong?

Last we left it you were getting ready to send over the docs. I need to update you that we have interest from another buyer. This person is overseas and they'd like to get a deal done as quickly as possible. My dad's all for moving ahead with him. Personally, I don't think it's right to do that without talking to you first.

I know you've got a lot on your plate, and I don't want you to think I'm breathing down your neck. But you understand we can't have him walk and then have you back out, too, and we end up with nothing. As you know, the property's with the original owner, it's never changed hands, and so it's rotten luck that we're in this situation. Between you and me, I would like you to come out the winner here.

Let me know what I can do to make that happen.

Take care.
Beau

I didn't answer him, went over to Instagram.

A notification flashed: Shasta Swann had accepted Clay Gardner's friend request.

She followed many more accounts than followed her. Peers were noticeably scarce. No one I could connect to Nick. The feed consisted of nature photos and training logs. Flowers, seabirds, Bowie the sheepdog; mileage in the captions, eliciting a few likes or heart emojis.

I scrolled back in time.

September 1, 2024.

Shortly after Nicholas Moore had set out on his journey of self-discovery.

His path revealed by two photos.

One: sunlight breaking through warped tree trunks. The Cathedral.

Two: fingers, intertwined. Left hand, smaller, feminine. Right hand, knobby, tan, tattooed across the knuckles in curlicued font.

H O L D

The caption read:

just because it ends
doesn't mean it's over

CHAPTER 31

texted a screenshot to Maddie Zwick, who confirmed that the male hand was Nick's. The tattoo combined with the one on his left knuckles to yield the phrase HOLD FAST—another sailor's mark, encouragement in times of trouble.

The storm will come. Grab a rope and cling for dear life.

I called Tara Moore.

She'd never heard of Octavio Prado, *Lake of the Moon,* or Swann's Flat. When I sent her the picture of Nick's hand, though, she yelped.

"Who is this bitch?" she said.

"She's a minor."

"Yeah? And? You trying to say something about my son?"

"No, just that—"

"Like it's *his* fault?"

"I'm not saying that."

"That don't mean nothing, they learn young . . . What's he doing with her?"

"I don't know how they met, but there's a reference to the town in the manuscript. I'm thinking Nicholas went there following in Prado's footsteps."

"Goddamn pussy-whipped idiot. What's her name? I'll get acquainted with her."

"No need for that. And to be clear, there's nothing that adds up to evidence of a crime."

"Oh bullshit, *bullshit*." She began to weep. "Goddamn fucking *idiot*."

"I know this is stressful, Tara—"

"He's dead."

"We don't know that."

"He is."

"Until we know for sure, it doesn't help him—or you—to assume that."

"It's *me*." She sobbed. "I *did* this to him. I lied to him about Warren, that's why he left."

"Not necessarily. He easily could've found something else to chase."

"A stupid book! Oh Jesus . . . You think I'm a bad mother."

"I don't."

"Then you're stupid, I am a bad mother. I'm a bad person."

"Tara, I'm going to get to work on this now, okay?"

Silence.

"Tara?"

". . . Yeah."

"Promise me you won't interfere."

"I promise. I don't know nothing, anyway." She huffed. "Story of my life."

AMY SAID, "*AGAIN?*"

"I didn't commit to going there. I said I'd work on it. Which I can do from here."

"But you want to go back."

"Do I think I'll get more in person? Yes. But not at the expense of making you miserable."

She blew out air. "Okay. Let's discuss the risks."

"On the plus side," I said, "Al Bock's my pal now. So I don't have to worry about getting shot."

"Not by him," she said. "That doesn't eliminate anyone else."

"You're right. The situation is more delicate. My plan is to meet with the local sheriff before I head to town. I need to speak to him anyway, to see what he knows. I'll ask him to check in if I'm not out within a certain amount of time."

"That only helps after the fact. He can't do anything in the moment if he's not with you."

"I'm also considering bringing backup."

"Who?"

"Regina Klein," I said. "I don't know if she'll agree. My gut is yes. She cares about the case."

"Hand it off to her, then."

"I could do that."

"But it's your case. And you care about it, too."

I nodded.

"One to ten," Amy said. "How worried do I need to be?"

"Seven-point-five. Six-point-five if she's with me."

"That's an awful lot of confidence to put in a person you met once."

"Once was enough."

"Then I want to meet her, too."

THE DOORBELL RANG.

"I got it," Charlotte yelled.

I said, "Wait for me, please."

"Let me look through the peep, Daddy."

I held her up.

She said, "There's a lady with glasses holding bags."

"Good job. You may open the door."

Regina stood on the porch, tiny, impish, wearing purple Keds, nails refinished the same color. One bag was a rainbow gift bag and the other was from Trader Joe's.

I ushered her in. "How was the drive?"

"Heinous."

Amy emerged from the kitchen with Myles on her hip. "I'm Amy. Thanks for coming."

"Regina. Thanks for having me."

"I'm Charlotte," Charlotte said.

"Hi, Charlotte. That's a pretty name."

"How old are you?"

"I'm thirty-seven. How old are you?"

"Four and three-quarters. My birthday is in nine days."

"That's exciting. Are you having a party?"

"It's a pirate party. We've having a pirate ship piñata."

"Fun. Can I come?"

"No. My brother is one and a half. He had his birthday. His name is Myles. He's a baby."

"I can see that."

"Why are you so short?"

"Charlotte," I said.

Regina knelt so they were eye level. "Do you know what oxygen is?"

"Air."

"That's right. You must be really smart to know that."

"Yeah."

"An interesting fact about oxygen is, the higher up you go, the less of it there is. Think about what happens if you go all the way up to space. Is there oxygen in space?"

Charlotte shook her head.

"Right. So I like it better down here." Regina inhaled through her nose. "Easier to breathe."

"That's not true. You're being silly."

"Not me, I'm never silly. Guess what? I brought you something."

"What is it?"

"Tuna fish ice cream."

"*Ewwww.*"

"What's wrong?"

"That's yucky."

"Your daddy told me it's your favorite."

Charlotte wheeled on me. "*No.* Daddy!"

"I must've gotten mixed up," I said.

"Okay, let me see if I have anything else." Regina rooted in the gift bag.

Amy glanced at me. *This is Mrs. Potty Mouth?*

Regina produced a wrapped box. "How about this?"

Charlotte peeled back the paper on a set of Magna-Tiles.

"Wow," Amy said. "What a fantastic gift. Thank you, Regina. Charlotte, what do you—"

Charlotte took off running.

"Charlotte, what do you say?" I called.

"Thaaaaank youuuuuu."

Regina presented Myles with a wooden stacking toy.

He clung to Amy, one finger in his mouth.

"I know," Regina said. "I wouldn't trust me, either."

The Trader Joe's bag contained flowers, Chardonnay, and chocolate.

"I tried to cover all the bases," Regina said.

"Yes, yes, and yes," Amy said.

"You didn't have to do this," I said.

"And yet I did," Regina said.

OVER DINNER, AMY asked Regina if she'd grown up in Santa Cruz.

"Nnn." She swallowed and wiped her mouth. "LA. I came up for undergrad, then went home to do my master's."

"What in?"

"Social work. I was with County Children and Family Services till I got burned out."

Amy nodded sympathetically.

"How'd you transition to being a PI?" I asked.

"I had this friend, a child advocacy lawyer. She hooked me up with a guy who taught me the ropes. I worked for him for a while. But I was sick of LA and I had all these good memories of Santa Cruz. I didn't realize that I only had those memories 'cause I was in college. Now I'm just a person, living in a place."

"Regina," Charlotte said, "you have to eat your broccoli if you want to earn dessert."

"Says who."

"Daddy."

"Well." Regina forked a floret. "Rules are rules."

Charlotte displayed her plate. "Can I be done, please, Daddy?"

"Yes," I said. "Do you want to play for a little?"

She ran out. Immediately Myles began waving his arms, flinging specks of salmon, knocking his sippy cup to the floor.

"All done?" Amy asked.

"Ah duh."

"Very good talking." She unbuckled the high chair, wiped him down, and set him on her lap to continue eating. He didn't want to sit still, began twisting and arching his back.

"You think he'll go to me?" Regina asked.

"Let's see," Amy said, handing him over.

He squirmed, but within a minute his head was on Regina's shoulder as she stroked his back.

"You're the baby whisperer," I said.

Regina smiled. "Do I earn dessert?"

SHE AND AMY sat outside, drinking and talking, while I did bedtime routine. From across the house I heard their laughter, brash and honest.

I stepped out onto the deck. The wine was down to an inch.

"We're trading war stories," Amy said.

"She rules," Regina said.

"I know it," I said.

Amy stood. "Wonderful to meet you, Regina."

"Likewise."

"Take care of my husband, please."

"Listen, I'm only human."

Amy laughed, pecked me on the cheek, and slipped inside.

"She's nervous," Regina said. "Do I need to be nervous?"

"A little bit probably wouldn't hurt."

"Then we need to set some fucking ground rules."

I took a chair. "How'd you learn to turn it on and off like this?"

"A childhood spent in musical theater." She rubbed her nose. "Rule number one: Full transparency, starting now."

"Cuts both ways."

"You first. Talk."

I did, for almost an hour.

She said, "You ran *over* her?"

"Not over. Into. A glancing blow."

"What the fuck, Clay? The fuck are you getting me into?"

"She's fine. The doctor checked her out and I haven't heard anything from them since. No lawyer letter. No calls. She accepted my friend request."

"I'm pretty sure that's a valid legal defense in zero of the fifty states."

"I know it's not ideal."

"No shit."

"Silver lining," I said. "It gives me an excuse to check in on Shasta while we're there."

"And what? You're just gonna casually segue into questioning her about this guy she had a thing with who also happens to be missing?"

"I'll ask where she got the necklace."

She put on an adolescent whine: "'This? My boyyyfriend gave it to me.'"

"'Okay. Who's your boyfriend?'"

"Don't ask her that. Why are you asking her that? That's fucking weird."

"Suggestions welcome."

"Before we get into any of that: Why assume what happened to Nick is connected to what's going on up there? Why can't it be that he met her, banged her, and took off?"

"It can," I said. "But she's still the last person to have contact with him, so we need to talk to her. I think we should at least explore the possibility that somebody didn't like him getting close to her. She's the majority landowner. The scheme runs through her. Nick waltzes into town, sweeps her off her feet—that poses a threat to their control."

"You've decided Little Miss is free of sin."

"No. But I told you, they've been at this for thirty-some years, way before she was born. She's not the one emailing me and pumping me for information. Beau Bergstrom is."

"Exactly why I don't like it," she said. "It feels like he's trying to smoke you out." She drummed the chair arm with her purple nails. "You think your cover's still good?"

"I'm hoping your being there will help shore it up."

"Me and my feminine fucking wiles. All right. How do we fold me in? Details."

"You're my sister," I said. "I want your opinion on the property."

"Are you shitting me? Sister? Look at me. Now look at you."

I conceded the point.

She said, "The only logical story—and it pains me deeply to say these words—is I'm your, ahem, *wife*. And, because I'm smarter than you and oodles more practical, I'm skeptical about this whole land idea. We already own a place in . . ."

"Tahoe."

"Tahoe. Why do we need more headaches? But I leave the door open just enough for them to think I could be convinced."

"How'd we meet?"

"The circus," she said. "We were both in the freak show."

"A mutual friend set us up. What kind of work do you do, Mrs. Gardner?"

"Fuck off with your patriarchy. I kept my name."

"All right, what name do you want?"

"Edison," she said, cracking up.

"Can you focus?"

"Ah. You're having second thoughts about me."

"And third."

"Regina Bloom," she said. "I'm a pediatric social worker. You fell for me because I'm so passionate about helping people. But. I have a secret dream."

"Impossible. You're married to me. What more could you want?"

"I write."

"Gives you and Beau something in common," I said.

"I don't share that with many people," she said. "But I feel comfortable around him."

"Why did you fall for me?"

"'Cause you're fucking loaded. Where'd we get married?"

"Tiburon."

"How romantic."

"It is. Amy and I got married there. July 4, 2020."

"You want to check with her before lending me her wedding day?"

"She's letting me drive off with you."

"She's a very trusting woman, your wife."

"Or she perceives you as no danger whatsoever."

"Touché," she said. "Are we staying overnight?"

"Probably."

"Are we sharing a room?"

"If we're married, I think we have to. I'll bring a sleeping bag."

"Bring earplugs. I snore. Okay," she said, "it's a start. We'll work on it."

"Your turn for transparency," I said.

Without hesitation, she said, "I lied about Warren Pezanko. He did answer my letter."

"What did he say about Nick?"

"He never spoke to him. He barely knew who I was talking about. He asked me to smuggle him titty pics."

"Are we ruling him out?"

"Nothing there," she said. "Your stuff feels stronger."

I nodded. "Anything else you want to tell me?"

"About the case? No. But we're not done with ground rules. Number two: Any money comes out of this, I get dibs."

"There's no money. Tara's broke."

"Go back to Chris Villareal. Get him to throw us a bone."

"He's not interested."

"He might be, if we bring him these fuckers' heads on a plate."

"I'll ask," I said. "You get first crack at expenses. Then me. Anything on top of that is gravy and we go fifty–fifty. Good?"

"Good."

I put out my hand but she held up a finger.

"Number three. We leave in ten days."

"It's not going to take that long to work up a backstory."

"Ten days. Not one day sooner."

"You have something you need to do?"

"No. You do," she said. "Your daughter's birthday party, moron."

THREE

CHAPTER 32

Ten days later I waited on my front steps in the predawn. Red and gold streamers fluttered from the eaves; a skull and crossbones was taped to the front door, along with an arrow directing guests to the backyard. *Arrrgh matey, party be in the stern.*

Regina Klein pulled up in a black rented Jeep Wrangler four-by-four.

I took my bag to the curb. The passenger window buzzed down, and she stretched across to hand me a gift-wrapped box. "For Charlotte."

"You got her a present."

"That was for dinner. This is for her birthday."

"Thank you."

I jogged back to the house and left the gift in the entry hall by Amy's boots. When I returned to the car Regina had moved to the passenger seat. Her eyes were closed.

"Wake me up in an hour," she said.

She was snoring before I hit the freeway.

TRAFFIC WAS LIGHT and I made good time. Up 580 and over the San Rafael Bridge to Marin, merging onto 101 toward Sonoma as the gray world began to differentiate. Driving with the radio off, my mind drifted to another road trip, seven years ago, with another partner beside me. We'd gone to visit a school where the students made the rules. One died; the school shut down.

I reached Petaluma with Regina still sawing wood and pushed on toward Santa Rosa, past a luxury outlet mall for saving money and a casino for losing it. Fast-food restaurants alternated with vast family vineyards, wine country in its many white-collar, blue-collar contradictions.

My phone buzzed in the cupholder.

Regina opened one eye. "Wha."

The caller ID read MAEVE FERRIS.

"That's Prado's agent."

"The fuck is she calling this early."

"She's in New York. Answer it, please."

Clearing her throat, she raised the phone to her ear. "Clay Edison's office . . . I'll see if he's available. One moment, please." She tapped MUTE. "Are you available, sir?"

"Cut that shit out."

Regina unmuted and tapped SPEAKERPHONE. "You're on with Mr. Edison."

"Hi, Maeve. Sorry. That's my colleague. You'll have to excuse her."

Ferris said, "Hello, Colleague."

Regina said, "Pleasure."

"What's up?" I asked.

"Our conversation set me reminiscing," Ferris said. "I have a few boxes left from my agency days. Tax forms, royalty statements, contracts, galleys. I went down to scrounge. Perhaps I'd kept Octavio's transfer receipts after all. No—but I did find a letter from him, the one instructing me to burn *Cathedral*. Would you like me to send you a photo?"

"Please. Thanks so much."

"One second. I'll text it."

I slowed onto the shoulder. Regina leaned over to share the screen. Her eyes were wide awake and alert.

An image appeared, typewritten words on creased paper.

> My pride and joy throw it in the fire.
> Dont try to find me good bye
> —O

The letters had a three-dimensional quality, and when I zoomed in I could see a streak of Wite-Out behind the word *good*.

"Was this done on an actual typewriter?" I asked.

"Looks that way," Ferris said. "It's odd, Octavio always worked by hand, why bother for such a short message? Where in the world did he get a typewriter? Not to mention the sloppiness. He was prickly about not sounding uneducated. Grammar, spelling—those things mattered to him."

"Could be he was in a bad way, mentally. The manuscript breaks down as it goes along."

"Yes. But something about this feels off. I suppose I didn't notice at the time because I was more concerned with what he was saying, rather than the phrasing."

"You told me the letter showed up after the manuscript," I said. "How long after?"

"Well. I . . . I don't remember."

"Do you have the envelope it came in?" Regina asked.

"I don't know. I can look. I'll have to check my storage cage, in the basement. Give me thirty minutes or so."

"Take your time," I said. "Thank you."

The call disconnected.

Regina sat up to peer through the windshield. "Where are we?"

"Near Healdsburg."

"I can take over but I need coffee first."

"Deal."

I drove into town, stopping at the first café and paying for breakfast: egg sandwich and drip coffee for me, oatmilk latte and dairy-free burrito for Regina.

"When did you become a vegan?" I asked.

"I'm not," she said, chewing. "I'm lactose-intolerant."

"Bummer."

"You know what's a fucking bummer? Two thousand years of anti-Semitism."

Maeve Ferris called, breathless and excited. "I found it. I'm texting it to you."

The envelope was addressed to her Seventh Avenue office. No return address.

But there was a postmark.

Millburg CA 955
9 July 2007 PM

"This is great," I said. "Thank you so much."

"Please let me know what happens."

"I will. Take care, Maeve."

Regina crumpled her burrito wrapper. "I'll drive."

AT TEN A.M. we rolled up to Fanny's Market. The bulletin board had been rearranged since my previous visit, new flyers added and others shuffled around. Nick Moore had been relegated to the far left side, his face covered.

Regina moved him front and center.

"You want to grab anything?" She mimed toking. "Munchies?"

WE PARKED IN the lot serving the town's public buildings. All shared an exterior scheme of yellow stucco and brown shingles.

The sheriff's substation was distinguished by the addition of heavy-duty steel screens along one side where the holding cells were.

A lone deputy staffed the counter. He took our licenses and ducked through a door.

While he was gone I browsed a much smaller corkboard advertising feel-good events. Highway cleanup, DUI checkpoints, have your kids meet the deputies.

There were a few missing persons posters, too, but nothing like the menagerie down the block. Which made sense, if your goal was to reach as many eyes as possible. More people needed snacks than they did the law.

The deputy returned to escort us back.

A sergeant waited in the hall. Mid-forties, black hair and a lantern jaw, intelligent eyes. He introduced himself as Mike Gallo.

"Thanks for talking to us," I said.

His smile was friendly but tinged with wariness. "Two of you."

Regina said, "It takes a village."

He saw us into his Every-Cop office: scabby carpeting, tubular steel chairs, a computer on life support. Binders piled five-high beside desk photos of teen boys and a handsome wife. The open window framed a view of the schoolyard through dual-purpose chain link. Keep the students in and the prisoners out.

We sat.

"What can I do for you?" Gallo said.

I passed him a clean copy of Nicholas Moore's flyer.

He nodded. "I've seen it over at Fanny's."

"Anything you can share?" Regina asked.

"Unfortunately not. Unless I'm mistaken he's not our case."

"Santa Cruz PD."

"There you go," he said. "Happens all the time, 'cause of the bulletin board. I appreciate what they're doing as a service to the community. I have three deputies covering five hundred square miles. I'll take any help I can get. But it's turned into a magnet for desperate folks. Not everybody gets that sticking the flyer up here doesn't automatically make it our jurisdiction."

"I hear you," I said. "I used to be a sheriff-coroner for Alameda."

"So you know what I mean."

"For sure. We do have indications Nicholas was in the area last year."

"In Millburg?"

"Swann's Flat."

"Uh-huh." Gallo's expression was hard to read. "What indications?"

We told him about Nick's obsession with Octavio Prado; about the stolen manuscript, the necklace, the TikTok. I showed him Shasta's Instagram post.

Gallo swiped back and forth between the two photos, trees and hands. "Shasta Swann. That's Kurt's daughter."

"You know her," Regina said.

"She used to go to school with my boys till they pulled her. I think they homeschool her now." He gave my phone back. "What makes you believe Mr. Moore is missing, as opposed to gone away on his own?"

"It's been fifteen months without contact," Regina said.

"Okay, but we have a lot of wandering types passing through. They show up at harvest, do a little trimming, make some cash, and skip."

"That wasn't Nick's scene," I said.

"My point is, nobody's keeping track of who's going in and out. This is Humboldt. People come here to be left alone."

Regina said, "What about John Does in the morgue?"

"None meeting his description."

"Abandoned vehicles?"

"Those we got no shortage of. Head up Alderpoint, it's practically a junkyard." Gallo looked at me. "What was the original reason, brought you to Swann's Flat?"

"Due diligence on a piece of property."

"Mm."

I said, "Kind of an unusual system they have going."

"Buyer beware."

I sensed an opening, though not its motives. "You get complaints?"

"Almost never," Gallo said. "And never anything of a criminal nature."

Almost.

"One resident I spoke to said he'd been harassed," I said. "Windows broken, so forth."

"Don't recall seeing a report."

"He didn't make one."

"Then there's not a whole lot I can do. You know that. Fact is, I can't remember the last time we took a call from them. It's another world out there."

"The Humboldt of Humboldt," Regina said.

Gallo smiled. "If you like."

"I also spoke with someone from your Coroner's Bureau," I said. "Owen Ryall."

"He's a good guy."

"He was telling me about the night Kurt Swann died."

Gallo's dark eyes slitted. "Not sure what that has to do with Mr. Moore."

"I get the sense that they have their own way of handling problems in Swann's Flat."

A bell split the silence.

Through the open window I saw kids trickle out onto the schoolyard, twenty or thirty of them, ranging from first graders to preteens. Not much of a peer group.

Gallo said, "I didn't offer you anything to drink."

"I'd love some coffee, thanks," Regina said.

"How do you take it?"

"Black. Unless you have oatmilk."

"Lemme see what I can scare up. Clay?"

"All set," I said.

"Back in a bit," Gallo said.

He left, shutting the door.

CHAPTER 33

A breeze ruffled Gallo's desktop. In the schoolyard, recess got under way, the kids pairing off except for one girl skipping rope alone.

"He's vetting us," I said.

"Or calling the Bergstroms to give them a heads-up," Regina said.

"Or searching for oatmilk."

"Shouldn't be that hard," she said. "It's everywhere now."

"That's the bougiest thing I've ever heard."

"Tell it to my colon."

At a quarter to, the school bell sounded again. Students began filing inside.

Gallo reentered, shut the door, and placed a foam cup in front of Regina. "Black it is."

"Thanks."

He lowered the window. "I moved here in 2007. There were hardly any families. Still aren't many. That school"—he tapped the glass—"was falling down."

He turned. "Who do you think paid to fix it up?"

"Kurt Swann," I said.

"Library needed new computers." He sat at his desk. "Someone had to pay for that, too."

"He's dead now," Regina said.

"Yes, ma'am, he is."

I said, "But they still have pull."

"Not with me," Gallo said. "Are we clear on that?"

He waited for acknowledgment from both of us before going on: "But I wasn't always the one sitting in this chair. Now, I want us to respect each other."

"Of course," I said.

"Good. So tell me. How much shit do you plan to stir up?"

"As much as we have to," Regina said.

I thought Gallo might get annoyed, but he smiled and shook his head. "I thought you might say that. So again, let me be clear: Everything I say, this point forward, is off the record."

I nodded. Regina made a *zip-the-lip* gesture.

Gallo straightened the disordered pages on his desktop. "This is when I was a rookie. I respond to a disturbance at the 76. Two trucks, a Dodge Ram and a tow truck, pushed right up against each other. A young woman, eighteen, nineteen, arguing with a pair of older guys. She tells me they hemmed her in so she can't leave. They don't deny it, but one guy says first off, she's his wife, and second, the Dodge is his, not hers. She stole it, so they followed her.

"I separate them, ask for IDs and registration. The first guy gives me his license and I do a double take. Kurt Swann, address in Swann's Flat. Bear in mind, I've been on the job about three months. I've seen the town on the map, but every place around here's named for some or other dead person. I didn't know there was any actual Swanns. He's smirking at me, waiting for me to connect the dots. The other guy, it's his tow truck."

"Dave Pelman," I said.

"Yeah. I ask the woman for her license. She doesn't have it. Doesn't have any ID. 'Okay, what's your name.' 'Leonie.' 'Is that your husband?' She won't answer. I'm trying to get her story and

Kurt's begging from over on the sidewalk: 'I love you, I forgive you, come home.'"

"Forgive her for what?" I asked.

"Who knows? But now it's looking like some sort of domestic dispute. She's jumpy, but she doesn't have any visible injuries. I offer to bring her to the station, speak with her in private. She won't budge. Clams up totally. I have her open the Dodge to get the registration from the glove box. Sure enough, it's in Kurt's name only. Then I hear something in the back seat. I peek over. There's two big suitcases and a baby in a car seat."

"She was leaving him?"

"Maybe. Maybe she was going to visit her mother and would've ended up coming back."

"Most of them do," Regina said.

Gallo nodded. "One thing's for sure: I'm out of my depth. I get on the horn to my supervisor."

"The guy who used to sit in that chair," I said.

"Correct. As I'm talking to him, Leonie goes and hands the keys over to Kurt. She gets in the Dodge with him and they drive off."

"Willingly?"

"So far as I can see. I'm not about to go chasing after them, 'cause—"

"There's a baby," Regina said.

"Correct. I head back to the station and tell the sergeant what happened. He shakes his head. 'Fucking rednecks.'"

"He'd dealt with Kurt before," I said.

"That was the implication. He doesn't have me do anything right then, but the next day he tells me to take a partner and do a welfare check. I remember being on that road for the first time, thinking anyone who'd live down there had to be out of their damn mind. Then we get to the house and ho-ly shit. Here's this supposed redneck, and he's living in a palace.

"Leonie comes to the door. You can smell the booze on her from five feet away. She says she's fine, please leave them alone. Kurt comes running from the stable, screaming his head off. 'You sonsabitches, step onto my land, threaten my family.' He herds her inside, slams the door, and runs around, yanking down the shades. Pretty soon the whole house is blacked out, and we can hear Kurt, ranting and raving.

"We try to radio in, but the reception's for shit. We're calling and calling and it's not going through. We don't want to leave before we've ascertained there's no danger to her or to the child. So we decide to split up: I'll stay behind, my partner will drive till he can get a signal.

"Before he can leave, a new vehicle pulls up and a young guy gets out, 'bout the same age as Leonie. He's smiling like it's the greatest day of his life. 'Why hello there, Deputy.'"

"That sounds like Beau," I said.

"Yup. He tells us Leonie called him and said Kurt's acting up. 'Lemme talk some sense into him.' He knocks. 'Open up, Kurt. It's me.' Door swings in, and I tense up, thinking he's gonna catch a face full of buckshot. But Kurt steps aside. Ten minutes later they both come out. Kurt's done a one eighty. Meek as hell, like the kid shot him up with a tranquilizer.

"Beau goes, 'These gentlemen don't mean you any harm. They're just doing their job. They just want to ask questions. Isn't that right? What can we do for you, gentlemen?'

"I tell Kurt I'd like a word with Leonie. Beau says, 'She's not feeling well.' 'I need to hear that from her.' 'Of course, Officer, right this way.' I'm talking to Kurt and this punk's answering. Then he tries to escort me in. Like it's *his* house. I said, 'Both of you, stay outside.'

"Leonie's laid out on the couch. She's got the baby in a playpen. She says, 'I never called you, I have a headache, please leave.'

Talking toward the front door, loud enough for them to hear her out on the lawn. She won't even look at me."

"She must've been terrified," Regina said.

"Yes, ma'am. The baby starts crying. Leonie doesn't move a muscle. It's howling and turning red. I said to her, 'Do you need me to pick her up?' *That* sets Leonie off. She jumps up and screams at me to leave them alone. *Screams.* I'm tripping over myself to get out of there."

Gallo tented his fingers. "So now me and my partner have a choice."

"Bust Kurt," Regina said. "He's free in forty-eight hours, goes home to take it out on her."

"Bust them both and see if she wants to seek protection," I said. "But she's not giving off a cooperative vibe."

"Plus there's the baby to think about," Regina said.

"Or?" Gallo smiled. "There's another option."

I said, "Apologize for the misunderstanding and be on your way."

"Bingo," Gallo said. "I didn't have any DV training. Was pretty much a kid myself. I'd like to think that if I had another opportunity, I would've known what to ask and how to ask it. But she never called."

"They usually don't," Regina said.

Gallo frowned. "True. But since then there's no evidence she's not fine."

I said, "Could we talk about the night of Kurt's death? Were you on the scene?"

"Everyone was," Gallo said. "It was an all-hands situation."

"The coroner's report is based almost entirely on Dave Pelman's account. Was he ever considered a suspect?"

"It never got that far. I can tell you we spoke to Pelman's ex-wife. She runs the hotel."

"Jenelle Counts?" I said.

"That's her. She told us Pelman had a thing for Leonie."

"Were they having an affair?" Regina asked.

"She didn't come right out and make an accusation. More hinting. And it's his ex talking, you gotta take what she says with a shaker of salt. In the end, the coroner was strong on it being an accident. We had to abide by that. As you, Clay, are no doubt aware."

"The report doesn't mention the Bergstroms at all," I said. "Were they interviewed?"

"Not by me."

"They weren't suspects, either."

"Like I said: accident."

"I'm asking your opinion."

"My opinion didn't matter. I wasn't the sergeant."

"You are now," Regina said.

"Yeah," Gallo said. "So I can imagine *his* thought process. Are these folks in Swann's Flat a buncha weirdos? You bet. So's everyone else in a hundred-mile radius. We got lots bigger problems, more so back then. Cartels muscling in, shooting each other up, setting fire to grow sites. Now you have this redneck, and his woman's losing her mind if you try to touch her baby. My opinion? Nobody's shedding tears over Kurt Swann."

CHAPTER 34

We left the station and set out west beneath gathering clouds, Regina at the wheel.

She said, "Takeaways."

"Beau having Kurt on a leash interests me," I said. "I've thought of them as a management-ownership arrangement. The Swanns hold title, the Bergstroms do the work. But this makes it seem like Beau and Emil have serious leverage."

"They know how the scam works, can bring it crashing down."

"Not without implicating themselves, and I can't see Emil doing that. He's an egomaniac. Self-interested, first and foremost."

"The land was doing nothing till he showed up," she said. "Meaning, Kurt's no business genius. It takes Emil to coax money out of it. That gives him power over Kurt."

"Probably makes Kurt resentful, too. And if he's a loose cannon, he becomes a liability."

Regina nodded. "How about this: Kurt suspects Leonie of cheating on him. He's jealous, beating on her. That brings the cops around, which makes the Bergstroms nervous. They have Pelman take Kurt out. Added bonus, they do Leonie a favor and put her in their debt."

"Why would Pelman agree to that?" I asked. "He's the one helped Kurt force her back to Swann's Flat in the first place."

"Both things can be true. If Pelman had a soft spot for her, he probably didn't want her leaving, either. But he also doesn't like how Kurt treats her, and when the Bergstroms give him a chance to get rid of a rival, he goes ahead."

"Or they paid him, simple as that," I said. "Or the Bergstroms weren't involved and Leonie got Pelman to do it herself."

"She seem capable of that?" Regina asked.

"She struck me as more high-strung than psychopathic. But I talked to her under unusual circumstances. I have no idea what she's like normally."

"If Kurt dies, Leonie inherits from him automatically. How does the land wind up in Shasta's trust?"

"He could've had Leonie sign a prenup and left everything to Shasta. Or transferred the property in his lifetime without telling her."

"That implies he didn't trust Leonie."

"Or he was lording it over her."

"Or, again, we're totally off base," Regina said. "Kurt had nothing to do with it. Leonie made the transfer."

"Why would she do that?"

"Say the Bergstroms do have dirt on her. Getting the land out of her hands creates a layer of insulation between her and them. And depending on how the trust is set up, it can also protect Shasta, at least to some extent."

"Be nice to know who the trustee is."

"Be nice to know a lot of things," Regina said. "Whatever the specifics, they've reached a working arrangement and are all making money. So at the moment it's not in anyone's interest to be contentious."

"Pelman, too," I said. "He's got the coolant concession."

"Think Jenelle will talk to us?"

"I think you'll do better with her than I will."

"Tell me something I don't know."

"After they executed Mata Hari, her head was preserved," I said. "But then it was lost and never recovered. It's still missing, to this day."

She stared at me. "What is wrong with you?"

"Did you know that?"

"No. Why would I know that?"

"You're welcome."

She faced the road and sighed. "You're gonna get me fucking killed."

AT BLACKBERRY JUNCTION we pulled over so I could drive the final stretch. Experience and all-wheel drive made a huge difference, and the trip went faster, the way second trips always do.

For me.

Regina was folded into a comma, taking strained nasal breaths.

"Do you need a break?" I asked.

She shook her head tightly.

"I might have some jerky left. Helps with nausea."

"Shut up," she gasped.

At the mile eight hairpin, I stopped and switched on the hazards.

Regina looked up. Sweat beaded her forehead. "What's going on?"

"This is where Kurt went over."

I parked and stepped carefully out to the memorial. The flowers in the Jack Daniel's vase had been recently replaced with a spray of blueblossoms, the bottle filled with fresh water.

Across the valley, over the ridge, the sky was lowering toward a rough gray sea.

Regina stumbled from the Jeep and bent to catch her breath, elbows on thighs. After a minute she joined me.

She examined the cross, the flowers.

Then she did exactly what I'd done: plucked a golf-ball-sized stone and tossed it into the void. It ricocheted off the cliffside and vanished without a sound.

"That's gotta hurt," she said.

"Not for very long."

HALF AN HOUR later we crossed the town boundary and proceeded through the rows of empty lots. Plastic markers flapped in the wind.

"I thought you were exaggerating," Regina said. "But this is creepy as fuck."

"Welcome to Swann's Flat."

"Last time I let you plan our honeymoon."

Our first stop was 22 Black Sand Court. For weeks I had been trying unsuccessfully to reach Al Bock. I wasn't worried about him, per se, but it felt wise to rendezvous with a friendly.

I turned onto his block. The wooden fortress loomed into view.

Regina sat forward. "Jesus Christ."

We were showing up unannounced, and I slowed to a crawl. Fifty yards from the fence, my eye landed on a motion sensor, mounted to the trunk of a lodgepole pine. The housing had been painted taupe for camouflage. I'd missed it the last time.

I braked. "He knows we're here."

She followed my gaze to the sensor. "I thought this guy was on our side."

"I'm pretty sure he is."

" 'Pretty sure.' "

I unbuckled. "Get behind the wheel."

"Hang on."

"Be ready to drive," I said and got out.

"Clay," Regina called. "What the fuck?"

I stuck my hands above my head. "It's Clay Edison, Sergeant Bock. Can you hear me?"

"Clay," Regina yelled.

"I'm approaching the gate, Sergeant. Okay? Here I come."

Behind the fence, King Kong snarled like a lawn mower.

I rang the bell.

Growling, barking, claws on wood.

I addressed the security camera. "Sergeant? Are you home?"

A honk spun me around. Regina was leaning on the horn and waving frantically toward the roadside, where Al Bock had out-flanked me and risen in a thicket, ten yards to my rear. He wore jeans and long-sleeved black T-shirt and was sighting on a hunting rifle, shuttling smoothly between me and Regina, the bright-green dot of a daylight laser scope flicking precisely from my chest to hers and back.

"Sergeant," I said. "It's Clay Edison."

He lowered the rifle. "You didn't tell me you were coming."

"I sent an email."

"Haven't checked it."

"I tried calling, too. It won't go through."

"Line's out."

Regina sat again. She was throttling the wheel, ready to roar up and collect me. Or flatten him.

"What's she so dang excited about?" Bock said.

"Meeting you, I think." I signaled to her that it was safe.

Bock came forward to shake my hand. For a man in his early seventies he was remarkably trim and fit, with a shaved head and a sharp jawline just beginning to pouch underneath. His grip was crushing, his palm one solid callus.

"What happened to the line?" I asked.

"One guess."

"A tree fell down."

"About a week after we talked," he said.

Regina climbed from the Jeep. "Nice place you got here."

"Thanks," Bock said.

"The ladies must love it."

"Don't get too many of those."

"Nooo." She gestured to the fence, with its razor wire and wall of bamboo. "But it's so warm and welcoming."

"Home sweet home. Al."

"Regina."

"I apologize if I startled you, Regina."

"You can make it up to me. Got any coffee?"

CHAPTER 35

The house was a silvered A-frame, sturdy and plain, empha-sizing security and self-sufficiency over aesthetics.

Bars encaged the windows. Solar panels tiled the roof. Bock's rustbucket Chevy sat by the chained driveway gates. Motion sensors with alarms and lights protected the vegetable beds and hoop houses where he grew his food, serving to deter animals as well as human intruders. The toolshed, outhouse, root cellar, and smokehouse were padlocked. State law limited him to two deer and one elk per season; throw in fish, small game, and the occasional field trip for wild boar, and he had more than enough to see him and the puppy through.

The surrounding forest contained additional sensors and trip wires, plus an electric fence.

"No land mines?" Regina said.

"Too expensive."

The front door was sealed—another diversionary tactic. King Kong, a ninety-pound brindle pitbull-mastiff mix, had quieted down, although he stuck to his master's legs, casting sullen glances in our direction as we went around to the rear. An outdoor shower stall faced the trees. Nearby Bock had cleared room for what he called "my social life": a sixteen-foot ham radio mast. The mountains prevented him from reaching points inland. Mostly he talked to ships and other hams along the coast.

He opened the back door—it was triple-locked—and stood aside.

"Welcome to my humble abomination."

The interior was rustic but cozy, consisting of an open main floor and a sleeping loft, furnished with basic, handmade pieces in unfinished cedar and pine. A dedicated cabinet housed his radio gear. Regina and I sat at the small eating table while Bock scooped coffee into a moka pot and set it going on the woodstove. King Kong stood alertly by his side.

No TV; no light fixtures. He woke with the sun and went to bed at dark. Every few months he drove to Millburg to stock up on essentials and check out the maximum of twenty library books.

Listening to him, I found myself wavering between envy for the simplicity of his life and pity for its isolation. A stale musk permeated throughout—one man's sweat soaked into every surface. While he was dressed neatly and well groomed, I could smell him, too, when he put out the mugs and sat across from us.

I asked how long it would take to repair the phone line.

"Twelve to fourteen weeks."

"You didn't want to do it yourself?"

"I offered to. They told me if I touch it they'll cancel my service. You know, I didn't have any trouble for years till you came around."

"Shoulda shot him when you had the chance," Regina said.

Bock smiled. "To what do I owe the honor?"

I showed him Nick's flyer. "Recognize him?"

Bock shook his head.

"We think he was in Swann's Flat last summer. He hasn't been heard from since."

"You never noticed him around town?" Regina asked.

"No, ma'am. I don't get out much, though."

I said, "He may have connected with Shasta Swann."

Regina said, "What can you tell us about her?"

"Shasta?" Bock said. "I see her time to time, riding her bike or walking her dog. Seems like a nice enough kid. I remember when she was born, 'cause it was a big deal. First baby on the peninsula in fifteen years."

"Who came before her?"

"DJ Pelman." He scratched King Kong's neck. "Truth be told, I don't know how happy she is."

"What makes you say that?" I asked.

"This is no place for a girl her age. It's one thing, you're a grown man, you make a decision. But ask me, it doesn't seem fair to do to her. Can't fault her wanting to get out."

"Did she express that to you?"

"Not in so many words."

Regina said, "But?"

"Well . . . This is years ago. I was down by the marina, getting ready to take my boat out. She comes riding over, starts asking me questions about joining up."

"As in the military?" I asked.

"Yes, sir. She wanted to know how old you had to be, where I'd gotten to live. I told her Japan and Korea, but mostly I spent my career in the same damn spot. I said, 'You want to see the world, there's better ways.'"

"How old was she when you had this conversation?" Regina said.

"Eight? Ten? I'm not the right person to ask about kids' ages."

"And she was already plotting her escape."

Bock nodded.

"She's still here," I said.

"Well, look," he said. "It's like that song. 'You can check out when you want, but you can't leave.' I think I got that wrong."

"Close enough," Regina said.

I showed him a copy of Octavio Prado's jacket photo. "What about this person?"

"Oh yeah. The writer guy."

The response was so swift that I was momentarily thrown. Regina's hand flew to her mouth.

I said, "You recognize him."

"Yes, sir. He helped build my house."

THE HELP WASN'T very helpful, Bock clarified. And it wasn't a house, either, not at that point; he only had the foundation and portions of the framing done.

"I used to fish more than I do now, so I was out on my boat two, three times a week. Usually I'd stop off at the hotel for a beer. He was at the bar."

"You're sure it's the same person," Regina said.

"Yes, ma'am, sure as the Pope eats macaroni. Only he wasn't calling himself—what's it?"

"Octavio Prado."

"He told me his name was Felix," Bock said.

"Last name?" Regina said.

"De Jesús," I said.

They both looked at me.

"How do you know that?" Bock said.

"It comes from his first book," I said. "It's the name of the protagonist. Félix de Jesús."

"He actually published a book?" Bock said.

"One."

"Huh. I thought he was fibbing."

"Did he say what he was doing in Swann's Flat?" Regina asked.

"No, ma'am. We chatted a little and then I was on my way. I saw him a few more times, sitting on the beach or whatnot. I didn't talk to him. I was busy.

"One morning I'm up on the ladder working, and I hear Godzilla barking. I hadn't built the fence yet. I had him on a hundred-foot chain. I look out, and there's a guy standing in the street. It's the guy from the bar. He wants to know if he can move his car onto my land."

"What'd he need that for?" I asked.

"He had to vacate the place he was renting. Then he was sleeping in the car for a few days but they said he couldn't park on the street anymore or they'd tow it."

"Who did?"

"Bergstrom. Or maybe Pelman. It's his tow truck. He does whatever Emil wants."

"Why did Prado come to you?" Regina said.

Bock shook his head. "I guess he tried everywhere else first. I told him, 'I was you, I'd take the hint and vamoose.' He wouldn't listen. He says he can't pay me, but he'll work for me if I feed him and let him crash. He didn't mind sleeping in the car, long as he could get it off the street. Another set of hands didn't sound too bad. 'Okay, let's give it a whirl.'"

"How'd that go?" I asked.

"'Bout as good as you'd think. I didn't know jack shit about construction, and I still knew twice as much as him. I was spending all my time making sure he didn't saw his fingers off. After a couple of weeks I told him no hard feelings, and he split."

"How well did you get to know him?" Regina asked.

"He wasn't a talker. Whenever I asked him about himself I got a different story."

"You called him the writer guy," I said.

"He told me he was working on a book. I asked what it was about. He goes to the car, brings this goddamn thing the size of an encyclopedia. Hands it to me. Like I'm gonna read it on the spot. I flipped through it. 'Nifty, let's get back to work.'"

"Sergeant, do you happen to remember if he had a typewriter with him?"

"Boy," Bock said. "I couldn't tell you one way or the other. The car, it was an itty-bitty blue Toyota, packed full of crap, bags and boxes. I don't know how he slept in there. Typewriter . . . ? Maybe. For all I know, he had a refrigerator."

"Where did he go when he left?" Regina asked.

"Well, I was getting to that. Not too long after me and him parted ways, I was taking the puppy for a walk. I go past Dave Pelman's place and see the same car sitting in the driveway."

"Prado's Toyota."

Bock nodded. "You don't get too many vehicles like that around here. Most everyone has a truck or SUV. I went over to have a closer look. It's empty, no bags, nothing. Pelman comes out, hollering that I'm trespassing. I asked him, 'Whose car is this?' He goes, 'It's mine.'"

"What did you make of that?" I asked.

"At the time, not much. I figured the guy was hard up for cash. He musta sold the car to Pelman before skipping town."

"How could Prado have left without his car?" Regina asked. "What about his stuff?"

"Yeah, no. Didn't sit right. I kept thinking about it. Few days later I go by again. The car's gone. I knock and ask Pelman about it. He plays dumb. 'What car?' 'You know what car, the blue Toyota.'" Bock mimed scratching his head. "'Ohhh, yeah. I stripped it for parts.'"

"You said Pelman does whatever Emil wants," I said.

"Yes, sir."

"Did Prado ever mention having conflict with Emil? Or anyone else in Swann's Flat?"

"No, sir," Bock said.

"Did he seem to know any of the other residents?"

"He never said so."

"What happened after you asked Pelman about the Toyota?" I asked.

"Nothing really."

"No one bothered you about it."

"No, sir."

"And Prado?" Regina asked.

"I didn't see him again."

"Sorry if this seems unrelated, Sergeant," I said. "What do you remember about when Kurt Swann died?"

"Just that it happened."

"Were there rumors?" Regina asked.

"Rumors?"

"That it wasn't an accident, for example."

"No, ma'am. I mind my own business."

Thunder rumbled in the distance.

"We should get moving," Regina said.

I nodded. "Thanks, Sergeant. We'll be in touch."

"Yes, sir. Can I ask what it is you plan to do?"

"Have to see how it goes. Right now we're just gathering information."

"Mm." Bock chewed his cheek.

Regina said, "Something you want to tell us?"

"I don't want to stick my nose in where it don't belong."

"That's okay."

"Well . . . I told you I used to drop by the bar. Those days, DJ was living with his mom."

"Jenelle," I said.

"Yes, sir. I got to know him some."

I readied myself for an anecdote revealing signs of early psychopathy—torturing animals, setting fires.

But Bock sounded wistful as he said, "He's a good kid. It's not his fault his dad is the way he is. I ain't gonna say to you he's a saint. But he means well. Whatever shit the rest of them's mixed up in . . . I wanted you to know that."

"Thank you," Regina said.

He nodded.

"Anything else?" I asked.

He paused. "Just be careful, okay? With the rest of them."

CHAPTER 36

Our primary interest was talking to Shasta Swann, but our cover story put us in town to look at property. We had to do what normal people did, in the normal order, starting with checking in.

The bell jangled as we entered the Counts Hotel.

Jenelle barreled through the saloon doors. "You're back."

"I'm back. And I brought the boss."

Regina introduced herself. "Clay had the best time. He can't stop raving about it."

She had donned a new persona: soothing, earnest, intimate; her voice satiny and the skin around her eyes crinkled with pleasure.

A childhood spent in musical theater, indeed.

Jenelle appeared flattered, and slightly flustered, by the assault of warmth. "I have the same room, if you'd like."

"Wonderful," Regina said.

I counted out six hundred dollars.

"Will you be wanting dinner?" Jenelle asked.

"Not sure yet," I said.

"Kitchen closes at seven." She handed me a key. "You know the way."

WE ONLY STAYED long enough to drop our bags and strap up. I went down the hall to the bathroom, changing into my vest, P365, and magnetic front shirt. When I returned to the room, Regina was dressed the same, with the addition of a pale-pink leather purse. It had chrome buckles, a slender strap, a cute embossed logo.

The ideal accessory for a fun weekend getaway.

Plus an invisible side pocket, near her shooting hand, concealing her Ruger Max .380.

She put in a fresh magazine and racked the slide. "Ready, honey pie?"

"Never readier, babycakes."

THE NEXT NORMAL thing to do on a property tour was to tour property.

Driving north on Beachcomber toward the Bergstrom mansion, I pointed out the mansions belonging to Maggie Penrose and the Clancys.

"You mean Shasta," Regina said.

"Technically."

"And literally. She's profiting here, too."

"Which she may or may not know."

"You really want to defend this girl."

"You really want to indict her."

"She's not *my* Instagram friend."

Beau Bergstrom's Range Rover was parked in the driveway. We'd assumed that making contact with any of the residents—other than Bock—would alert all of them to our presence. But he answered the door with a look of genuine surprise.

"Clay."

Maybe Jenelle hadn't had a chance to call him. Or she'd never intended to.

He recovered quickly, putting out a hand. "Great to see you, brother."

"You too," I said. "My wife, Regina."

"It's a pleasure, Beau," she said.

Yet another new voice. Soft, breathy, coy.

Eyelashes batting at warp speed.

And the Oscar goes to . . .

"The pleasure," Beau said, "is all mine."

He stood back with a bow. "After you."

The interior layout was predictable. Central living room with spiral staircase, kitchen and dining room off the garage, corridor leading to first-floor rooms. When it came to furnishings, the Bergstroms' taste was masculine and impersonal, heavy on black leather and mirrors. Lucite pool table, one-armed bandit. It looked like what it was: a late-nineties bachelor pad, writ large.

"Drink?" Beau said.

"I'd love some water," I said.

"Could I use your restroom?" Regina asked.

"But of course," Beau said. "Down the hall to the right."

She left, and he and I stepped into the kitchen.

"Apologies for dropping out of the sky like this," I said. "The schedule's been insane."

"No worries," Beau said, filling a glass for me. "How was Hong Kong?"

"Busy. Ever been?"

"Can't say I have."

"You gotta go," I said. "Worth it for the dim sum alone . . ."

I filled him in on my adventure, piling on unnecessary detail, letting the impatience build behind his smile.

"Terrific," Beau said. "Listen, Clay, did you see my last email?"

I nodded. "I was going to reply, but I thought it'd be easier to talk face-to-face. And Regina wanted to see the property in person."

Beau clucked his tongue. "I hate to be the bearer of bad news, but we just accepted an offer from the other party."

"Oh no. You're kidding."

He shook his head grimly. "Wish I was."

"Shit. She's gonna be so disappointed."

"I feel bad about it, Clay. I didn't hear from you, so—"

"No. I get it. You have to do what you have to do."

Regina reappeared.

"Excuse me," she said. "Lady issues."

"The property's sold," I said.

"Oh *no*." Her face was a tragedy mask. "Really?"

"Unfortunately," Beau said.

"Ugh."

"I wish you'd called first. I coulda saved you the trouble of driving all the way up."

"It's okay," I said. "We'll make the most of it while we're here. Right, honey?"

"There's really nothing we can do?" Regina asked.

Beau sighed, pinched the bridge of his nose. *These people.* He was an actor, too.

"Okay, look," he said. "The draft contract went out last week. It's under attorney review. My dad went up to Eureka to meet with him. They're supposed to finalize and sign tomorrow morning. That gives us a window where we can still pull out without losing money. But a small one. Why don't the three of us go over together right now? You can see it for yourself, see how you feel. Maybe you won't like it, and we have nothing to discuss."

"And if we do like it?" she said.

"I'll call him and plead your case. But no guarantees. Fair?"

"More than fair," I said.

"Thank you," Regina said. "*So* much."

"It's up the way, mile and change," Beau said. "We could hoof it, but I don't want to get caught in a downpour."

"We'll take our car and follow you," I said.

———

I STARTED THE Jeep. "Lady issues resolved?"

"Peachy," Regina said.

"Find anything?"

"I only had a few minutes to poke around. But there's an office. With a typewriter."

THE APPEAL OF 185 Beachcomber was self-evident: The lot was situated behind a deep, high berm, with 270-degree views encompassing ocean, mountains, and forest. On a clear day it would be spectacular; as it was, the mist imparted an otherworldly quality, suspending us in midair.

"Mamma mia," Regina said.

Beau said, "She's a real gem."

I wondered if he realized he was quoting his own copy.

"The elevation makes it feel private," Beau said, "even though the water's right there."

He walked us around, well set in salesman mode. While the loggers' dormitories were no longer standing—they'd been picked apart for salvage—the natural stone foundations remained.

"They're much bigger than I pictured," Regina said.

"Crew numbered about eighty men," Beau said.

"More people than live here today," I said.

"Way more. They worked in shifts, four days in the field and three at the pier."

"No days off?" Regina asked.

"Sunday morning, for church."

She gazed dewily up at the hills. "It's a miracle they didn't chop down the whole forest."

"Nature always wins. It's all protected land now, so you'll never lose that view."

"How'd they get the logs down?"

"Steam engine," he said, tracing the path out of the mountains. "I showed Clay on our hike. Tracks used to run to the pier, and there was a lumber chute off the end. The cove's too tight for ships to pull up directly. What they call a dog-hole port, 'cause only a dog could turn around in it . . ."

While I'd heard his patter, Regina hadn't. Her *ooh*s and *aah*s encouraged him to lay it on thick.

"The history is so fascinating," she said.

"Couldn't agree more, Regina," Beau said.

We were threading through the pine grove, descending a gentle slope.

"Especially the way you tell it," she said. "It really makes the place come alive."

"I told your husband, it's a passion of mine."

"Clay said you're writing a book."

"Ah, gee. I don't know I'd call it a *book*. Watch your step."

"Thanks . . . I do a little writing, myself."

"Is that right?"

"Mostly poetry."

"Where do you get your inspiration?" Beau said.

"Everywhere," she said. "The world is such a beautiful place. You just have to open yourself up and let it in."

The slope ended at a stone overhang. Beneath was a space about ten feet wide and half as deep, forming a natural windbreak and shelter. Crushed mussel shells sparkled in the soil. Cookfire soot smudged the ceiling.

"Most of the year the Native Americans lived in the hills," Beau said. "They came down for the summer to take advantage of the sea harvest." He grinned. "The original beach house."

Regina squinted at a rock face. "Is that . . . a *painting*?"

Two deer, rendered in fading red pigment; the testimony of an ancient mind.

"Oh my God," she said.

"How's that for inspiration?" Beau asked.

THE WIND WAS picking up as we traipsed over the damp grass. Stray droplets pricked my face. At five thirty p.m., the sun was fighting a desperate and losing battle, clouds blackened like the bottom of a scorched pot. A vein of light flared over the water, illuminating the ocean for miles and leaving the darkness heavier than before.

"So?" Beau said. "What do we think?"

I glanced at Regina. "Honey?"

She smiled shyly at Beau. "I think you should talk to your dad."

Beau chuckled. "Thanks for making my life easy."

"What do you want me to say? It's incredible."

"All righty. I'll do my best. I'll call you after I've spoken with him. You're at the hotel?"

"For tonight, at least," I said.

"If it doesn't work out," Beau said, "maybe tomorrow we can have a look at some of those other properties you saw last time."

"How would you feel about that?" I asked Regina.

She gave a thumbs-down.

"The woman knows what she wants," Beau said.

"Always," I said.

"I'd love it if you could show me around a little," Regina said, "like you did for Clay. Love to see what you're working on, too."

"Nothing would make me happier," Beau said. "Careful, now. Slippery."

He extended his arm gallantly to escort her down the berm. "I see you learned your lesson and rented a four-wheeler."

"It didn't help," Regina said.

"'Scuse me for saying so, but someone got her cherry popped."

"Big time."

CHAPTER 37

I t was drizzling as we arrived at the Clancy residence. Regina and I hurried onto the porch. Bowie began barking before I'd knocked.

Coming.

Leonie opened the door, one hand on the dog's collar. She stared at me.

"Hi, Mrs. Clancy. This is my wife."

Regina introduced herself. "Great to meet you."

"You, too," Leonie said. Stock niceties, reflexive. Then reality kicked in and she reverted to form: "What's this about?"

"We're in town for a few days," I said. "I wanted to check in, see how Shasta's doing."

Bowie lunged, forcing Leonie to grab at the doorpost. Her body wobbled, her eyes were bleary. "Better. Thanks."

I held up a pair of Apple AirPods, new in the box. "These are for her."

"To replace the ones she lost," Regina said.

"Oh," Leonie said. "That's . . . It's very kind of you."

I said, "Would you mind giving them to her?"

Regina and I smiled simultaneously. What a lovely couple.

Our plan was to forge a connection with Shasta—an opening to exploit, if not now, then at some later date.

It worked faster and better than expected.

Leonie said, "You can give them to her yourself."

WE TRAILED HER as she dragged the dog through the foyer and into the living room. An open wine bottle and stemless glass sat on the coffee table. Cooking smells drifted from the kitchen, where an exhaust fan bellowed.

Leonie released Bowie. He ran to me, rising on his hind legs to greet me.

"Hello again, Big Guy," I said, rubbing his head.

"Lee? Is someone there?" Jason Clancy came to the kitchen doorway, wearing an apron over corduroys and a green broad-cloth shirt, sleeves rolled to his elbows. "Oh. Hey."

"You remember Clay," Leonie said.

"Yeah, of course. Good to see you again. Sorry, I'm covered in fish . . . Jason."

"Regina."

"They brought something for Shasta," Leonie said.

"Right," Jason said. "Cool."

"Would you mind if I used your restroom?" Regina asked.

"Down the hall."

"Thanks."

"I'll let her know you're here," Leonie said, starting up the stairs.

With both women gone, Jason turned to me. "Beer?"

"Sure. Thanks."

He wiped his hands on his apron, went behind the bar, and popped open two Sierra Nevadas. "Couldn't stay away, huh?"

I smiled. "We came to look at a property."

"Oh yeah?" He handed me a bottle and sat on the couch, patting the cushion for Bowie, who curled up next to him. "Which?"

"One eighty-five Beachcomber."

"I didn't know that was for sale."

"Beau Bergstrom took us to look at it. Sounds like there are other offers, though."

"Huh. Well." He tilted his beer toward me. "Good luck."

Leonie returned. Shasta was two steps behind, barefoot and dressed in loose gray sweatpants. The puka shell necklace had been replaced by a thin silver chain tucked beneath a Rolling Stones big-tongue T-shirt.

"Hi there," I said.

"Hey," she said. "Thank you so much."

"You're welcome. We didn't know if you got new ones already."

"No, I've just been using my old wired pair. This is great."

"How're you feeling?"

"Fine. Full recovery."

"Back on the bike?"

"We're taking it slow," Leonie said.

"I have to build up my stamina," Shasta said. "I wasn't allowed to ride for six weeks."

"We agreed we wanted to be careful," Leonie said, reaching to brush hair from Shasta's face.

Shasta tilted away in annoyance.

"You got a new necklace, too," I said.

"Just the chain," Shasta said, fishing the rooster pendant out from her shirt. "I was going to get the same thing, with shells, but I kinda prefer how this looks."

Regina reentered. "Hi. You must be Shasta. I'm Regina."

"Hi," Shasta said. "Thanks for that."

"You're very welcome."

"Who's watching the kids while you're away?" Leonie asked.

"Clay's mom," Regina said.

Jason said, "They're thinking of buying one eighty-five."

Leonie raised her eyebrows. "Oh."

White light bleached the room, followed by a peal of thunder that rattled the windows and a crash of rain.

Bowie began to howl.

"Easy, pal," Jason said, stroking his head.

"Well," Leonie said. "Thank you for—"

Shasta said, "Do you guys want to stay for dinner?"

I looked at Regina. "Well—"

"You can't go out in this weather," Shasta said. Cheeky smile. "You could have an accident."

I laughed.

Regina said, "That's so sweet, but we wouldn't want to impose."

"You're not. We have plenty of food. Right?" she asked Jason.

". . . Yeah," he said.

"Great," Shasta said. "I'll set the table."

"I'll help you," Regina said.

"Can I give you a hand?" I asked Jason.

"Cut tomatoes?"

"I think I can manage that."

Leonie picked up the wine bottle and refilled her glass.

AS SOON AS we sat down to eat, Bowie began running in circles, herding us in our chairs, forcing us closer and closer to the edge of the table.

"Can you please crate him," Leonie said.

"It's instinct," Shasta said. "He can't help it."

"Am I a sheep? Look at this. *Bowie.*"

The dog rested his paws on my back and began nuzzling my neck.

"Down." Leonie rapped the tabletop. *"Down."*

"Don't worry about it," I said.

"Bowie," Shasta said. "Come."

She induced him to settle at her feet by dangling a piece of rockfish.

Jason Clancy was an accomplished cook and a first-rate provider: He'd caught the fish himself and grown the vegetables. The wine, a Sauvignon Blanc from a Humboldt vineyard, was quickly finished and another bottle uncorked. Leonie drank the most, although Shasta did her part, surreptitiously topping off her half glass when her mother wasn't paying attention.

Regina said, "Everything's delicious."

"Thanks," Jason said.

Leonie said, "You can see why I married him."

"How'd you two meet?" I asked.

"Online," Jason said.

Shasta reached for the wine.

"Excuse me, young lady," Leonie said.

"You said half a glass."

"You've already had more than that."

"It complements the food." Shasta poured a full glass, nosed. *"Fruity."*

Leonie looked to Jason for help.

"Kitten," he said.

Shasta, ignoring him, said, "How much is Beau charging you for one eighty-five?"

"Shasta," Leonie said.

"What."

"That's not polite."

"We're all adults here," Shasta said.

"You're not."

"Not yet."

"I'm just asking a question."

"It's none of your business."

"I mean," Shasta said, swirling her glass, "we could be neighbors, so it kind of is."

I said, "We haven't settled on a price yet."

"Why would you want to live here?"

Leonie said, "They like it, obviously."

"It's beautiful," Regina said.

"There's lots of beautiful places," Shasta said.

Jason said, "More salad, anyone?"

"Yes, please," I said.

Shasta said, "How old are your kids?"

"Four and one," I said, accepting the bowl.

"Are you planning to raise them here?"

"Shasta," Leonie said.

"I'm just asking."

"We were thinking it would be part-time," Regina said.

"Where will you send them to school?" Shasta asked.

Leonie's jaw tensed.

"Where did you go?" I asked.

"Millburg. But I stopped when I was in third grade. Now I do everything online."

"Otherwise you'd have to drive three hours each way," Leonie said.

"That's a lot," Regina said.

"It's better like this," Leonie said. "You can go at your own pace."

"Hurray for my own pace." Shasta twirled a finger, tossed back her wine, and reached for the bottle.

Leonie snatched it away. "No more. Eat something."

"I'm not hungry. We've had the same thing for like two weeks straight."

"Oh, I'm *so* sorry for you, that must be *so* hard."

Thunder boomed.

"Excuse me," Regina said. She pushed back from the table and left the room.

"So, Clay," Shasta said. "How'd you get that scar?"

"For God's sake," Leonie hissed.

"No, it's fine," I said.

I told the window warehouse story.

"Badass," Shasta said.

"Thanks, but really it was just stupid."

"Do you want to see mine?"

Before I could respond she propped her foot on the table and pulled up her sweatpant leg, exposing her shin. The newly grown flesh was pinkish and raised.

"I'm sorry," I said.

"No, I like it," Shasta said. She grinned. "It's the most interesting thing about me."

"Stop that," Leonie said. "Right now."

"Or what?"

With a grunt Leonie shoved Shasta's leg to the floor, startling Bowie.

Mother and daughter glared at each other.

Jason cleared his throat. "Maybe you need a breather, kitten."

"Fuck you," Shasta muttered.

"What did you say?" Leonie demanded.

Silence.

"Apologize. *Now*."

"I apologize, Jason," Shasta said.

Regina came back, looking sheepish. "Sorry about this. But: Can I borrow something from you? It's a lady issue."

Shasta stood up. "I got you."

"Thanks."

Bowie trotted after them as they crossed into the living room and started up the stairs.

Leonie said, "I'm sorry you had to see that."

I said, "It's fine, really."

I heard Regina's voice. Bouncy, child-like.

I love your necklace.

"Here's my advice," Leonie said. "Don't have teenagers."

"We'll try," I said. "But I'm not sure how we can avoid it."

"Just kill them the night before they turn thirteen. Go into their rooms and put a pillow over their faces."

Jason said, "I'll get dessert."

CHAPTER 38

We got free of the Clancys, thanked them for their hospital-ity, and dashed to the car through the sheeting rain.

Regina slammed the passenger door and flopped back. "Family values."

"How'd you do?"

"I was in Shasta's room for less than a minute. I didn't see anything connected to Nick."

"What'd she say about the necklace?"

"Gift from a friend."

"Not a boyfriend."

"She said friend, I didn't press," Regina said. "You saw how she tried to discourage us from buying. Think she knows about the scam?"

"Or she hates it here because it's been a miserable childhood."

"All that power play stuff with her mother? I'm pretty sure she knows." Regina paused. "I feel for her."

"Me too." I started the car.

With no streetlights and few stars, visibility was limited to ten feet, and I crept along, following the reflection of the headlights against the rusted guardrail.

"How 'bout that cave painting Beau showed us?" Regina said.

"Awe-inspiring," I said. "I didn't realize he was an artist, too."

"Oh yeah, a regular fucking Renaissance man."

I laughed. "Priorities for tomorrow."

"For me, it's Shasta."

"Agreed. We need to speak to her away from her parents."

"Bright ideas on how to go about that?" Regina said.

"She's gonna leave the house at some point," I said, "to ride, or to walk the dog. We stake her out and 'happen' to run into her."

"Didn't you do that already?"

"Ha ha ha. Are you done?"

"Not on your life. Continue."

I said, "We strike up a conversation with her. Keep it light. If she seems open, shift it to growing up in Swann's Flat, her social life. Then we try to guide her to Nick."

"We can't come on too strong."

"Definitely. If we can't find a way to get there, we tee her up to try again. 'Could you swing by the hotel later? We wanted your opinion on something.'"

"You sure that'll work?"

"She's a teenager," I said. "She thinks her parents are idiots. Two adults, wanting to know what *she* thinks?"

Regina nodded. "We also need a typewriter sample from Beau."

"Let's see what he says about tomorrow and figure out how to proceed."

"And Al? Do we trust him?"

"I can't see him being the one to harm Prado, but I've been fooled before."

She said, "I thought it was strange, him preemptively defending DJ Pelman. Something to ask Jenelle about."

"Bright ideas for that?" I asked.

"Watch and learn."

————

JENELLE COUNTS HAD inverted the dining room chairs on tables and was sweeping up.

She said, "There's some soup left, if you want it."

"I'd love a glass of wine," Regina said. "It's been a long day."

"White or red?"

"You choose. And a glass for you. For your trouble."

Jenelle smiled. "I won't say no."

"Why don't you go on and shower?" Regina said to me. "I'll be up in a bit."

I saluted. "Good night."

"'Night," Jenelle said. Happy I was leaving.

I PHONED AMY from the landline.

"We're here and we're fine," I said.

"Thanks for letting me know."

"Kids okay?"

"Great."

"Are you okay?"

"Anxious, but I'll survive."

"I'll check in as often as I can."

"Thanks, honey. Good luck."

"I love you, Amy. So much."

"I love you, too."

I showered and dressed for bed. Rolling out the sleeping bag, I sat to type up my notes.

Over the sound of the rain I could hear Jenelle's belly laughs drifting up through the floor. It reminded me of how rapidly Regina had established rapport with Amy.

More than a childhood in musical theater. A gift.

The phone rang. I set the laptop aside and lifted the receiver. "Hello?"

"Hey hey," Beau said. "Good news. Just spoke to my dad. I

had to twist his arm, but he agreed to hit the brakes on the other deal."

"Dude. You're the greatest."

"Only the best, for the best," he said. "He's gonna meet with the lawyer in the morning. They'll draw up the preliminaries. All goes well, he should be home midafternoon, and we can sit down and get this done."

"Thank you."

"Glad it worked out. Leaves us some time for a morning activity."

"What'd you have in mind?"

"We could head up to the old sawmill," Beau said.

"She'll love that."

"Then that's what we'll do. Seven thirty at the hotel?"

"She likes to sleep late," I said. "We'll come over to your place when she's ready."

"Okey doke."

"Thanks again, Beau."

"You're more than welcome, my friend. You have yourself a good night."

The wind rose to a shriek. The room lights flickered.

I crossed to the bay window and parted the curtains.

The marina was underwater. Waves spumed against the peninsular edge, froth surged over the plaza, obliterating the boundary between land and sea.

REGINA TIPTOED IN around midnight.

I removed my earplugs and sat up. "How'd it go?"

"I gotta new bestie."

Unable to question Jenelle directly about Dave Pelman, Prado, or Nick, she'd steered their conversation toward the male species. Concentrating on me and our "marriage."

"I shared that we're going through a bumpy patch. My anxiety. Your erectile dysfunction. All the juicy deets."

"Thanks for that."

"I'm very committed to my craft."

"Did she reciprocate with her own personal stuff?"

"It took a bottle and a half, but then the dam blew. Her parents built the hotel. They were among the first to buy, back in the sixties. She grew up here. She said there used to be more permanent residents, but over time they died or moved or got bought out."

"Bought out, or pushed out?"

"I'm not sure there's a difference," she said. "She's skittish about the Bergstroms."

"They've threatened her, too?"

"That's not the feeling I got. More general unease than outright fear."

I said, "Like living in a dictatorship and knowing you won't lead the rebellion. But that doesn't mean you're complicit. I was sure she was going to call Beau after we checked in, to warn him we were in town, but he looked caught off guard."

Regina nodded. "She depends on the Bergstroms but doesn't like it. I asked her about tourist season. It doesn't exist. There's no way she's staying afloat without help."

"They're subsidizing her."

"Or, Shasta is. Technically."

I said, "Al Bock told me no one lives here unless the Bergstroms want them to. What purpose does Jenelle serve?"

"The few visitors do need lodging, she's there. It gives the appearance of a regular old vacation destination."

"She doesn't make waves," I said, "no reason for the Bergstroms to upset the status quo. What'd she have to say about Dave?"

"He moved here as a kid with his mom."

"The beauty queen."

"He and Jenelle were never legally married. He knocked her up and ran off."

"Stand-up guy."

"She didn't seem bitter. Then his mom got sick and he came back. Jenelle said he tried to rekindle it. 'I'm a changed man,' that kinda bullshit. She kicked him to the curb."

"Smart lady."

"She is. I like her."

"Trust her?"

"As much as I trust any of these folks."

"Low bar," I said. "Did she describe the relationship between Dave and Kurt?"

"Nope, and I couldn't find a way to bring it up. Who we *did* talk about was her on-again, off-again, of the last twenty years."

"Emil?"

She Xed her arms and made a buzzing sound.

I stared. *"Al?"*

"Ding ding ding ding ding."

"Whoa."

"Wild, right? And I wasn't even asking. She goes, 'Is your other car okay? Did you get the mirror fixed?' I told her the maniac who shot it out paid for the repair. She goes, 'Aw, he's not so bad, once you get to know him.' I could see she was trying not to laugh. I prodded, and she's all, 'No big deal, once upon a time me and him had a little thing.' "

"Maybe why he feels protective toward her son."

"I had the same thought."

"If Al did do something to Prado," I said, "would she know about it?"

Regina shook her head. "I don't know. Hard to tell if this thing between her and Al is the real deal or just a product of circumstance."

"They're both lonely."

"Everyone here's lonely," she said. "That's why they talk."

"I thought you didn't believe in all that psychology bullshit."

"I believe in what works. Did you hear from Beau?"

I told her the plan. "He wanted to meet here but I said we'd come to the house."

"You run interference while I sneak into his office?"

"Lady issues *are* a bitch."

She laughed. "And Daddy Emil? What's our play with him?"

"Stick to real estate, give him plenty of rope, and see if he says anything incriminating."

"And when he hands us papers to sign?"

"We tell him we'll bring it to our own attorney for review."

"You don't think that'll make them suspicious?"

"If I were them, I'd be more suspicious if we didn't want a lawyer to look at it."

She sat for a while, saying nothing, digesting. "It's late."

She took her pajamas and toothbrush, and went out. I stuck in my earplugs and rolled over.

CHAPTER 39

The next morning Jenelle looked tired and hungover, avoiding eye contact with us as she set out breakfast.

"Will you need the room again?" she asked.

"I'm not sure," I said. "Can we let you know?"

"Noon. Full day after that."

"Okay. Thanks."

"This is all so good, by the way," Regina said.

Jenelle nodded and retreated to the kitchen.

WE ATE OUR fill and went to the room to prep.

Regina said, "New strategy: You skip the sawmill Meet up with us later at the house, once Emil's there."

"Why?"

"Beau's a lech. I'll get more out of him, one-on-one. Plus it frees you up to talk to Shasta."

"We can do that together, afterward."

"No matter what you say, I think it's gonna spook the Bergstroms when we balk. If they start getting hostile, we might have to clear out in a hurry. We need to be efficient."

"You said yourself we can't force things with Shasta."

"Okay, but better something than nothing. If you're really getting nowhere, you can drop Nick on her. She has a conscience, she may spill."

"It has to be a game-time decision," I said. "I'm not going to try unless I'm confident it won't backfire."

"Up to you. Worst case, we leave, spend a few months building a relationship with her over the internet. Given her age, that might even work better."

"Or they all close ranks and we miss any shot we have with her."

"They could do that anyway."

I said nothing.

"Fortune favors the bold," Regina said.

"Okay," I said. "I'm in."

"What's your excuse for begging off?"

"An old knee injury acting up."

"I guess that works."

"You have a better idea?" I asked.

"I was thinking a severe attack of ED."

I DRESSED IN the bathroom and met Regina on the landing. She'd undergone another transformation, selecting an outfit best described as Schoolgirl Hiker Minx: leggings with mesh cutouts, snug tank top exposing a crescent of firm midriff, pigtails. The addition of a Patagonia fleece retrieved her from the realm of pure male fantasy. The gun purse hung unobtrusively at her side.

She twirled a braid. "How do I look?"

"Like a woman whose husband has erectile dysfunction."

THE STORM HAD abated overnight, leaving puddles and flotsam strewn across the marina: kelp, driftwood, starfish slowly dying beneath a blanket of low-lying fog. Curdled clouds arched from horizon to mountaintop. The receding surf had deposited sand to the top of the cove ramp. No wind, but evidence of its wrath was everywhere: bait kiosk flayed of shingles, boat covers peeled back like torn fingernails.

We drove north on Beachcomber. Broken branches littered the road.

Our knock at the Bergstroms' went unanswered. A persistent scraping noise drew us around to an unfenced yard that bled into open fields. Aside from the barn and sheep pen were stables, a chicken coop, and a rabbit hutch.

And, incongruously, a large, kidney-shaped swimming pool, tarped to keep out debris.

A piece of cinema Hollywood, chiseled into the landscape. Like Emil himself.

The scrape was coming from the coop. DJ Pelman crouched by a bloodstained tree stump, sharpening a hatchet with a file. His jeans had slipped to expose three inches of plumber's crack. Beau Bergstrom, dressed in a canvas chore coat, watched him like an overbearing supervisor.

I whistled. "Morning."

Beau looked up, returned the greeting, and started toward us, circumventing the pool. "Wasn't expecting you for a while."

"Up and at 'em," Regina said.

"We can come back if you're not ready," I said.

"I was born ready," Beau said.

DJ slunk over, hitching his waistband. The hatchet dangled in his fingers. "Wassup."

"That thing looks dangerous," Regina said.

He said, "It is if you're a chicken."

Beau said, "Shall we?"

I said, "Actually, I have to take a rain check."

Regina gave a strained smile. Not the first time she'd been disappointed by her lame husband. "His knee's acting up."

"Oh no," Beau said. "That's too bad."

"Yeah," I said. "It's the wet weather, brings it out."

DJ snickered. "Like uh actual rain check. Get it?"

"Good one, Deej," Beau said flatly. "Well. Sorry to lose you, Clay. Fret not, though. I'll take good care of her."

Regina said, "Speaking of which, can I use the little girls' room?"

"Took the words right out my mouth. Patio's unlocked."

"Thanks. Back in a jiff."

Beau sneaked a peek at her receding shape, then grinned and punched me lightly on the shoulder. "What're you gonna do with your newfound freedom?"

"Relax. I might drive around and take some pictures. Sky's beautiful today."

"Always happens after a storm," DJ said.

We continued to make small talk. Regina was gone for three minutes, five. Ten. I could see Beau's attention beginning to drift, eyes darting to the house. Where'd she gotten to?

At last the door slid open and she appeared.

"Sorry," she called, trotting over.

"I was getting worried you fell in," Beau said.

I said, "All set?"

"All set," she said, giving me a slight nod. *Got it.*

She cranked up the wattage on her smile and trained it on Beau. "What's on the agenda?"

"Before we get going, I thought I'd show you some of what I'm working on," he said.

"Sounds great."

"What time should I be back?" I asked.

"Figure two, two thirty. My dad'll be getting in around then. Hey, though," Beau said, "I just thought of something. Once we get this all squared away, you guys should stay for dinner."

Regina said, "We wouldn't want to impose."

"Aw, it's no trouble. We gotta eat anyway. Might as well celebrate."

DJ flipped the hatchet and caught it by the handle. "Just as easy to kill two."

I said, "Sure, thanks."

"Right on," Beau said. He bowed to Regina. "After you, m'lady."

She giggled and curtsied. "Why thank you, kind sir."

We moved off in three directions: Beau and Regina toward the patio doors, DJ to the coop, and me toward the street. As I turned the corner of the house I heard an alarmed squawk, then a *thunk*, then silence.

I DROVE TO the Clancys', pulling over with a few hundred yards to go and grabbing my camera bag from the footwell. To reach the entry road, Shasta would have to pass this way.

I attached the telephoto lens to the EOS and stepped out to the railing.

I snapped pictures of the ocean, the same monochrome shot, over and over.

At nine thirty-four a.m., the Clancys' garage door raised.

I zoomed in.

Shasta walked out a bike. She had her helmet on, but rather than a unisuit, she wore jeans and a flannel and was carrying a backpack.

She put in her brand-new AirPods, clicked in her cleats.

I swung the camera back to the water. I wanted to look busy when she rode up.

Oh, hey there. What a coincidence.

She turned left out of the driveway, heading south, into the fog.

Away from me.

"Fuck."

I ran and jumped behind the wheel.

I'd tailed my fair share of vehicles, but never a bike. Out of the blocks I miscalculated, laying on the gas too hard. But she wasn't pedaling at racing cadence; there was a restrained quality to her movements, not lazy but deliberate, as if she knew she had a long way to go.

At the marina she bore left and wound inland. The storm had felled numerous trees. Shasta sailed around them with ease.

I hung back, letting her shrink into the mist before lumbering onto the muddy shoulders, praying not to get stuck, praying I could catch sight of her before she made another three turns and I lost her.

Turkey-Tail Road.

Yarrow Lane.

We were approaching the southeastern quadrant, nearing Al Bock's place.

Why would she have any reason to go see him?

She didn't, glided past his block and kept going, her stroke quickening as she rounded onto Whitethorn Court.

I inched up.

It was a skimpy, steep cul-de-sac, one third paved, the rest reclaimed by nature. Rainwater formed mirrored disks in the uneven ground.

Shasta had dismounted and was pushing the bike along a grassy verge. Through the zoom I watched her stop and remove her cycling cleats, changing them out for a pair of hiking boots from her backpack. She put away her AirPods, took out a pink water bottle, and walked into the trees.

I got out of the Jeep and jogged up the verge.

She'd propped the bike against an alder, stuck the cleats on the handlebars.

Panning the camera over the dark, wet depths, I spotted her

sixty yards ahead, high-stepping, her gait methodical and confident.

I waded forward, into the brush.

SLOW GOING.

Dense vegetation and rolling mist provided cover for me but made Shasta tough to track. I had no water of my own, no map, no compass, no sense of progress or a destination.

Gradually the terrain lifted us out of the dripping coastal habitat and into the foothills.

She never hesitated, never looked back.

After an hour and a half of climbing she disappeared over a ridge.

I hurried up, sneakers sucking in the mud.

At the ridgeline, I understood where we were and where we were headed.

A valley gaped below. On the far side, green peaks capped a wall of exposed rock. The entry road was a scrawny yellow scar that pushed out into the void to form a violent hairpin.

Shasta was far downslope, switchbacking fast.

I checked my watch. Eleven forty a.m.

To have any chance of making the meeting with Emil, I ought to turn back now.

What Would Regina Do?

What the fuck do you think, Mr. Potato Head? Move it or lose it.

IT TOOK THIRTY minutes to reach the valley floor, another thirty to cross it. There Shasta turned north, parallel to the cliff. The canopy was too thick for me to see up to the entry road, but I knew that it must be directly above.

A quarter mile along, she stopped and dropped down behind a shrub.

I slanted through the trees, getting as close as I could without drawing her attention. She had taken off the pack and was leaning on one knee, staring at the earth as though hypnotized.

After several silent minutes she rose, threw on the pack, and departed.

I waited for her to recede before moving up.

I saw her boot prints, bent stalks slowly recovering their height.

Beneath resurgent ground cover, the soil had subsided to reveal the outline of a grave.

She'd left wildflowers.

Per the coroner's report, Kurt Swann's body had landed right around here. But there was no headstone, and I couldn't see such a remote location as the permanent resting place of a town elder—certainly not after search-and-rescue had gone to the effort of removing him.

A detailed scene examination would have to wait; Shasta was already out of sight, and I doubted I could find my way back to the car on my own.

I took rapid-fire photos and set out.

I'd covered about a hundred yards when she spoke somewhere to my right.

"Why are you following me?"

I turned. She stood in shadow, half hidden by a redwood, aiming a pistol at my center mass.

I said, "Can you please put that down?"

"No."

"I'm not going to hurt you."

"Why are you following me?"

"I wanted to talk to you."

"You're following me. That's not talking."

"Who is that, back there? Is it Nick?"

She stepped forward, keeping the gun high. "Who are *you*?"

Breathing fast, voice shrill, edging toward catastrophe.

I said, "I work for his mother. She asked me to find him."

"She doesn't care about him."

"I know she made mistakes. But I promise you: She cares. And she's hurting."

The gun shook. Compact automatic. Not enough to stop a bear. I wasn't a bear.

"Please, Shasta," I said.

Tears pooled in her eyes.

She let the gun drop to her side.

"Thank you."

She nodded, wiped her face with the heel of her hand.

I said, "Do you want to tell me about it?"

Another nod, sad and slow.

offered to sit, but she wanted to walk. An athlete: She felt calmer with her body in motion.

She said, "I was riding out to Blackberry Junction. He was coming in the other direction."

"Driving?"

"No, on foot. He had this ginormous hiking pack and he wasn't wearing a shirt. I think he waved. I wasn't really paying attention. I get focused when I ride, you know?"

"Oh, I know," I said.

She laughed softly. "Yeah. On my way home, I saw him again, sitting in the dirt. He was really grungy, and scrawny, with pale stripes on his shoulders from the pack. He's got this necklace on"—she touched her own chest—"and he's shaking his water bottle into his mouth, to get the last drops. Honestly, it was kinda pathetic. So I stopped."

"You felt bad for him."

"Totally. And . . . I mean, we get hikers, but it's never anyone my age. Like, okay, maybe you're a homicidal maniac, but at least that's something *new.*"

I smiled.

"He asked how much farther to Swann's Flat," she said. "I go, 'Seven point two miles,' and his face just . . . collapsed."

Maddie Zwick had described him in similar language.

"I knew he'd never make it without water," Shasta said. "I poured my bottle into his."

"Kind of you."

"I had to. I felt responsible. I said, 'Pace yourself. In about five miles, you'll see a stream to your left. But it's not drinkable unless you filter it.' He's all, 'Thank you so much, you're a lifesaver.' I asked why he needed to go there. He told me he's looking for someone. 'Who? I know everyone.' He opens his pack and starts taking out stuff. Rations, matches, a flashlight."

"Camping supplies," I said.

She nodded. "At the bottom there's a pillowcase with these huge bundles of paper, held together by rubber bands. He unties one and starts turning pages. I couldn't read it because he was going so fast. Finally he finds what he's looking for. Pencil drawing, about this big."

Displaying her palm.

"A woman's face," she said. "I asked who she is. He said he didn't know her name. 'How do you expect to find her, then?' He shrugs. 'I'll figure it out.'

"Then he gave me a funny look. He goes, 'Do you know her?'

"It was such a strange thing to ask. The drawing—it was really shitty. One eye was way too big and her jaw was all crooked. It didn't look like it could be an actual person. But."

Her breathing had accelerated again.

"I did know her," she said. "I knew, right away. It was my mom."

She stopped, downed a big gulp of water, offered me the bottle.

I drank. I was parched; I also wanted to help her regain a sense of control.

"Thanks," I said.

I gave the bottle back and we resumed walking.

"What did you think when you saw the drawing?" I asked.

"I was imagining things. I was dehydrated, or low blood sugar. But . . . I know what my mom looks like."

"Did you tell Nick that?"

"No way. Are you kidding? I just met this guy. I have no idea who he is. What if he— I don't know. Wants to hurt her."

"I agree with you, Shasta. I'd do the same thing."

"Yeah. So. I told him I'd never seen her before. And he says, 'I thought you knew everyone.' 'Not her.' He's staring at me, like he knows I'm lying. He didn't say anything, though. He just started putting the pages away. I asked him what is all that. 'A book.' 'You wrote it?' 'My dad did.' 'Who's your dad?' 'Octavio Prado.'

"Then he gives me that same funny look. 'You've heard of him.' 'No, sorry.' And it's the same thing: I could tell he knew the truth." She paused. "I guess I'm just a bad liar."

"You did know about Prado," I said.

She nodded. "I read *Lake of the Moon*."

"When?"

"A couple years ago. It was the summer we had all the wildfires. I couldn't train or be outside for too long. I felt so bored, I was losing my shit. We don't have a lot of books, but Maggie has tons, and she lets me borrow whatever I want. I rode over, and . . ." Faint smile. "I could hear her, upstairs, singing in the bath. I yelled that I'm here for a book. 'Okay, go ahead, I'll be down in a minute.' I went to the garage and started looking through the shelves."

"What drew you to *Lake of the Moon*?" I asked.

"It was short."

I smiled. "Always a plus."

"And the author was from Fresno. That's where my mom's from."

I said, "Leonie is?"

"She was born there."

"How'd she get to Swann's Flat?"

Shasta shook her head. "She won't talk about it. She gets really mad if I try to ask. I only knew about Fresno because my grandma came to visit once. She wanted us to move back."

"How old were you?"

"Eight or nine? The two of them got into this huge fight. My grandma was like, 'You can't do this to Shasta, it's not good for her to grow up this way.' And my mom goes, 'I'd rather die than set foot in that hick town,' which is ridiculous, if you think about it, because . . ."

"Look where you are."

"*Exactly,*" Shasta said, her relief palpable: I got it.

"Did you ever talk to your grandmother on your own?"

"That was the only time I met her. I wasn't allowed to call. She used to send me birthday presents and my mom would throw them in the trash."

"That sounds tough."

She nodded. "I never met my grandfather. My mom hates him. She said he's a sicko. I don't even know if they're alive, either of them. I googled them but, you know. They're old, so."

"I'm sorry, Shasta. This is a lot."

"Yeah. It's all right. Thanks, though."

"What did you make of *Lake of the Moon*?" I asked.

"Well, I just started looking at it when Maggie comes into the garage. I show it to her, and she literally *runs* over and grabs it out of my hands."

"Did she say why?"

"No. She made me take *Wuthering Heights* instead. 'You'll like this better, I loved it when I was your age.' And it was so, so not her to act like that. She's never been strict with me. So now I'm like, I *have* to read this."

"Of course."

"I came back later, when she was out on her walk. I go into the garage, but the book's not there. She left a gap on the shelf. Like a warning. It pissed me off. First you *assume* I'm going to try and steal it. And I mean—yeah, okay. I did. But still. It proved she didn't trust me. And like, stop, please. I'm not five. I can use the internet."

"You ordered it."

"With my mom's account," she said. "Then I had to make sure she and Jason didn't find out. 'Cause obviously there's something radioactive about this book. It became this whole complicated thing, 'cause we don't get our mail delivered, we have to pick it up from the post office in Millburg. DJ drives out and collects it, then he gives it to Jenelle, and we pick it up from the hotel. Usually Jason goes, but for the next month I volunteered to do it. He just thought I was being helpful." She mimicked him: " 'Gee, thanks, kitten.' "

I laughed. "Nothing stops you."

She shrugged, gave a half smile.

"Okay. So now you have the book."

"I didn't get why Maggie was acting so weird. I kept waiting for some massively inappropriate scene, but it was just cursing and a tiny amount of sex. I've read much worse."

"Did you like it?"

"Kinda? The main character felt real, not some adult pretending to be a teenager. And the parts about Fresno were interesting. I wanted to ask my mom about it but I didn't want to upset her. I stuck it under my bed. One night I'm doing homework in the kitchen and she barges in, holding the book. 'Where'd you get this?' Like it was a bag of crack. She called me an ungrateful little bitch, and . . ."

Shasta broke off, her face hard.

She said, "She slapped me."

"That's awful."

"It didn't hurt that much. Just . . ." Shasta swallowed. "She yells. A lot. Especially when she's drunk. So, all the time, basically. But she really doesn't do . . . that."

Our feet squelched in the soft forest floor.

"So, yeah," she said. "That's how I knew about Octavio Prado."

"You didn't tell Nick that, either."

She shook her head. "I asked where he's planning to sleep. 'I'll figure it out when I get there.' I said, 'There's a bridge by the town sign. Meet me there tomorrow. Eight a.m.'"

IN THE MORNING he was waiting for her.

She led him through the maze, pedaling as slow as humanly possible. Nick told her he'd spent the night in the woods. He was talkative and animated, stopping repeatedly to take pictures of the abandoned lots.

"It's just like he described," he said.

"Who?" she asked.

"Prado. He calls it 'purgatory by the sea.'"

A cottage stood at 6 Anemone Lane. Shasta opened the front door and waved him inside.

Bare, dusty rooms.

"Who lives here?" Nick asked.

"No one."

From her satchel she took three sandwiches wrapped in waxed paper. His eyes went wide. He tore open the paper and ate greedily, stuffing halves into his mouth and licking peanut butter from his fingers. When he was done he exhaled with contentment.

"Better?" she asked.

"Much. Thanks."

On the kitchenette counter she laid out the remaining half loaf, the peanut butter, three cans of sardines, dried apricots, bottled water, and toilet paper. The faucets didn't work, but there was an outhouse.

She asked what else he needed.

"I'm good. Thanks."

"Sorry there's no bed."

"It's great. Thank you."

"You don't have to keep saying that," she said.

"Yeah, I do," he said. "'Cause you keep doing nice things for me."

Her cheeks flushed. "Can I see it again?"

No need to specify what "it" was.

They sat facing each other on the splintery floor. Nick dug out the manuscript and found the drawing for her.

Shasta had lain awake most of the night, picturing the woman and comparing her with Leonie. She hoped that a second viewing, in the cold light of day, would make plain her error. But the resemblance was impossible to deny. If anything it seemed stronger.

She brushed the surface of the paper. "You really don't know her name?"

He shook his head.

"Why don't you ask your dad?"

"He's not around."

"How do you know she's a real person?"

"I just do."

"What if you're wrong?"

"I'm not."

"But what if you are?"

"I'm not."

"Okay, but," she said, "this is stupid. What makes you so sure she's here? What if she doesn't want to talk to you?"

He leaned forward. Their knees touched. She thought he was going to kiss her but he took the drawing from her and held it next to her face.

She recoiled. "What are you—*stop*."

She leapt up, began pacing in agitation. "Seriously. What's your problem?"

She walked to the window. The glass was cloudy, the world beyond a copy of itself.

He started to speak, quietly, then building steam. *Lake of the Moon.* The links between Prado's life and his own. The manuscript, hidden away, forgotten till he'd rescued it.

He took pages, presented his evidence: the first postmile, another by the highway exit for Swann's Flat Road. The town was never named, but there was a hastily drawn map of the peninsula, along with a doodle of a swan. Nick was confident he was in the right place.

As for the title, *Cathedral,* he admitted that he didn't know what it referred to.

"I do," she said.

His mouth fell open.

She grabbed her satchel. "I'll meet you at the bridge. Tomorrow morning at six."

"We can't go now?"

"It's too far. You have to promise me you won't leave the house before then. You have to stay inside. That's the deal."

"Why? Where are you going?"

"Promise," she demanded.

He promised.

SHE RODE STRAIGHT to Maggie's, found her working in the garden.

"Hello, my lovely."

"I need to talk to you."

"Nice to see you, too."

"Can we go inside, please?"

Maggie's expression turned serious. "Yes. Of course."

They sat at the breakfast table. Maggie poured iced tea. "Fire away."

"I once asked to borrow a book. *Lake of the Moon.* You wouldn't let me. Why?"

"I'm sure I had a good reason."

"What was it?"

"Oh well. I suppose you were too young."

"I came back for it and it was gone. Did you hide it?"

Maggie scoffed. "Shasta."

"Did you?"

"If I did, I don't remember."

"I don't believe you."

"Well, that's your choice."

"I got my own copy. There's nothing terrible in it."

Maggie said nothing.

"Where is it now?" Shasta said. "I want to see it."

"You said you read it."

"I want to see yours."

"What difference does that make?"

Shasta stood up from the table. "I'll find it myself."

"Wait," Maggie said. "Wait, please."

Shasta crossed the house to the exam room, began pawing through cabinets and drawers.

Maggie came to the doorway but made no attempt to intervene. "I wish you'd be patient."

Shasta finished searching and started out. "Excuse me."

Maggie moved aside.

In the office, Shasta discovered the book tucked behind the issues of *JAMA*.

The title page was inscribed.

2 leelee 4 eva
op 5.7.07

"What was she to him?"

Maggie hesitated. "An old friend."

"From Fresno."

Maggie nodded.

"Did she love him?"

"Shasta, I really don't think I should—"

"*Did* she?"

Maggie lowered her head. "Not enough."

EARLY THE NEXT morning Shasta met Nick at the bridge. She stashed the bike by the roadside, handed him a thermos of coffee, switched her cleats for boots.

Just to reach the trailhead they had to hike almost an hour. His pace was aggressive, and she worried he'd tire himself out. But he was full of energy. For the first time in weeks he'd slept well, he said, and it was much easier to move without the pack. He'd hardly put it down since leaving Santa Cruz, using it as a pillow, afraid the manuscript would get stolen.

She asked about his journey. He told her he'd had a car but quickly saw that gas was going to eat up all his money. He sold it and started hitchhiking. It only took him a few days to reach Fort Bragg. From that point traffic died out, and he ended up walking most of the next ninety-odd miles. He didn't mind it. The lulls gave him time to reflect.

"What does your family think?" she asked.

"It's just my mom. She doesn't care."

Then he really got into what his mother was like.

Going to school without lunch because she was too fucked up to buy food. A case of lice that went untreated for a year.

He'd suffered way worse than she had. Shasta felt reluctant to talk about herself in comparison. But he drew her out. When he asked a question it seemed to her that he truly wanted to hear her answer. Was *excited* to hear.

She described Leonie's mood swings. Two bottles of wine a day. Crazy rules: Shasta turned seventeen in a few months and still didn't have her learner's permit.

"She says I can bike everywhere I need to go. The road's too dangerous to drive."

"That sucks."

"Whatever. Next year I can do what I want."

"You should leave now."

She smiled.

"For real," he said. "Just get your shit and go."

"I can't."

"Sure you can. I did. What's the issue? You want to go to college or something?"

"I haven't applied. I haven't really thought about it. Neither of my parents went."

"So?"

"I don't know. I've never been anywhere."

"Uh, yeah. That's the point of leaving."

She laughed.

"You just have to start moving," he said. "It'll make sense."

THEY WALKED AND talked for hours, thoughts overlapping, sentences shingling.

It wasn't like she didn't have friends. She belonged to a homeschooling group that met twice a month, the same kids for years. She chatted online.

But this was different. *He* was different.

Real.

"*Yes,*" he said.

They had stopped for a snack break. The sun was high, Nick's chest glistening as he stood atop a boulder and spread his arms toward the sky.

He howled. Smiled at her.

Shasta smiled and rolled her eyes and crouched down to open her satchel.

"Do you want me to carry that?" he said. "You've had it the whole time."

"It's okay." She turned away to dig through its contents. More snacks, extra water.

A pistol. She wasn't completely naïve.

Unzipping an interior pocket, she took out a snapshot.

Her mother as a younger woman.

She held the photo out to Nick.

He hopped down to look.

When he raised his eyes to her they had a strange, feverish quality.

She nodded to him, and they set out together without speaking.

THEY HELD HANDS at the center of the Cathedral. She could feel the pendant, still warm from the heat of his body, lying against her throat. Above them the sky glimmered like a tossed coin.

He said, "You have to ask her."

Shasta didn't answer.

"He could be your father, too."

She had a father, though. Two. The brooding masculine presence who existed only in pictures; Jason, with his awkward laugh and his bottomless patience. She loved them both and said so to Nick.

She hoped he could see that. She needed him to see that.

He said, "Show me."

FROM THE TRAILHEAD it was ninety minutes to the memorial: the father she'd never known.

The bouquet, California poppies and morning glories, was still healthy; she'd placed it on a ride the previous week. She used her sleeve to dust off the cross, and they stood shoulder to shoulder, surveying the valley like conquerors. They'd been hiking all day. Nick didn't appear tired in the least. For the first time he seemed at ease.

She wasn't. Her insides stewed with conflicting emotions.

Safety and comfort.

Something more.

She could smell the salt dried on his skin.

She brought her face up to his for a kiss.

He shied back, smiling. "Hey."

She mumbled an apology.

"Don't," he said.

Don't what? Apologize? Be mad? Try that again?

She stared at the dirt, humiliated.

"Hey," he said. "Don't worry about it."

"Leave me alone."

"Shasta. Come on."

He reached for her. She yanked free, moved away from him. "Leave me *alone.*"

"Shasta," he said.

He stepped toward her. His ankle wobbled. He grabbed at the cross to steady himself and his foot landed near the edge.

The ground beneath him collapsed.

He vanished.

His cry was faint and short-lived. In the stillness that followed she could hear her own blood.

THE SUN WAS setting as she rang the bell at Maggie's house.

The door opened.

Maggie saw her streaked, swollen face and said, "Oh my darling girl."

She gave Shasta a glass of water, took her upstairs, and helped her into bed.

Shasta sank back into the pillows. She shut her eyes, feeling the mattress sag as Maggie sat by her side. Fingertips gently combed her hair.

"Tell me."

———

SHE TALKED UNTIL the room grew dark. Then she lay still and quiet, listening to the surf crash.

"I was the first person to hold you," Maggie said. "Did you know that?"

Shasta shook her head.

"It's true. I pulled you out and held you before I gave you to your mother. You were so small you fit in my two hands."

Shasta smiled.

"Do you want something to eat?" Maggie asked.

"I'm just tired."

"Get some rest. We'll talk about it in the morning."

"Bowie needs to be walked," Shasta said.

"I'll let them know."

"Tell them I'm sorry."

"Sleep, now."

SHE WOKE LATE, still wearing her soiled hiking clothes, and padded downstairs to the kitchen.

Maggie was at the breakfast table with her mother and Jason.

The three of them stopped talking when she entered. The way they looked reminded her of a word from AP World History: tribunal.

Maggie said, "Good morning, young lady. How are you feeling?"

Jason pulled out a chair. "Please sit, kitten."

Her mother said nothing.

Shasta shuffled to the table.

"You must be starving," Maggie said. "What can I get you?"

"Coffee."

"Coming right up."

"Here," Leonie said, sliding Shasta a plate of toast.

"I'm not hungry," Shasta said.

"You need your strength."

Shasta picked up a piece of toast. It was cold.

Maggie brought a mug. "There you are."

The coffee was lukewarm, too. The three of them had been there awhile. A conclusion had been reached. Jason delivered it.

"It wasn't your fault."

That made her feel worse. Whose fault was it, if not hers? She *wanted* it to be her fault.

"What do I do now?" she said.

"You don't do anything," Leonie said. "We're handling it."

Shasta knew what that meant. They'd do nothing.

She said, "Shouldn't we, I don't know. Call someone?"

"Who would you like to call?" Leonie said.

"I don't know. His mom?"

"Do you have her phone number?"

"No, but . . . The police? Don't they need to know?"

Maggie said, "It's better not to involve them."

"So what," Shasta said. "We can't just . . . Leave him out there."

Jason said, "I'll get the map, and you can show me where he is."

"I'm coming with you," Shasta said.

Maggie and Jason exchanged a look.

"You don't need to do that," Maggie said.

"I want to."

"I think you've gone through quite enough already."

"He's *dead*."

"It was an *accident*," Leonie said.

"No." Shasta buried her face in her hands. "No."

"This is not your fault, kitten," Jason said.

"Don't say that. You don't know that."

"That's what you told Maggie," Leonie said.

"No," Shasta said, shaking her head.

"No? It wasn't an accident? Did you lie to her?"

"I—" Shasta uncovered her face and focused on Maggie. "Why did you tell them that?"

"Because it's the truth," Leonie said, "and beating yourself up won't bring him back."

Maggie said, "The important thing, now, is to protect you."

"I don't want to be protected," Shasta said. "I didn't ask for that."

"The thing is," Jason said, "this affects all of us. Not just you."

"How."

"What?"

"How does it affect you."

Now they were smiling at her, all three of them. Fearful, frozen smiles.

"You've had a terrible day," Leonie said. "Why don't you take a nice hot shower."

"I don't want to take a shower."

"It'll make you feel better."

"I don't want to take a shower, I want you to tell me what's going on."

Jason said, "Kitten—"

"Stop it. All of you. Just stop."

Maggie said, "She deserves to know."

Leonie glared at her.

"It's only a matter of time."

"Shut up," Leonie snapped. To Shasta: "Go take a shower."

"No," Shasta said.

"I'm not asking you. Go."

"No."

Silence.

"Last year," Leonie said, "you wanted a new bike. Do you remember what it cost?"

"I don't know. A lot."

"How much?"

"You don't have to lecture me about money."

Leonie slammed the table. Plates jumped. *"How much."*

"I . . . I don't know."

"Eleven thousand dollars."

"Fine."

"No. Not 'fine.' You want to know? You *deserve* to know? Then close your spoiled brat mouth, and pay attention. Your *bike*," Leonie said, ticking off on her fingers, "your *horses. Bowie.* The *food you eat.* Everything you have, that *we* have, it comes from somewhere."

"Stop, all right? I get it."

"I don't think you do. Our *house.*" Leonie pointed to Maggie. *"Her* house, and everything that *she* has. Everything you see, when you walk outside. It *comes from somewhere.*"

Each word took a bite out of her heart.

"Do you know what a trust is?" Maggie asked.

Shasta shook her head.

"This land belonged to your grandfather. He gave it to your father, who gave it to you. That land is what helps pay for things."

"For *everything,*" Leonie said.

"Right now," Maggie said, "I help make the decisions for you. Until you turn eighteen."

Shasta looked back and forth between them, her mother and the woman who'd first held her. She felt sick, she felt dizzy, her throat had gone dry. "Then what happens."

"You make the decisions," Leonie said.

"It's going to be fine," Maggie said. "You're a smart girl."

Shasta said, "What if I don't want to?"

Nobody answered.

A new and frightening awareness spread through her.

They were afraid. These three adults she'd always relied on.

More than afraid. Terrified.

Of her.

What she might say.

What she might do.

Of her power.

Electricity rippled over her skin.

She looked at Jason. "I'm coming with you."

THE FOLLOWING DAY the two of them drove to Whitethorn Court. Jason parked on the grassy verge, took a shovel from the trunk, and unfolded a topo map, marked with the route and a square quarter-mile area beneath the roadside memorial.

They moved swiftly over the ridge and through the valley. It was a rare windless day, screaming hot.

He said, "Your mom loves you. I know it probably doesn't always feel that way, but she does. And she's had it hard. Take it from me."

Shasta said nothing.

They picked their way along the base of the cliff till Jason drew up short.

A scrap of fabric hung limp from a snapped branch.

"Wait here," he said.

He climbed through brambles; came back shaking his head. "You don't want to."

She pushed past him.

"Shasta. Please don't."

Thorns pricked her hands as she parted the thick, woody stalks and saw it.

The body was in pieces. The face was pulp.

She doubled over and vomited.

Jason laid a hand on her back. "It's okay. You're okay."

They buried him, taking turns with the shovel.

———

SHE STOPPED EATING, stopped training, lost weight.

Leonie wanted her to take an antidepressant. Maggie agreed that it wouldn't hurt.

Every day Shasta put one pill into the toilet. Soon enough Leonie caught her, and from then on she made Shasta swallow in front of her and stick out her tongue.

ONE RAINY NIGHT at dinner, she said, "Is Octavio Prado my father?"

"Why would you think that?" Leonie said.

"Because he loved you," Shasta said.

Her mother killed her wine. "That doesn't mean anything."

BY LATE APRIL, the roads had begun to dry out.

Shasta climbed on her bike and headed for the mountains.

The extended layoff had hurt her conditioning. She started off too fast. She got to the top of the first hill and felt ready to keel over.

You just have to start moving.

She pedaled harder.

Past the cross.

Past the place where she'd first talked to Nick.

Normally she turned around at Blackberry Junction. Leonie didn't like her going farther.

It'll make sense.

Shasta pushed on, legs cramping, back cramping, heart threatening to explode.

She rode all the way to Millburg, stopping at the market to refill her water bottle.

His face was on a poster. In one photo he wore the necklace. Tara's name and contact information were listed.

Shasta started to take a picture.

Then she stopped. What could she possibly say, six months after the fact?

She remembered, too, the stories he'd told her. His crazy, drug-addicted mother.

She put her phone away and rode home.

BY JUNE SHE was nearly back to form. That day she made it to the Junction in an hour twelve—not her best time, but not her worst, either.

On the return trip, it occurred to her that she hadn't thought about Nick for a few days.

Maybe the pills were doing their job.

The song she was listening to ended.

A car was coming in the opposite direction. She couldn't see it yet but she could hear it, up around the bend.

Lately she'd been wondering what it would feel like to die.

Jump off a cliff. Walk into the ocean where the riptides were bad.

Take a gun to the forest; kneel down.

She didn't understand where these thoughts were coming from. Even on her worst nights, right after the accident, when she fantasized about punishment, she never gave herself a death sentence, but a lifetime of remembering.

But she'd stopped remembering, hadn't she?

The car was getting close, its engine straining.

She wouldn't have to *do* anything. Just keep pedaling and let it happen.

Another accident.

She leaned into the curve.

I SAID, "AND there I was."

"I saw your face," she said. "You weren't some monster. Just a guy with a beard. I thought, *How stupid is it? Dying like this?*"

"You swerved."

"Too slow."

"I'm grateful you did."

"Me too."

"I'm sorry you had to go through all of this, Shasta."

"Thanks."

"Thank you for being honest with me. I know it was hard."

She nodded.

"When I first brought you home, your mom was furious with me," I said. "Then she backed off, suddenly. Was that you?"

"I told her I'd go to the cops about Nick if she didn't drop it."

"Thanks for that, too."

"You're welcome," she said.

"Some of the details you shared about the manuscript, like the second milepost—they aren't in the scan that I have, or at least I didn't see them. It would be helpful to take a look at the original. Do you know what happened to it? Is it still at the cottage?"

"I sort of forgot about it, because of everything that was going on. I went to look for it and it was gone. The backpack, too. I guess my mom or Jason took it."

"Would they have destroyed it?"

"Probably. I can ask."

"Let's wait. My priority is speaking to Nick's mom and making sure he gets a proper burial."

"Okay." She paused. "What's she like?"

"Tara? She's had it hard, too."

Shasta said nothing.

"I want to be upfront with you," I said. "Regina and I are probably going to have to inform the authorities about Nick's death."

"Am I in trouble?"

"I can't answer that. If what you told me is true—"

"It is." She faced me. "I swear."

Her eyes did not move from mine.

"What about Maggie?" she said. "Is she in trouble?"

"I don't know, Shasta."

She nodded. Accepting punishment out of force of habit.

WE REACHED WHITETHORN Court.

Shasta took off the necklace. The pendant swung as she offered it to me. "Give it to Tara?"

I put the necklace in my pocket.

"I'm sorry it's not the original chain," she said.

"I think it's all right."

She knelt to unlace her boots.

I asked, "You want a lift home?"

"I'm good."

"Okay. Good luck, Shasta."

"Can I ask you something?" she said. "Is Regina really your wife?"

I laughed. "No."

"Thank God." She kicked off the boot, worked her foot into a cleat. "You guys make a terrible couple."

CHAPTER 41

Quarter past three. Beau and Regina would have long finished their hike. Emil would be back from Eureka. They would be sitting around, wondering where I was.

I saw no reason to linger now that we knew the truth about Nick.

The bell jangled as I entered the hotel.

DJ Pelman looked over from his barstool.

"Hey," I said.

His lips parted.

Jenelle Counts called from the kitchen: "Hello?"

"Just me," I said.

I took the stairs three at a time, packed up Regina's stuff and mine, returned to the main floor with bags in hand. Jenelle was behind the bar.

"You're leaving?"

"'Fraid so."

She tilted her head. "Something wrong?"

"Not at all, we just need to get rolling." I laid the room key on the counter and tugged out my wallet. "Six hundred?"

She didn't answer right away. "Don't worry about it."

"You're sure."

"On the house."

"Thank you." I turned to DJ. "My apologies to the chicken."

He stared blankly. "What?"

"The chicken you killed. For dinner."

"Oh . . . Yeah. Yeah, it's all good." Weak smile. "Rain check."

"Say goodbye to your wife for me," Jenelle said.

I grabbed the bags. "Will do."

I PULLED UP to the Bergstroms'.

The Range Rover wasn't in the driveway.

The front door opened. Emil appeared on the porch.

He took off his hat and began waving it at me.

Q: *What do you do if you feel unsafe?*

A: *I leave.*

But I couldn't. Not without Regina.

I got out of the Jeep and started up the front walk.

Emil stood with his hips thrust forward, fingers hooked through his belt loops. He was sporting a Canadian tuxedo: denim jacket one shade lighter than his jeans. The belt buckle winked.

He grinned. "The man of the hour."

"They're not back yet?"

"Looks that way. I thought you were with them."

"I stayed behind. My knee's acting up."

"Sorry to hear it. Got just the remedy for that. Come on in."

I followed him to the hyper-masculine living room. He selected a bottle from the bar cart.

"Scotch, neat."

"You remember."

"The old bean's still good for a few things." He poured for me, fixed himself a bourbon. "Take a load off."

We sat opposite each other, him in an easy chair and me on the sofa.

"Slainte," he said, raising his drink.

As I brought the scotch to my lips, I saw him observing me over the rim of his glass, this jolly avuncular figure, focused not on his drink but on mine, his eyes bright and expectant.

My own focus shifted. Sharpened.

I laid the tumbler aside. "You know what, I'll hold off so we can all celebrate together."

"That's the spirit," Emil said. "Anything else, while you wait? Lemonade?"

"I'm good, thanks."

"How was your day?"

"Quiet. How was Eureka?"

"Intolerable," he said. "Makes me twice as grateful to get home."

"I appreciate your flexibility."

"You've got Beau to thank for that. He's taken a real shine to you."

"It's mutual."

"Too bad about your knee. May I ask what happened?"

"Old tennis injury."

"Huh. You're such a tall guy. I would have guessed basketball."

A new smile split his meaty face.

"Must be tough to find the time to play," he said. "Extra tough if you're holding down a second job."

"How's that?"

"Private equity," he said, "and private investigation. Hard work. Time consuming. What's your hourly rate, Clay Edison?"

I said, "Too high, apparently."

He roared with laughter. "I respect a man doesn't take himself too serious."

"Where'd I screw up?"

"Talked to Kathleen."

"Interesting," I said. "She made it sound like there was no love lost between you two."

"Me and her, no. But a mama's heart is true. You threaten her baby, out come the claws."

He shot his bourbon, set it down. "Well, look, friend. We have a nice, peaceful community, and we intend to keep it that way."

I stood. "I'll get out of your hair, then."

"We're not done."

"I am."

"Sit your ass down," he said.

A shape slid into the kitchen doorway; I turned, reaching into my shirt for the P365, and found myself confronting a shotgun-wielding Dave Pelman.

"Hands," he said.

My fingertips brushed the grip.

I might be able to draw and squeeze off a shot.

I might get tangled up in fabric.

The outcome hinged on how quickly I moved, how accurate he was, what was chambered in the shotgun.

A deer slug: Hit or miss.

Buckshot: Didn't much matter.

Too many unknowns.

"Hands," Pelman repeated.

"I'd do as the man says," Emil said.

I withdrew my hand from my shirt.

They had me lie on my stomach and lace my fingers behind my head. Pelman trained the shotgun on me while Emil knelt on my back and zip-tied my wrists.

"I think there's been a misunderstanding," I said.

"Terrific," Emil said. He rolled me over and confiscated the P365, along with my phone and keys. "I look forward to getting that cleared right up."

———

THEY FORCED ME outside and into the Jeep's cargo hold. Pelman climbed in the back seat, leaned over, and pressed the shotgun to my scar.

A door slammed. The engine started. We began to move.

Curled up against the luggage, I could see a sliver of sky, treetops swaying.

I felt behind me for the zipper of Regina's bag.

Maybe I could get my hands on something sharp. A nail clipper. Tweezers.

The edge of the shotgun barrel bit into my flesh.

Pelman said, "Uh-uh."

After about ten minutes the Jeep pulled over.

The cargo hatch opened.

Emil waved me out with the P365.

We were on a narrow street, parked opposite a wooden house. Beau's Range Rover sat at the curb. I couldn't see a street sign, but the tow truck in the driveway told me it was Dave Pelman's residence and garage. Gray Fox Run, somewhere in the southern half of the peninsula.

The adjacent lots were pure forest. The house itself was largish but crude, patched with raw lumber. Chain link enclosed a sodden brown lawn. A pair of squeaking weather vanes bickered. Rooster versus winged pig.

Pelman prodded me toward the driveway.

I moved through the trembling shadows of pines.

To the rear sprawled acres of junkyard: dirt piled with hubcaps, hoses, tires, rusted-out frames and panels, scrap, perforated canisters of motor oil and coolant and paint, gasoline in five-gallon jugs. Rainbow slicks floated on mud. A pathway made of pallets brought us to a swaybacked barn.

Emil hauled the door wide. Darkness yawned.

I paused on the threshold, breathing grease and solvent.

A jab to the spine sent me stumbling.

Blades of light leaked through gaps in the siding. More trash heaped in the dank corners. I passed beneath low-hanging rafters. Nailed to them, like hunting trophies, were license plates from California and a dozen other states. I wondered which belonged to Octavio Prado.

At the far end of the barn, Regina sat in a steel folding chair. Her wrists were duct-taped to the frame, her ankles to the legs. There was a cut above her left eye. Dried blood ran from one nostril and over her lips. She was shirtless, shivering, although they'd let her keep her bra and covered her shoulders with a filthy towel.

Her pink gun purse hung on a wall hook among an array of hand tools.

Beau occupied a second folding chair. He smiled. "Look who decided to join us."

He got up. His S&W500, the bear stopper, was holstered on his belt.

Rush him. Head-butt him.

And then what?

My hands were tied.

He put me in the open chair and duct-taped my ankles to it.

"Listen up," he said. "I'm gonna undo your hands. Take off your shirt and vest and throw them on the ground. If you make a move, if you do anything I don't like, Dave'll shoot her in the head. Then I'll break your fingers, one by one, and shoot you. Are we on the same page?"

"Yes."

"Terrific."

He took down a pair of tin snips, circled behind me, giving me a wide berth.

Grab the tool.

Grab his gun.

Emil and Pelman were out of reach, triangulating with firearms. Regina was immobilized.

I was strapped to the chair.

The only weapons we had were our tongues.

Beau cut the zip-tie and stood back. "Go on."

I opened the magnetic shirtfront. "You're not even going to buy me dinner?"

Once I was bare-chested, he taped my arms to the chair and assumed his place at his father's side. Dave Pelman, faithful servant, stood in readiness with the shotgun.

Emil said, "Now, where were we? Oh yeah: You were going to clear up a misunderstanding. Go ahead, Clay Edison. Enlighten me."

"It's strictly business," I said. "We're just here for due diligence."

"Pretty darn diligent, sending two of you," he said. "Expensive. Who is this person, with money to burn? I'd love to meet him."

I resisted the urge to look at Regina. I didn't know what she'd told them.

"Here's how I see it," Emil said. "You show up outta nowhere, peddling some bullshit about land. You go around, asking all kinds of questions, from all kinds of folks. Now you're back again."

He removed his hat, scratched his pate. "I don't want to be cynical, Clay. But it feels to me like it might be more than strictly business. Son? Care to illustrate?"

Beau unfolded a sheet of paper and displayed it.

Rows of typed characters: upper and lowercase letters, numerals, and punctuation marks. She'd covered the whole keyboard, plus an additional three lines for direct comparison.

My pride and joy throw it in the fire.
Dont try to find me good bye
—0

"I don't know what that is," I said.

"Why don't you ask your little gal pal?" Emil said. He gestured to the purse. "It was in her pocketbook."

Regina remained expressionless.

"You shoulda gotten rid of that contraption years ago," Emil said to Beau.

"You're right, Pops. I'm sorry."

"Live and learn." Emil sighed and replaced his hat. "I must admit, Clay, this pattern of dishonesty wounds me deeply."

"Funny," I said. "I met a whole bunch of folks who feel the same way about you."

"Ah. Now we're getting somewhere. Which of those individuals do I have to thank for the gift of you?"

"Bill Arenhold."

It felt good to see Emil struck dumb, however briefly.

"My word. There's a name I haven't heard in a while. How's he doing?"

"Not great. I'm pretty sure you knew that, though."

"Be fair, now. You can't blame me for everything. Billy was a loser and he took the loser's way out."

"He couldn't have been that bad. He helped you find this place."

"Any idiot can pick up a pencil," Emil said. "Only one Picasso."

"What about Kurt Swann? Also an idiot?"

"Inbred moron." Probably without realizing it, he glanced at Pelman. "Greedy, too."

"Must be exhausting, having to deal with so much incompetence."

"It's a plague," Emil said.

"We spoke to the sheriff," I said. "If we don't check in with him by tomorrow morning, he's going to come looking for us."

"I reckon you'd better think fast, then."

"About what?"

"Coming clean. We'll give you a little respite to consider."

He and Beau started out, leaving Pelman as sentry.

Regina lifted her head. "Hey, Beau."

He turned back.

"You should really call your mom more," she said. "She misses you."

A change washed over him, smile twisting, shoulders bunched.

He strode toward us.

"Son," Emil said.

Beau grabbed Pelman's shotgun by the barrel.

"No," I yelled. *"No no no."*

He wound up the weapon like a baseball bat and swung, crushing the butt of the gun into Regina's midsection.

Audible crack.

She gasped and jackknifed. The chair tipped forward. She landed on her face and rolled sideways and vomited in the dirt.

Beau handed Pelman the shotgun and left with his father.

The door rumbled shut.

"Regina," I said.

She retched and heaved. The towel had fallen off, exposing her.

I began scooting my chair toward her.

Pelman said, "Uh-uh."

"Then pick her up."

He said nothing.

"Asshole. Pick her up."

"Shut your mouth."

It took a while for Regina's breathing to calm. She tried to rock herself to a sitting position but couldn't manage it and lay still.

"Sorry about the typewriter." She spat blood. "Live and learn."

SILENCE AMPLIFIED ALL the small sounds: pinecones knocking on the roof, the creak of the chairs as we twisted against our bonds.

Dave Pelman squatted on a milk crate and sucked at his teeth.

"It doesn't matter what we tell them," Regina said. "They have to kill us."

"Hush," Pelman said.

She wriggled around to face him. A huge purple bruise tattooed her flank. "You really think they won't sell you out to the cops? They're using you. Again."

He didn't respond.

"There's two of them," she said. "One of you. Their word against yours."

He cricked his neck.

"How many promises has Emil made you, over the years? How many has he kept?"

Pelman propped the shotgun against the wall, approached Regina, and leaned down, his face inches from hers.

"Hush," he whispered.

He returned to the crate and picked up his gun.

THE BARN DOOR rumbled open.

Beau went to Regina and roughly set her chair upright.

Emil said, "Time's up. Have we come to our senses?"

"What do you want to know?" I asked.

"Start with who's footing your bill."

"Start with go fuck yourself," Regina said.

"Right," Emil said. "I can see you still need some convincing. David? Ladies first."

Pelman aimed the shotgun at her.

He paused. Lowered the gun.

"David," Emil said. "Is there a problem?"

"Not in here," Pelman said. "I don't want the mess."

Emil gave a forbearing smile. "Let's be quick about it, please."

Beau cut us from the chairs, starting with our legs. He duct-taped Regina's left ankle to my right, then moved on to our arms, which he bound behind our backs and joined at the wrists.

Cumbersome process, a hint of farce. Emil's smile grew progressively testier.

My lot in life: abiding idiots!

Finally we were ready to go. Beau gripped me by the biceps and put the S&W to my temple. Emil held on to Regina, the SIG Sauer in her ear. Pelman brought up the rear, goading us with the shotgun.

They marched us out to the junkyard.

Emil said, "Where's going to make you happy, David?"

Pelman pointed to the forest backing his property.

We started through the trees, the five of us in tight formation. The difference between Regina's stride length and mine had us tripping over each other.

I tugged at her wrists.

She glanced at me sidelong.

I tugged again, twice.

She blinked rapidly, her jaw pulsed. She didn't understand. What did I want?

Make a break for it?

To the left?

Before I could try again, Pelman said, "Okay."

He drove the butt of the shotgun into the soft tissue behind my knee. Pain tore through the joint. It caved, and I sank down in the mud, taking Regina with me.

"Last chance," Emil said.

Pelman leveled the shotgun at Regina. His finger tensed on the trigger.

A bright-green dot freckled his nose.

His face exploded.

CHAPTER 42

Stage set slaughterhouse:

Bone and blood and brain, misted like a winter's day breath; the shotgun arcing skyward, tethered to the dead man by his finger through the trigger guard.

Regina, head averted, eyes clenched.

Beau Bergstrom cowering in the muck; his father, rigid with disbelief, mustache bristling, arms outstretched to ward off the assault, SIG Sauer flung from his grasp and hovering in midair.

Then everything was moving.

Emil's pistol hit the ground, followed by Pelman's body. The impact set off the shotgun and blew a hole harmlessly through a patch of dogwood as songbirds and squirrels and raccoons erupted from the underbrush and took flight amid a cascade of white blossoms.

Beau rose up, firing wildly at the unknown, five earsplitting booms. The front of his jeans was soaked.

Emil turned and fled.

"Dad," Beau yelled.

A bullet caught his left shoulder and dropped him.

"*Dad.*" He kicked his heels, propelling himself backward, trying to return fire. But he'd spent the revolver's capacity; it hammered loudly on the empty chambers. "*Wait.*"

He scrambled to his feet and crashed off into the brush right as a third shot plugged into the mud and sent up a splash.

Seventy yards away, Al Bock leaned out from behind a stout tree trunk, began darting from blind to blind.

I yelled, "Clear."

He hustled toward us. Over his T-shirt and jeans shirt he'd added camouflage body armor and a matching cap. "Are you hurt?"

"No," Regina said. "Hurry."

He freed us with his hunting knife. I grabbed the SIG Sauer, Regina took the shotgun, and the three of us ran through the woods, skirting a junkyard ambush, spilling into the street.

Emil rocketed past in the Range Rover.

Regina raised the shotgun and blew out his rear window.

He sheered, fishtailed, accelerated away.

"Dad."

Beau stumbled onto the front lawn, clutching his bleeding shoulder, right in time to see his father escape around the block.

Regina swung the shotgun toward him. "Stop, motherfucker."

He spun and ran up the driveway.

"Get Emil," Regina said and took off after Beau.

Al glanced at me, then followed her.

EMIL STILL HAD my keys, including the one for the Jeep. All that was left was Pelman's tow truck. I sprinted to it.

The door was unlocked. Keys in the ignition.

It was that kind of town.

I backed into the street and floored it.

The truck was sluggish, and Emil had a two-minute head start. I didn't know exactly where I was, either, or where he would go. But I had the mountains to orient me and sufficient knowledge of his character to believe he would act to save himself, above all.

I drove toward the entry road.

At the town boundary I crossed the bridge. The paving ended.

Fresh tire tracks sliced uphill through the mud.

One mile on I'd had no further sign of him, and I began to think I should turn back, get to a phone, and call the sheriff.

Then I saw him.

He was driving prudently in deference to the slippery conditions. Through the shot-out rear window I glimpsed the brim of his Stetson like a dark halo.

He checked over his shoulder but didn't speed up. He had the advantage and he knew it.

We passed the spot where I'd hit Shasta; passed the memorial; took the hairpin at five miles per hour.

At the next flat patch his back tires spun and he lurched ahead.

I leaned over the wheel, urging the truck on, sweat coursing down my bare torso.

The gap between us widened.

He disappeared around a blind curve.

An instant later I heard a massive crash.

I braked hard, slewing to a standstill with my bumper kissing oblivion.

Silence.

Gun drawn, I slipped from the truck, advanced.

A faint hiss became audible.

I cleared the curve.

An incense cedar lay in the road. It had toppled diagonally to expose its rotted root system. Emil had jerked the wheel, but there was nowhere to go, and in trying to avoid the tree he'd plowed into it head-on. I could see his listing silhouette. Metal ticked.

"Put your hands on the dash," I yelled.

No response.

I orbited in, crunching over glass pebbles.

A branch—eight inches in diameter, still attached to the trunk—had pierced the windshield.

I kept the gun up and opened the driver's door.

The branch was about twelve feet long. It had been violently shorn of bark, filling the vehicle with the smell of gasoline and pencil shavings. The jagged, broken tip had speared Emil through the abdomen, pinning him to the seat before bursting out the other side.

He sat in a pool of blood, chin to chest, breathing fast and shallow. Blood sprayed the dash and the instrument panel. The ceiling dripped with it. Bits of foam and upholstery blanketed the rear seats. The blood-spattered Stetson was overturned in the footwell.

"Emil."

He didn't answer. I wasn't sure he'd heard me.

I said, "Your turn to come clean."

His chest stopped moving.

I said, "You abandoned your son. Twice. The last memory of you he's going to have is you running away and leaving him to die. Now he knows what I know, and what everyone else who's ever met you knows: You're a coward and a loser."

His mouth opened as if to speak. A bubble of blood welled out.

It popped.

He slumped.

I touched his neck. Nothing.

I used a twig to recover my possessions from his jacket pockets, mindful not to get blood on my hands.

BACK AT GRAY Fox Run, Al Bock leaned against the Jeep, rifle on his shoulder.

I jumped from the tow truck. "Is she okay?"

"In the barn."

I limped up the driveway to the junkyard. My knee throbbed. I'd been suppressing the pain; now it was surfacing, with a vengeance.

The barn door was ajar. Regina sat on a folding chair. The shotgun rested on her lap and she was gazing down at Beau Bergstrom's body.

His chin jutted toward the rafters. Blood saturated the dirt. The entry wound in his chest dwarfed the rifle wound in his shoulder. Definitely a deer slug.

"Emil?" she said.

"Dead."

"Terrific."

She stood, grabbed her purse off the wall, and walked out.

CHAPTER 43

A
l had come on foot. We took the Jeep to his house on Black
Sand Court. Along the way, I described the crash.

"The road's blocked."

"I'll have a look," Al said. "Other business first."

I pulled into the cul-de-sac.

"Stay put," he said.

While he was gone Regina and I got clean shirts from the trunk
and dry-swallowed ibuprofen. I brought her up to speed on Nick.

"Poor kid," she said.

The gate opened. Al beckoned to us.

INSIDE THE A-FRAME, DJ Pelman was bent over at the eating table,
doughy face in his hands. Jenelle Counts sat beside him, rubbing
his back and murmuring to him like he was a child of five rather
than a man in his thirties.

Bock brought chairs for Regina and me but remained standing
with King Kong at his heel.

"Son," he said gently.

DJ uncovered his face. His eyes were bloodshot.

Bock said, "Not gonna wiffle and waffle. I'm responsible for
your dad being dead. Not these two. You got no quarrel with
them. You're mad, be mad at me. But there was no choice. He was

about to slaughter the innocent and after that they'da probably slaughtered him. Got it?"

Silence.

"You understand me, DJ?"

Jenelle said, "He does."

"Be nice to hear it from him."

DJ said, "Yeah."

Bock turned to us. "You also need to know something. You're alive *'cause* of DJ. He told his mom what Beau was up to and she told me. So you got them to thank."

"Thank you," I said.

Regina said nothing. I wondered what Beau had done to her. If DJ had participated, prior to his attack of conscience.

Bock said, "Anybody feels the need to get something off their chest, now's the time. Otherwise we'll put a fork in it and move on."

I said, "I have some questions for DJ."

He reacted with surprise to his own name. "Uh. Okay."

"Octavio Prado."

"Who?"

Regina said, "The writer."

"Oh," he said.

"You don't have to talk to them," Jenelle said.

"No," DJ said. "It's . . . It's okay."

"You didn't do anything wrong, baby."

"Mom. It's okay." He licked his lips. "What about him."

"Everything you know," Regina said. "From the beginning."

"Um . . . yeah. So . . . so, Beau heard from his dad about this guy come to town. He wanted to go meet him."

"Why?"

"He thought it was neat. He never met a real writer. The guy . . . Shit. What's his name?"

"Prado."

"Prado," he repeated, as if studying for a final exam. "He had a house he was renting. We went over, and he let us in. Beau was asking him questions. Like, where do you get ideas?"

"Did Prado tell you why he was in Swann's Flat?" I asked.

"He said he was looking for God." DJ shook his head. "That, I remember 'cause it was a pretty weird thing to say, you know?"

"Sure," I said. "Did you see a manuscript?"

"A what?"

"Loose pages," Regina said.

"Oh. Yeah. That. Yeah, he showed it to us. Like this shitload of paper. I thought it looked stupid but Beau thought it was the greatest thing ever. He was *real* excited. Went home and started writing his own story. He was working on it for a while, then me and him brought it over to . . . To *Prado*. This time he didn't look so friendly, you know? He goes, 'I have to work, leave it and I'll get to it in a few days.' He was sort of blocking the doorway, so we couldn't see in. But you could tell there was someone else in there with him. Beau told me, 'Go around and look through the window.' I go and it's Leonie Swann."

"What were she and Prado doing?"

"You mean . . . doing *it*? Uh-uh. Nothing like that. Just sitting on the floor, talking."

"What was the mood?"

"Huh?"

"Were they happy? Sad? Angry."

"I mean," he said. "I dunno. I just ran out of there. I didn't want to get caught."

"All right," I said. "What happened next?"

"Beau went to ask Prado about his story. He was happy 'cause Prado liked it. After that he started visiting him a couple times a week, bringing him things to read."

"Did you go, too?"

"Not usually. It was boring. I didn't have nothing to say, and the two of them together was . . ." DJ interlaced his fingers. "I mean, he's a lot smarter than me, Beau is."

Jenelle said, "Beau used to make fun of him. Telling him he's dumb, he'll work for him one day like Dave worked for his daddy."

DJ colored.

Jenelle patted his arm. "You got nothing to be ashamed of, baby."

"Whatever, it's . . . I don't care."

I said, "Did you ever see Prado and Leonie together again?"

"Just the once," DJ said.

"Kurt was jealous of him," Jenelle said.

"Prado?" I asked.

She nodded.

"You know that how?" Regina asked.

"I saw it myself. He was having dinner at the hotel. Kurt busts in, grabs him off the stool. 'Stay away from my wife.' He threw him out on his ass and told him to get gone. Then he told me I'm not allowed to rent him a room."

"That's when Prado went to you," Regina said to Al.

He said, "I suppose so."

I said, "But you didn't know about him and Leonie. Or the incident with Kurt."

"No, sir."

I turned to Jenelle. "And you didn't tell Al about what you'd witnessed."

She shifted uncomfortably. "We weren't together then."

"All right, DJ. Let's keep going. Beau and Prado are spending time together."

"Yeah."

"Did something change?"

"I mean." His knee was jogging rapidly. "Sort of."

"He was just a kid," Jenelle said.

Regina and I let the silence stretch.

"Okay, so what it was," DJ said. "Me and Beau, we're hanging out at the garage. Prado rolls up, asks to buy some gas. He's leaving town. Beau's all, 'You can't leave,' and Prado says he has to, they won't let him stay no more."

" 'They' meaning Kurt," Regina said.

"I dunno. I guess. Beau's like, 'Lemme talk to my dad, he'll fix it.' The guy got scared. 'No no, don't do that.' It started off like that, but pretty soon it got out of hand. He's like, 'Gimme the fucking gas,' and Beau's all, 'Don't sell it to him.' They're yelling at each other. Then Prado, he goes, 'Fuck you, you're a needy little bitch, you suck, your stories suck.' Beau heard that, he just . . ." DJ shuddered. "Snapped. He grabbed a, a wrench, and . . ."

He trailed off.

"You see?" Jenelle said. "I told you it wasn't his fault."

"My dad heard them fighting," DJ said. "He comes out, sees the guy lying there with his head bashed in. He phones Emil to come over. When he got there, Beau tells them he didn't mean to kill the guy, it was an accident. Emil said, 'You oughta be more careful.' But he was looking at me when he said it. Like it was me done it, not Beau."

"What happened with the body?" I asked.

"My dad took it out on the boat and threw it in the ocean. He had me clean out the guy's car. Took forever, it was so full of shit. I had to keep emptying the burn barrel."

"And the manuscript?"

"I didn't get to it yet before Beau turns up, asking what did I do with it. I told him it's in the trunk. He had me take it to the post office and mail it."

"How did he know where to send it?"

"There was like a little book in the car, with addresses and stuff. Beau kept it after he killed him. Like a souvenir."

"Did he tell you why he wanted to send in the manuscript?"

"He said it's a good book, people deserve to read it. I brought it with me next time I went to pick up the mail. Then, like a week later, he started freaking out. He was worried they'd find him and he'd get arrested. He told me drive back and get it from them. The lady told me sorry, too late. So I went home. But Beau was antsy as hell for a long time."

"Waiting for the cops to show up."

DJ nodded. "His dad musta noticed. He sat Beau down and started asking him questions till he blabbed. Emil had him write a letter, pretending to be the guy, so they'd think he wasn't here no more. I guess it worked, you know? 'Cause they never came."

He sat back. "That's the only time I know of Emil hit him. When he made Beau write that letter."

"Not after killing Prado," I said.

"Nah. That didn't bother him. But after the mail thing, he gave Beau a black eye. Broke his tooth, too. Beau was like, 'I'm gonna kill that motherfucker.'" Faint smile. "I told him, 'You get used to it.'"

Jenelle bit her lip. DJ looked at her.

"Aw, it's all right," he said.

"I'm sorry, baby."

"Mom. Don't. Hey. Hey. It's all right."

He drew her into his arms, shushing her as she wept quietly.

Al Bock turned to me and Regina. "Let's get up there before we lose the light."

CHAPTER 44

We caravanned out to the crash site.

While Al examined the tree, Regina stared at Emil's skewered body. The first blowflies had arrived, congregating around his mouth and nostrils. The bloodstains on his clothes, the upholstery, and the ceiling were dry, though the pool surrounding him remained semi-viscous, clumping up and losing its shine.

She tilted her head back, breathing deeply to control her nausea.

"Remind me how long you were a coroner," she said.

"Thirteen years."

"Ever seen anything like this?"

"No."

"Well," she said. "First time for everything."

Al rendered his verdict: No way could we open the road before dark.

"You can stay with me tonight," he said. "We'll come back at dawn. Either of you know how to work a chain saw?"

I said, "I've cleared brush."

"Mm. We'll get it done. Now let's see to whatever hurt the two of you have."

———

MAGGIE PENROSE ANSWERED her door and started. The three of us made a motley sight—dirty and bloody and mismatched.

I said, "I need to borrow your phone."

Al said, "And she needs to be looked at."

"Nice to meet you, Doc," Regina said. "My ribs are broken."

Maggie said, "Come in."

She wasn't alone. Leonie and Jason Clancy sat on the living room sofa.

The tribunal. Best guess, the topic was Nick Moore and damage control.

Regina said, "How's everyone's day going?"

"Please," Maggie said, showing her toward the exam room.

I said to Al, "Fill them in?"

"Yes, sir."

I hobbled to the office.

AMY SAID, "I was starting to worry."

In the background was the benign tumult of an ordinary evening at the Edison household. Running water, Charlotte narrating loudly, Myles babbling along to *Cocomelon*.

"I'm okay," I said. "Can you find some privacy?"

"One second . . . Mom? Take over, please?"

I heard her mother's voice say, "Is everything all right?"

"Absolutely fine, just gimme a sec."

A door shut. The background noise cut out.

"What's going on," she said.

By the time I finished she was crying.

She said, "I don't know if I can take this anymore."

"I'm sorry, Amy."

She let out a shaky breath. "Is Regina okay?"

"Probably broken ribs. The doctor's checking her out."

"I can't believe this is happening again."

Again.

"I'll be safe till the morning," I said. "I'll leave once the road's clear and call as soon as I get service."

"We're not done talking about this."

"I know. Is there anything else you want me to do, right now?"

"Just be careful. If you really can."

"I can. I will."

"Fine," she said and hung up.

I dropped the phone in its cradle. My head ached, my knee ached, my heart pumped broken glass.

THE MOOD IN the living room had changed.

Maggie and Jason perched on the sofa like guilty schoolkids. Al Bock stood at attention. Regina had a bandage over her eye and was sitting at the bottom of the spiral staircase, an ice pack pressed to her side.

Leonie paced by the ocean-view windows, buzzing with feral energy.

"What the hell are we supposed to do now?" she said.

Spiky clarity in her voice. I hadn't heard it before.

She was sober.

"Those fuckers," she said, pointing to nowhere, "took care of *everything.*"

"Times change," Regina said.

Maggie said, "Just so you know, we didn't create this situation. Kurt did."

"You accepted it," I said. "You kept it going."

"For *Shasta,*" Leonie shouted.

"*Grow up,*" Regina yelled, twice as loud.

Leonie froze, startled.

Out over the water, gulls circled and screamed.

I said, "Where's the manuscript?"

Leonie crossed her arms and gave me her back.

"Jason?" I said.

"Uh." He glanced at his wife's impassive form. "Our place."

"I'll take it, please."

He nodded. Heaving up from the couch, he started for the door.

"Lee," he said. "You coming?"

Leonie didn't answer.

I said, "She's eighteen soon. It'll be out of your hands."

Leonie snorted. "It's never been in my hands."

IN THE CAR, Regina said, "What did you tell Amy?"

"The truth."

"Interesting choice."

WE WAITED IN the Clancys' driveway for Jason to carry out a cardboard box marked HAY & DEW VINEYARDS.

He set it gingerly in the Jeep's cargo hold. I opened the flaps on a deep stack of yellowed paper. The cover page was scrawled in pencil.

cathedral

a novel?

octavio prado

Feeling the presence of another person I looked toward the house.

Shasta was watching from an upstairs window.

She waved.

I waved back. So did Regina.

Jason frowned. He shook his head at Shasta, as if to shoo her away. But she stayed put, arms folded resolutely over her chest, just like her mother.

DINNER CHEZ BOCK was venison stew, cooked up with canned beans and homegrown vegetables. Al hovered by the stove, tending the pot and slipping meat scraps to King Kong. Regina took fresh clothes and went to use the outdoor shower. I sat at the table with the manuscript.

A yelp from outside: "*Fahhaaack* that's cold."

Bock smiled to himself.

As I turned pages, I noticed a significant difference from the PDF Eli Ruíz had sent me. The electronic version consisted of around nineteen hundred sheets. The paper original was far longer. Twice as long, in fact.

Whoever had made the scan had copied the fronts.

And skipped the backs.

One cheer for the UC Merced Work Study program.

Regina stumbled inside, hair wet, a bundle of dirty clothes under one arm. "That sucked."

"Improves circulation," Bock said.

"Fuck circulation."

He chuckled. "Stew still needs some time," he said to me, "if you want to give it a go."

I replaced the manuscript in the box and took clothes from my bag.

Regina padded to the kitchenette. Hooking a strand of hair over her ear, she leaned in for a sniff. "Tell me that's dairy-free."

THE NEXT MORNING Al was gone before we were awake. He'd taken King Kong and left a note instructing us to meet him at the crash site.

We loaded the Jeep and drove out.

Pink light streaked the hills like an infection. The warming earth steamed.

As we drew close I heard saws buzzing.

The tow truck rested on the shoulder, light bar flashing. Behind it tilted the Range Rover. The fatal branch was sawn flush with the windshield. Condensation blurred the side windows; a fly tornado filled the interior.

King Kong chased squirrels through the trees.

Al had made good progress on the fallen cedar, opening a three-foot gap.

It helped that he'd brought help.

Regina said, "Are you fucking kidding me."

A sweat-soaked DJ Pelman stood atop the trunk, wielding a giant Stihl.

He saw us and killed the motor.

Al did the same. He tugged out his earplugs and approached.

Regina and I both got out.

She took her gun purse and walked off in the other direction without a word.

He shook my hand, watched her go. "Morning."

"Morning. You guys work fast."

"Yes, sir. I think we'll be done by nine, give or take."

"Can I do anything?"

He mopped his brow. "Only brought the two saws."

I FOUND REGINA a hundred feet down the road, sitting on a log.

"The fuck is that dumb asshole doing here?" she said.

Personally, I thought it was a smart move. Get DJ involved; give him a job; defuse the anger through partnership and physical labor. But Regina didn't look like she was in the mood for strategic nuance.

She felt for the purse at her side.

Jammed her hand into the gun pocket and left it there.

The saws roared to life.

TWO AND A half hours later the gap was wide enough to squeeze the Jeep through under Al's guidance.

I lowered the window. "Thank you, Sergeant."

"Take care of yourself."

DJ stood a ways off. Sawdust dyed his skin and hair orange.

"Thanks," I called.

He gave a shallow nod.

"You'll keep an eye on him for me," I said to Al.

"Yes, sir."

Regina got out to hug Al and rub King Kong on the belly. Throwing one sharp glance at DJ—he didn't react—she returned to the passenger seat.

"Drive," she said.

A MILE OUTSIDE Millburg I got reception.

Amy answered on the first ring: "Are you okay?"

"Yes. We're out of there."

"Thank God. When will you be home?"

"In time for dinner, hopefully. I'll text you if that changes."

Regina said, "What are you making?"

Amy laughed. "Peanut noodles."

"Great," Regina said. "Set a place for me."

WE STOPPED AT the 76 for gas, drove to Fanny's Market.

Before heading inside for coffee and provisions, Regina stepped to the bulletin board to untack Nick Moore's flyer.

The screen door opened, and Sergeant Mike Gallo exited holding a bag of Funyuns and a travel mug emblazoned with the Humboldt Sheriff's seal.

He smiled at me from beneath a cream-colored Stetson. "I see you two made it out alive."

Regina turned, flyer in hand.

Gallo's gaze lingered on her bandaged eye. His smile faded.

"How much shit did you stir up?" he said.

"Nothing they can't handle themselves," I said.

A beat. Gallo nodded. He touched the brim of his hat. "Drive safe."

FOUR

Tara Moore sat on her living room sofa, rubbing the surface of the pendant.

"He was happy," she said. "With her."

She looked up at us. Grief had softened her face, her voice.

"Yes," Regina said. "He was."

"And it's a pretty spot she chose."

"Beautiful," I said.

"Do you have pictures? Can I see it?"

I said, "Once we sort everything out, we'll send you some."

"Maybe I could go visit, sometime," Tara said. "I'd like to meet her. I think that would be nice. Don't you think it'd be nice?"

Regina nodded.

Tara said, "I think it would."

She crushed the pendant to her chest, folded over with a moan.

Regina got down on the dusty carpet and held her as she sobbed.

ROY TRUJILLO, IN his office at UC Merced library, let out a low whistle. "Holy Moses."

The manuscript was stacked up on his desk—all three thousand, eight hundred forty-six handwritten pages of it.

He pressed his palms together. "Appreciate you, friends."

"Any chance we can get reimbursed for our expenses?" Regina asked.

Trujillo smiled regretfully. "Not sure we have room in the budget for that."

REGINA AND I said our goodbyes in the parking lot.

"It's been real," she said.

"Real what?"

"I'll let you fill in the blank, Poirot."

EN ROUTE TO San Leandro, I phoned Chris Villareal.

"Hey, Clay. Good to hear from you. How's it going?"

"They won't be cheating anyone again."

The line went quiet.

He said, "Do I want to know?"

"Sorry," I said. "You're breaking up."

He laughed. "Okay. Say I wanted to express my gratitude. What would you suggest?"

"Talk to my colleague. I'll send you her info."

"Got it. Anything else?"

"Referrals are always appreciated."

THAT SPRING, I cleaned out my bogus social media accounts. I hadn't logged into Clay Gardner's Instagram in months, and I decided to look in on Shasta Swann.

She'd posted two weeks prior. Wearing a UC Santa Cruz sweatshirt; beaming and holding up a letter.

I got in! #GoBananaSlugs

I messaged her congratulations.

The next day she replied with her number and asked me to call her.

"Great news," I said. "You must be so excited."

"You have no idea."

I smiled. "Are you going to race triathlon?"

"They don't have a team, just a club. I have tryouts for cross-country and swim."

"I know a couple of swimmers there. Happy to put you in touch."

"I think I'd rather do it on my own."

"Fair enough."

"Listen, I wanted to thank you," she said.

"What for?"

"Saying things I needed to hear."

"I don't think I did much."

"You did. It cleared up a lot for me. So. Thanks."

"You're welcome. How's your family?"

"I mean. They're fine." She paused. "I asked my mom again. If he's my father."

"Prado."

"She said no, he wasn't. My dad was my dad and he loved me."

"Okay. How do you feel about that?"

"I'm choosing to believe her. For now," she said. "I might change my mind. If I do, maybe I'll hire you."

I laughed.

"I could do it, you know. I'm eighteen, I have money."

"That's right, happy birthday."

"Thanks. It was pretty crazy. I had this big meeting with all these lawyers. They were acting all polite, bringing me water, like I'm a celebrity. Then they heard what I had to say and looked like they were going to shit themselves."

"What did you tell them?"

"I'm getting rid of the land."

"You're selling it?"

"It's going to be a nature preserve."

"Wow. That's a major decision, Shasta."

"Yeah. But it's what I want. And there's still plenty of money for me. Bank accounts and stocks, that kind of thing. So it's not like I'm Mother Teresa or anything."

"Good for you, then. What happens to your parents?"

"They can stay for the time being. Maggie, too, and Jenelle. The whole thing's super complicated. The lawyers said it's going to take like twenty years."

"The longer it takes, the more they make."

"Right?"

"Welcome to adulthood."

She laughed. "Anyway, I'm glad you got in touch."

"So am I," I said. "How's DJ doing?"

"Okay, I think. He moved in with his mom. She seems happy to have him."

"And Al?"

"Him?" she said. "Mad, as usual."

I FOUND A press release, issued by the John Muir Conservation Center, announcing a joint partnership with the County of Humboldt and the Swann's Flat Board of Supervisors.

The transfer would take place in stages, over an unspecified period, with current owners compensated out of a privately established trust fund. Among the center's ultimate goals was the reintroduction of native species, including the critically endangered Point Delgada limpet.

A local paper had rehashed the story under the headline LOST COAST HAMLET TO BECOME PUBLIC LAND. Most folks cited felt positively about the change.

Most.

Albert Bock, a Swann's Flat resident of almost two decades, vowed to fight the initiative.

"They want my house, they can come and take it over my dead body," he said.

AMY SAID, "I saw Regina today."

I pressed PAUSE. On-screen, a cute couple held hands on a balcony overlooking turquoise water. A graphic displayed the price in euros. "Really? Where?"

"Mountain View. It's halfway. We met for a ladies' lunch."

"I didn't know you were in touch with her."

She nodded, sipped her wine. "We text sometimes. Work. That kind of thing."

"Right," I said. "How is she?"

"Good. She asked me to give you a heads-up. She's wiring you some money."

"What money?"

"From your client. She's sending your half."

"How much is that?"

"I didn't ask."

"Okay. It'll be like Christmas come early." I reached to un-pause the TV. "Thanks for letting me know."

Amy said, "She thinks I'm being selfish."

"About what?"

"Your job. She thinks I need to let you do it."

"Hang on." I put down the remote. "Hang on. That's absurd. You are the least selfish person I know."

"She says you need to be free to operate without fear, and that walking around preoccupied about me actually makes you less safe."

"Amy. Stop. She is way out of line, here. She has no business getting involved."

"No, she doesn't. But she did."

"Okay, but—"

"Clay." She put her hand on my wrist. "Please listen."

I said, "I'm listening."

Her hand moved to my cheek, stroked softly. "We're so alike, you and me. Almost everything important, I know how you feel, because I feel it, too. I don't even have to ask. We're so lucky to have that."

I nodded.

"But there's this one part of you," she said, "this core part, that drives you to run toward things I would run away from. I don't understand it. I've tried, but I don't think I ever will. It scares me, and makes me feel distant from you."

"I know."

"But I also admire it. And I'm grateful for it, because the world needs it, and it's rare. I love it, because it's you. I knew it was there when I married you."

"That was before we had kids."

"Yes. And I want them to know—when they're ready—that their daddy is the best, bravest man in the world. They deserve to know that. It will help them. I'm not encouraging you to throw yourself in harm's way. I know you never would. But I don't want you to be someone you're not, either. I love you, for you, even if that means feeling uncomfortable sometimes."

"I love you, too," I said. "And thank you for saying that. It means a lot. But—"

"No buts, okay? We'll make this work." She smiled. "Just. Don't overdo it."

"How do I gauge that?"

"I'll inform you. Regularly."

We both burst out laughing, shedding tension.

I pointed to her wineglass. "Refill?"

"Yes, please."

When I returned from the kitchen, the TV was off.

"Don't you want to find out what happens to our friends in Majorca?" I said.

"House number two, 'The Villa in Need of Love.'"

"We haven't seen the third option yet."

"Trust me," she said.

She took the glass from me, put it on the table.

"All the signs are there," she said and kissed me.

ACKNOWLEDGMENTS

Avi Klein, for his wisdom and generosity.

Raphael Shorser, for his excessive attention to detail.

ABOUT THE AUTHORS

Jonathan Kellerman has lived in two worlds: clinical psychologist and #1 *New York Times* bestselling author of more than fifty crime novels. His unique perspective on human behavior has led to the creation of the Alex Delaware series, *The Butcher's Theater, Billy Straight, The Conspiracy Club, Twisted, True Detectives,* and *The Murderer's Daughter.* With his wife, bestselling novelist Faye Kellerman, he co-authored *Double Homicide* and *Capital Crimes.* With his son, bestselling novelist Jesse Kellerman, he co-authored *The Burning, Half Moon Bay, A Measure of Darkness, Crime Scene, The Golem of Hollywood,* and *The Golem of Paris.* He is also the author of two children's books and numerous nonfiction works, including *Savage Spawn: Reflections on Violent Children* and *With Strings Attached: The Art and Beauty of Vintage Guitars.* He has won the Goldwyn, Edgar, and Anthony awards and the Lifetime Achievement Award from the American Psychological Association, and has been nominated for a Shamus Award. Jonathan and Faye Kellerman live in California.

jonathankellerman.com
Facebook.com/JonathanKellerman

Jesse Kellerman won the Princess Grace Award for best young American playwright and is the author of *Sunstroke, Trouble* (nominated for the ITW Thriller Award for Best Novel), *The Genius* (winner of the 2010 Grand Prix des Lectrices de *Elle*), *The Executor,* and *Potboiler* (nominated for the Edgar Award for Best Novel). He lives in California.

jessekellerman.com
Facebook.com/JesseKellermanAuthor

ABOUT THE TYPE

This book was set in Sabon, a typeface designed by the well-known German typographer Jan Tschichold (1902–74). Sabon's design is based upon the original letter forms of sixteenth-century French type designer Claude Garamond and was created specifically to be used for three sources: foundry type for hand composition, Linotype, and Monotype. Tschichold named his typeface for the famous Frankfurt typefounder Jacques Sabon (c. 1520–80).